PROTECTING JESS

PROTECTING JESS

KARNA SMALL BODMAN

ARCADE
CrimeWise

An Arcade CrimeWise Book

Copyright © 2025 by Karna Small Bodman

All rights reserved. No part of this book may be reproduced in any manner without the express written consent of the publisher, except in the case of brief excerpts in critical reviews or articles. All inquiries should be addressed to Arcade Publishing, 307 West 36th Street, 11th Floor, New York, NY 10018.

Arcade CrimeWise books may be purchased in bulk at special discounts for sales promotion, corporate gifts, fund-raising, or educational purposes. Special editions can also be created to specifications. For details, contact the Special Sales Department, Arcade Publishing, 307 West 36th Street, 11th Floor, New York, NY 10018 or arcade@skyhorsepublishing.com.

Arcade CrimeWise® is a registered trademark of Skyhorse Publishing, Inc.®, a Delaware corporation.

Visit our website at www.arcadepub.com.
Please follow our publisher Tony Lyons on Instagram @tonylyonsisuncertain

10 9 8 7 6 5 4 3 2 1

First Edition

Library of Congress Cataloging-in-Publication Data is available on file.

Jacket design by Erin Seaward-Hiatt
Cover image from Getty Images

Print ISBN: 978-1-64821-107-2
Ebook ISBN: 978-1-64821-108-9

Printed in the United States of America

PRINCIPAL CHARACTERS:

JESSICA TANNER ("JESS")—Deputy Director of the President's Council of Economic Advisors, the White House

WILLIAM BLACK ("BILL")—Assistant Chief of Protocol, Department of State

OTHERS:

JACKSON L. EVERLY ("J. L.")—Chief of Staff, the White House

HAROLD CARRUTHERS ("HAL")—Chairman of the President's Council of Economic Advisors, the White House

STEPHEN DIZIO ("STEVE")—Undersecretary of State for International Security

KAY HELLER—Special Assistant to the President for Public Liaison

SYLVESTER LEVENTHAL—Secretary of State

CHET OSBORN—Station Chief, American Embassy, Brasilia

ALICIA SILVERTON—Deputy Chief of Protocol, Department of State

ESTELLE VIERA—Assistant to the Secretary of State

FOREIGN NATIONALS:

ROBERTO MENDEZ—President of Brazil

ANTONIO SERRA—Vice President of Brazil

EDWARDO RABELO—Vice President of Brazil's Security Chief

PAZIO—Brazilian drug kingpin

DOMINGO—Pazio's lieutenant

PROLOGUE

Outside Rio de Janeiro—2015

"You're looking at about fifty million bucks' worth coming across that river."

Bill Black focused his night vision goggles. "Even if we bust them tonight and confiscate the shipment, with their profit margin, it'll just keep coming."

"You got that one right," Chet Osborn said, crouching down behind a large boulder. "Those guys pay about fifty dollars for a kilogram. Then it's shipped for about two hundred and fifty and is sold for up to six grand in Rio and Sao Paulo."

"Figures," Bill said. "With close to two million cocaine addicts in Brazil, I hear it's the number two market. After the good old US of A," he added. "And they pay a lot more than six thousand for that two-plus pounds in New York and even more in Europe and the Middle East."

Chet checked his watch. "We've got a little time before those boats get across. Gotta be patient." He turned to Bill. "By the way, glad the agency sent you down for this one. We need all the help we can get. I hear that you've got a new gig coming up. You'll still be on our team though, won't you?" Chet inquired, sounding a note of concern.

"No problem. There's a new man heading up International Security at State. He arranged the appointment as a great cover. It'll get me into all sorts of places. I'm sure they'll keep sending me down here if something else comes up."

"Speaking of coming up, we've got the Summer Olympics in a while. You can be sure there will be more trouble, more raids, more everything, and I know you're pretty up to speed, pardon the term, on this whole trafficking thing."

Bill leaned back against the rocks overlooking the river and shook his head. "It's more than that. You're stationed at our embassy, working with the government down here, but have you been keeping up with all the drug stuff going on in the States?"

"Pretty much," Chet said.

"Whatever you've heard, it's getting worse. Some time ago a dose of heroin might have been five percent pure. Lately they've been finding it can be fifty percent pure on the street. That means thousands more are dying from overdoses."

"I know. Your kid sister. Right?" Chet asked.

"You remember. She was hit by a teenage driver so high he had no clue where he was. Killed her, but he survived the wreck. I couldn't believe it," Bill said. "Nearly killed my folks to go through all of that. Me too. Loved that girl. Told myself I'd do anything to get all those drugs off the streets, even if it's one shipment at a time." He grabbed his goggles again. "All I can do now is focus on the bastards who bring it in."

"They're getting close to shore now. I'll radio my guys." Chet gave the command while he and Bill checked their ammunition and crept forward. "They'll be shining the spotlights any minute now. Let's go."

They began running down the hill as a dozen local police joined the ambush. The lights came on, temporarily blinding the skippers. Chet and Bill took up positions fifty yards away and watched as the Brazilian officers shouted orders. Chet pulled out his binoculars. "Wait a minute, could that be?"

"Who?"

"We may have ourselves one of the big boys this time. Looks like Pazio's brother," Chet said, pointing to the lead boat. "Pazio has a huge drug smuggling operation with more dealers and hangers-on than you can count. But he does rely on his brother. I've heard they're very close."

"Must be if that kingpin sends his brother to handle shipments like this," Bill said.

"Since this is a big one, sure looks like it. Keep an eye on him. They've got trucks up on the road over there. Don't let him get away," Chet commanded.

The police fired over the heads of the traffickers and ordered the men to surrender. One yelled, "Nao dispares!" *Don't shoot.* But three of the dealers made a dash to the right and headed up toward the road. Bill took off after them, gun drawn, shouting as he ran.

They kept going, dodging through the forest until the brother abruptly held out his hand, signaling a stop. He drew his gun and fired at Bill just as he ducked behind a large tree. Pazio laughed and called out, "Voce nao pode para-nos." *You can't stop us.* All three fired again, turned and raced toward their trucks.

Bill tore off his goggles and sprinted after them. He didn't want to kill them. He wanted to take the brother into custody. If they could get him, they might be able to get Pazio. He was part of the prize. He might lead them to the FARC leaders, the Colombian terrorist group that raked in close to a billion in profits every year from the drug trade. It didn't matter that the government kept trying to negotiate with that Marxist organization. They still kept producing and shipping. It never seemed to stop.

As the trio got closer to the first vehicle, the brother turned, took another shot, and dove to the side of the truck, out of Bill's line of sight. The other two men jumped inside and motioned to the driver to get going. Bill aimed at the front tire. The truck swerved, hitting the brother then screeching to a halt.

The two men jumped off and ran to their comrade, cursing and pointing toward Bill. "Voce nature-o. Que voce nao val esquecer. Voce e um homem morto!"

Even though it was their own truck that ran over Pazio's brother, his comrades had shouted, *You killed him. We won't forget. You're a dead man!*

CHAPTER ONE

The White House—Summer 2016

Jessica Tanner scanned the president's schedule on her computer. She didn't have much time. She had been working on the papers for his briefing with the Council of Economic Advisors. As Deputy Director of the Economic Council, she needed to double check the talking points she had written for her boss and stop thinking about her date that night. She wondered if she would get out of the White House in time for the evening she had planned with Ken Daley.

Ken certainly was attractive. He worked out constantly, dressed well, and his aftershave was okay. At least he didn't marinade in it like a few guys she'd met. Then again, some of her friends called him the Ken-Doll. Looks great, kind of like an ad in *GQ*. That was better than Urban Outfitters. But there wasn't much sizzle. It seemed that so much was missing in their relationship. Like any sort of agreement on ideas and issues. When you live and work in the nation's capital, issues *are* your life. At least they are a lot of the time, and Ken was no philosophical soulmate. That much was obvious.

It seemed as if every time they went out, after he had taken the trouble to select the wine, he went on to adroitly push for some White House attention for his group, the Renewable Energy Committee, or REC. She called it the wreck. And she didn't appreciate it when almost every date included a bit of lobbying for some new ethanol subsidy or other, as if the price of corn weren't high enough already.

Why can't I find a guy who wants me for who *I am, not* what *I am?* She wondered. *Then again, here in the Capital, it seems that everyone wants to date a title or a resume because everyone has an agenda. Ah yes, welcome to Washington.*

A buzzer interrupted her thoughts. She pushed the button, "Yes?"

"Just wanted to remind you about those talking points for the nine o'clock," her administrative aide said.

"I'll have them done in just a sec. Thanks."

Jess was the first one to arrive in the Roosevelt Room, across from the Oval Office. She took her usual seat in one of the brown leather chairs at the large, mahogany conference table and glanced over at the clock on the mantel just below the famous painting of Teddy Roosevelt as a Rough Rider. She saw that she had a few more minutes before her boss and other members of the Council would arrive. She liked to be early for meetings, or most anything else. It gave her a chance to catch her breath from her usually hectic schedule and also to review her notes. She never came to a meeting without notes. Nobody in the White House did.

The president would arrive in about five minutes and sit across the table in the one chair that was slightly taller than all the rest. It was the same drill in the Cabinet Room down the hall. One chair is higher. At least she got to sit in on some of the Cabinet meetings, the ones having to do with economic policy, even if she did have to grab a seat along the wall where they never passed the M&Ms. That was fine, though. She was just glad to be included in those sessions so she could keep up to date on the latest decisions. After all, in the White House, knowledge is power.

She stared at the row of flags on the wall in front of her and wondered if they were here when this room served as the president's office back in the last century before the Oval Office was built in 1909. Probably not. There were flags all over the place, and these were probably much newer ones.

"Morning, Jess," her boss said as he walked into the room and set his leather folder down at a place directly across from the president's chair. "Good points this time."

"Thank you, Hal," she replied, brushing a strand of ash blond hair off her forehead.

"I especially liked the way you tied the new CBO figures into our projections for third quarter GDP growth."

"I was glad to see that the Congressional Budget Office came up with similar numbers ever since the president's new tax cut bill started taking effect."

Harold Carruthers smiled at his protégé as other economists flooded into the room. He had always said he was delighted to find a student from the Chicago School of Economics who was such a supply-side genius to fill out his team.

The others on his staff were all exceptional or else they wouldn't be there. But Jessica was something else altogether. Not only was she attractive, which had already caused some grief when a couple of the staff had tried to make a move on her, but she was almost irreverent when it came to discussions of economic policy.

While most of the others basked in their lofty status as members of the Council and had plastered their walls with diplomas and honorary degrees, Jess had never referred to herself as "Dr. Tanner," though she held the degree. She often repeated a phrase her father had used to describe a PhD. He said that as far as he was concerned, it stood for "piled higher and deeper." She always said it with a grin, though.

Jessica and the others pushed papers aside and scrambled to their feet when the door opened, and the president and his chief of staff walked in. "Good morning, Mr. President," everyone seemed to say at once.

The president smiled and took his seat, and the others followed suit. He looked down at his briefing paper for the meeting and then up at Harold. "Why don't you bring us up to speed on these new numbers,

Hal? It looks like some of my policies are beginning to bear fruit. Lord knows we need it. The country's been hungry for far too long."

"You're right, Mr. President," the chairman replied. He then went on to list the new predictions about GDP growth. Before he could make his next point, he began to cough. Jess quickly poured a glass of water from a silver pitcher in the center of the table and handed it to him. He took it and gave her a grateful nod, but he coughed again, spilling some water on the shiny surface. Jess grabbed a napkin from a tray and dabbed up the spill.

"I'm sorry, Mr. President," Hal choked. "It's just something that cropped up recently."

"Take your time, Hal," the president said sympathetically. He turned to Jessica. "Miss Tanner let's give Hal a moment here. Do you want to continue? I assume you have the same numbers."

It often happened that top staff asked Jessica for briefings and updates when Hal was busy. Everyone knew she did a lot of the research and wrote most of the memos. As Hal's deputy, that was her job. "Uh, certainly, Mr. President," she replied. She went on to summarize their findings and predictions. "Sir, it's the consensus of our council that your tax cuts are helping job growth, but we have a recommendation that you also consider a further cut in the capital gains tax rate."

"Yes, we can work on that," the president said with a wave of his hand. "My problem is with the Ways and Means Committee." Turning to his chief of staff, he said, "J. L., let's get moving on legislation about cap gains. I know we've been kicking that one around, and it might be a good idea to float it on the Hill and see what kind of flack we get this time."

"Certainly, Mr. President," Jackson Everly said, reaching for his pen. As he jotted down some notes, Jessica could see the presidential cuff links he always wore with crisp white shirts in contrast to his light brown complexion. Here she was in another meeting with the President of the United States. How lucky could a woman get to have a job like this?

While she was thanking those lucky stars for a dream job, she had a fleeting thought about how great it would be to have a dream date. She was always surrounded by economists, accountants, and analysts. Was it wrong to wish for a change of personality once in a while? Instead of spread sheets, a little spice perhaps. She glanced back at the president. *Stop dreaming. Concentrate on the meeting,* she thought.

Hal coughed once more and stood up. "I'm sorry, Mr. President, I'd better leave you. Don't want to spread any germs. That is, if I've got any."

"Go check in with the doctor's office in the EOB," the President said. He got up as well, which was the signal that this meeting was over.

As Jess was gathering her briefing papers, another staffer whispered, "What's the matter with Hal? I've never seen him look so . . . so . . . ashen."

Jessica leaned over and answered in a low voice, "I heard him like that a couple of times but nothing this bad. Then again, maybe it's allergies or something."

"Let's hope so. He's got a brutal schedule coming up."

"I know. Believe me, I know. Everything from Congressional testimony, a meeting this week with that African Finance Minister during their State Visit, possible new legislation, and the big conference in South America. And on that note, we'd better get back to work and cover for him."

CHAPTER TWO

The State Department

"Okay, people, listen up," the Deputy Chief of Protocol shouted. Alicia Silverton was trying to get the attention of two dozen staff members who were talking and checking their iPhones. When the chatter in the room subsided, she stood at the front, hands on her ample hips and continued. "We've got just three more days before the next State Visit, and I don't have to remind you how important this one is to the president's Africa policy. Not only because of their oil and mineral resources, but their strategic location."

"Remember the strategic location of that loin cloth the last time a leader from a sub-Saharan country went to the Oval Office?" Bill Black murmured to a colleague at the back of the room. "He was carrying a spear, and the Secret Service went ballistic." The other guy stifled a laugh and gave Bill the thumbs up.

"Can you please refrain from jabbering back there?" Alicia said, trying to regain control of the meeting. "Now, as I said, we all have our assignments, and it's especially challenging since the chief is overseas at that funeral."

"Right. You die, we fly," Bill whispered once more. Then, getting the evil eye from his boss, he shifted in his seat and feigned rapt attention.

Alicia pointed to a woman in the front row. "Double check with the White House on the arrival ceremony. This man is the newly elected president, so that means only a 19-gun salute, not the 21 guns reserved for kings and queens." The woman nodded and took notes.

"Last time we had a queen here," Bill murmured again, "it was Queen Elizabeth. The President asked her to dance, and the Marine Band played 'The Lady is a Tramp.'"

"Yeah, I read about those screw-ups in our policy book," the other young man whispered. "We don't control the Marine Band, though."

"That's enough from you two," Alicia stammered. She double checked her list and went on with the briefing. She covered the display of flags, the reception ceremony, facilities for visiting officials at Blair House across the street from the White House and the five extra rooms reserved at a luxury hotel downtown for additional foreign staff. She explained that the visiting president's aide had complained bitterly about the "meager" accommodations with only five extra hotel rooms besides Blair House, but he had been told that this restriction applied to all visiting dignitaries, and their delegation was, of course, welcome to rent as many additional rooms in any Washington hotel as their budget would allow.

As she droned on, Bill marveled again how this bitchy woman had managed to

nail her appointment as Deputy Chief of Protocol. Then again, as the daughter of a key senator on the Foreign Relations Committee who was a major backer of the president and personal friend of the Secretary of State, he figured this was the highest-ranking job they could find for her that didn't require Senate confirmation. She'd never make it through that process with her shrill manner and questionable escorts around town and probably in her bedroom. When he thought about it, it amused him to reflect that the House panel was called the House Foreign Affairs Committee and the Senate's was called the Senate Foreign Relations Committee. So, the Senate had "relations," but the House had "affairs." So did a lot of the State Department staff, according to the latest gossip.

Even with Alicia's State Department perch as his nominal boss, she didn't bother him too much. He had managed to carve out his own niche and had the chance to manage a lot of overseas travel assignments since Alicia was afraid of flying, though she wouldn't admit it. She usually found an excuse to stay in town and attend most of the embassy receptions and dinners.

He surreptitiously checked his iPhone again and saw the message he had been waiting for. He quickly punched in "Got it. Usual place," and looked at his watch. He had to get out of this inane meeting. Since he was Alicia's number two in the Protocol Office, it was mandatory, according to her rules, that he attend all staff meetings, so he had stayed and listened. Sort of. He knew the drill. He was paid to know the drill, but right now he figured that since the upcoming Africa visit was more or less covered, he could slip away and deal with some bigger problems.

He stretched out his six-foot-one lanky frame and glanced out the window onto C Street near Virginia Avenue, in the area known as Foggy Bottom. He saw that clouds were moving in. A big storm could certainly complicate an arrival ceremony if it produced more than fog. Right now, he was more concerned about his own arrival at a clandestine meeting. And he had to make it fast.

CHAPTER THREE

The White House

"**G**ood afternoon, Miss Tanner. I see you have arrived before Miss Heller. Shall I seat you now?" the Maitre d' of the White House Mess asked as he reached under his walnut podium to extract two navy blue menus.

"Sure. Guess I'm a few minutes early," Jessica replied, following him past the replica of the USS Constitution encased in Plexi-glass that was displayed on a long table at the entrance to the most exclusive restaurant in the country. At least that's how the staff felt about it. The wood paneled room in the basement of the West Wing next to the Situation Room had been serving Presidents and their top advisors since the '50s, and Navy Stewards competed for the coveted jobs of running the place.

As she walked past the large round staff table that seated twelve at the front of the room, Jessica saw a contingent of NSC staffers chatting with members of the Legislative Affairs team. When she didn't have a specific lunch reservation, she always tried to grab a seat at that open table since it was a great place to mingle with people from other departments, find out what was really going on and pick up the latest rumors.

When it came to policy and gossip, the one taboo about guests in the White House Mess concerned members of the press. No one, and that meant no one, was ever supposed to invite reporters, even if they happened to be personal friends, to have a meal in that room, since they might overhear something, anything that could lead to the leak of a story.

Jess sat down at a small table for two along the side wall adorned with a row of paintings of naval ships. The room could seat about fifty and yet had a cozy, intimate feel with its plush beige carpet and tables set apart and covered with white linen cloths. It was a total contrast to most of the other downtown spots where all the seats were usually jammed together on a wooden or tile floor with no carpet and a deafening noise level. Many of the newer, popular bars and restaurants were so modern in décor that Jess often described them as being nothing more than sticks and glass. She preferred slightly quieter places where she could actually talk to someone rather than those high energy clubs where DC's twenty- and thirty-somethings often hung out. She never figured out how anyone could have a decent conversation in one of those places.

Jess loved a good exchange, although the constant bickering with Ken had become rather tiresome. She was contemplating how she was going to handle his expected moves tonight when her friend walked up.

"Hi, Jess. Sorry to keep you waiting," Kay Heller said, slipping into an opposite chair. "It's starting to rain, so I had to dash over from the EOB too. Seems like nobody ever bothers with umbrellas on our side of West Exec. We just run back and forth all the time."

Jess took in Kay's somewhat harried look with her long brown hair a bit wind-blown and a few damp spots on her dark green blazer and pencil skirt. Kay took a napkin and dabbed her face. "What I wouldn't give for a cubicle here in the West Wing instead of the big offices we all have in the EOB. Of course, yours is bigger. You've even got a fireplace and a balcony."

"I know," Jess said. "We'd all give it up to be here. Proximity to the president is the name of the game in this town. But still, we're just across the driveway, and we spend a lot of time here anyway. At least we're not over in Virginia or Maryland with some of the other agencies."

"Good point," Kay agreed.

They perused their menus. When the waiter appeared, Jess ordered a fruit plate while Kay opted for the cobb salad with dressing on the side. "No wonder you stay so thin," her friend remarked when the waiter slipped away. "You should eat more protein."

"I suppose," Jess said. "I did see a recipe for bacon ice cream in a magazine."

Kay grinned. "You don't have to go that far. But what's with the fruit plate routine?"

"I just don't have much of an appetite right now. I feel so slammed with everything that's going on. And I'm worried about Hal. I think he's caught something really bad. I don't know, maybe it's just the flu or a cold. Hope that's all it is. But I don't want to dwell on our shop, tell me what you're up to. You guys over in Public Liaison seem to get assignments we can at least laugh about."

"You're right about that," Kay said. "Sorry about Hal. Let me know how he's doing." Jess nodded, and Kay went on. "Let's see. We get so many requests from nutty groups that want to meet with the president, or at least with someone they think has some influence around here."

"What now?"

"In addition to the request for a presidential visit to Gilroy, California, for the Annual Garlic Festival, I just got one saying that when the president does his next swing through the Mid-West, he should come to Wisconsin to see the National Mustard Museum."

Jess was taking a sip of her ice water and almost choked on it. "Get real."

"Oh yes. I learned that there are fifty-two different kinds of mustard. They even have mustard custard."

"Any hot dog stands around?" Jess asked.

"And the funny thing is that some of these crazy groups are actually granted access to our top staff every once in a while."

"Come to think of it, I did see a meeting on the chief of staff's schedule that sounds like one your shop might have vetted. Isn't there some sort of environmental group coming in this afternoon?"

"You got it. We did send it over for consideration. I wanted to get it out of my shop and let another pair of eyes take a look. I have no idea why his scheduling staff let this one in. I thought they'd decide to push it off to EPA. Trouble is that there are a bunch of holdovers in that agency who do nothing but write new regulations, so I guess someone figured out that we could at least give them a short meeting here, listen to their gripes and then just file it away without causing more paperwork."

"What's this one about?" Jess asked.

"It's some group that wants a new habitat conservation plan for a bunch of endangered species. And this time they say they want protection for red-cockaded woodpeckers. But nobody wants to add a line item for that one because our people found out that another one, something called the ivory-billed woodpecker, was found in Arkansas, and that one was supposed to be extinct. So, it's kind of a trade-off right now."

"I can't believe we're wasting time on that stuff," Jess said.

"It won't be too much time. The chief will host it. The president will just do a two-minute drop-by and then get out of there. Guess he's trying to protect his left flank or something."

"Must be."

The waiter brought their entrees, and Jess decided to change the subject. "By the way, whatever happened to that new guy you said you met at Old Ebbitt Grill the other night? The one from Florida."

Kay took a bite of her salad and chuckled. "Oh, that one. I have to admit he was gorgeous. Tall, dark, great tan, and he was in incredible shape. So, when we got to talking and he asked me out, I thought, 'why not?' He seemed harmless, and we were going in a group. We hooked up last night. Same time. Same place."

"That sounds good. So, what does he do?"

"That's the weird part. He said he was a flagpole straightener."

Jessica burst out laughing. "What the heck is that?"

"He said that with all the hurricanes and tropical storms in Florida, he has a lot of business. Not very geographically desirable for me though," Kay admitted.

"Oh Lord. I think you can do better than that."

"You'd think. But there seems to be a dearth of men in this town. I think they're outnumbered by women something like eight to one. Well, I read that article in *The Washington Post* last week about how DC is a magnet for all the bright poli-sci majors around the country, and the majority of them seem to be women on the hunt."

"Guess you're right. And now in the midst of this ratio, I'm rethinking my whole thing with Ken."

"Really?" Kay said, raising her eyebrows. "Why?"

Jessica toyed with the strawberries on her plate and replied. "Oh, I don't know. I mean, he's nice enough and all of that."

"And he sure looks the part with all that platinum hair and big shoulders. Why would you want to dump him?"

Jess paused for a long moment, gathering her thoughts. "It's just that we never seem to agree on anything."

"I have to admit that he may have the physical equipment, but I've often wondered if he has the intellectual equipment to keep up with you," Kay said.

"It isn't exactly that. I mean, he's smart enough. It's just that he thinks he's smart on all the wrong subjects."

"Like what?"

Jess leaned forward. "You know he runs that association that's always lobbying for another government grant or committee or bureau to solve everything."

"Which is just about the opposite of everything you've been preaching," Kay said.

"You got that right," Jess agreed. "I mean the other night he said that businesses create oppression and governments create prosperity."

"Yeah, this town is full of guys like that."

"And get this, he thinks it's okay to give government workers a day off on Christmas, but it's not okay to say 'Merry Christmas.' Go figure."

Kay smiled at her friend. "Guess it's not a perfect James Carville and Mary Matalin duo. But hey, they made it work."

"I don't think I'm that lucky. In fact, we've got a dinner date tonight—that is if I ever get out of this place at a decent hour—and I'm thinking about cutting it off."

"And then what are you going to do on Saturday nights?" Angela asked in an earnest tone.

"I guess we could go find a good movie. That is unless you want to spend more time with your Florida beach boy."

"No. He's going back to Miami. But when it comes to movies, I don't think there's anything good playing right now. At least not anything that isn't filled with special effects, explosions, and aliens. Even on TV, I looked at the schedule to see if there was anything to DVR, but they're showing re-runs of shows like *The Adventures of Sharkboy and Lavagirl* or *Mega Python vs. Gatoroid*."

Jess laughed and shook her head. "Okay. We forget movies."

"By the way, if you have a bit of extra time this weekend, do you suppose you could stop by and help me fix a lamp? It doesn't work, and you're so handy with tools I figure you might have an idea."

"It probably just needs to be re-wired or have the switch replaced. Should be easy. When you say I'm handy with tools, I wonder if we both can figure out a way to re-tool our private lives?"

"I have an idea," Kay said. "I heard about a great cooking class in Georgetown where we might pick up a few pointers."

"Now, there's a thought," Jess said. "Come to think of it, that just might be the only way I'll ever get some spice into my life."

CHAPTER FOUR

The Boat Center—Washington, DC

Bill ducked out of the rain and sat down on a bench just inside the storage warehouse at the Boat Center along the Potomac. Stacks of eight-man shells, kayaks, canoes, and singles were lined up inside the two-story building. He liked coming here. It wasn't that far from his office since it was on Virginia Avenue, just past the Watergate. He often came at dawn when there weren't many people around. Sometimes he'd take a single scull out on the river when it was calm and cool. That's when he could think about his assignments, his crazy schedule, or just nothing at all.

He heard that the president had rowed in college, though he didn't do it anymore. The Secret Service probably nixed that idea. Bill had rowed in college too, easily passed the swim tests and ended up taking a Navy Commission for four years. He loved the ships, the travel, even the strenuous training. But most of all, it was the camaraderie, the sense of belonging to something bigger than himself and a cause better than himself. It sounded a bit hokey when he thought about it. On the other hand, this town was filled with people loyal to some cause or other. That's why he had been drawn to it. And when he was recruited for his current job, he had jumped at the chance.

He checked his watch, sat back, and waited for his contact.

"Glad you could make it out of your meeting," the Special Agent muttered, taking a seat on the bench next to Bill.

"I can usually get away with a bit of notice. Alicia is always so busy planning the next event or primping for some delegation, she doesn't pay much attention to the rest of us."

"So this arrangement is working?"

"About as well as could be expected." Bill glanced at the member of his CIA team and asked, "What have you got for me today?"

"More trouble down south."

"Again? What kind of trouble?"

"We've been coordinating with Drug Enforcement on the latest cocaine shipments like we did before. But right in the middle of our latest investigation, the cartel kills another judge. At least it looked like the cartels at first. Now our contact says that he got word from an inside source that it might have been off-duty police who have been acting as death squads."

"Sounds about par for the course," Bill said. "Where do we fit in?"

"We've got more chatter about a possible major hit. This time it won't just be judges. Looks like someone is aiming at the top man."

"The President of Brazil?" Bill exclaimed.

"Maybe."

"Last time I was down there, people were saying he's a good guy," Bill said. "On our side and all of that. Didn't he just manage a bunch of raids in Alameo and round up a whole bevy of drug lords?"

"You mean in addition to the big one you helped with last year?" the agent said. "That turned out to be a pretty neat operation. People celebrated for days. I mean everyone except the buyers and sellers. Right now, their president is saying he's got to get tough. He's got to clean out drug labs and deal with the gang wars before the Summer Olympics."

"I can see that. So, you're saying that if he doesn't do something drastic, a lot of people won't want to go to a place with one of the highest murder rates in the world," Bill observed wryly.

"You got it."

"I still don't see where I fit into the mix."

"As I said, we're still working with DEA, tracking drug shipments, and trying to hunt down their henchmen. But with this new threat, we just don't have enough field forward people to prevent an assassination, if that's what they're planning. Their security types are overworked, and most of them can't be trusted anyway. We just heard from the station chief at our embassy down there that one of the president's confidantes, a man he does trust, is asking for our help."

"You mean Chet Osborn?" Bill asked.

"Yeah, Chet. You worked with him before. Good man," the agent said.

"What about DOD?" Bill asked. "Every time I look around it seems that they're moving into more and more of our operations. Talk about turf fights. You've got their Special Forces operating secretly overseas, you've got Delta Force, the Rangers, the Seals, Marines . . ."

"Yes, but most of them are still tied down in Pakistan, all over the Middle East, the Far East, even the Philippines. Or else they're worrying about nuclear proliferation in God-knows-where. Not much presence in South America, you know. Besides, if we put an operation together for something like stopping a planned assassination, this is going to take an up-close-and-personal connection, not a Seal Team Six."

"Guess you're right about that," Bill said. Then he stopped, paused for a moment, and brought up what he thought was a rather obvious concern. "They're looking for help from us. Well, from me, I guess. But on something like a possible assassination attempt, remember, this isn't an episode of that TV show where they send a lone agent somewhere to entirely change the game. All on his own."

"Yeah, but the thing is, Chet thinks you could be a big help to him. You've been in country. Rio, not Brasilia. You know the language. You know our people. The only problem—and this could be a big one—is that ever since you took down Pazio's brother . . ."

"He was run over by his own truck," Bill protested.

"I know. But there's word on the street that Pazio still holds *you* responsible."

"That op was near Rio. Their president is in Brasilia, the capital. Besides, I can handle myself. Just tell me the assignment."

The agent checked his cell and looked over at Bill. "We're doubling down on our local sources, watching the chatter and cell phone intercepts. If more of this pans out, the agency says you'll be the next man out. I just wanted to give you a heads-up." He stared at Bill for a moment and asked. "If we need you, do you think you can get away without causing a stir?"

"I'll have to think about that," Bill said. "I'll check around and see what else we've got going in that part of the world. Maybe I can put something together. We'll have to coordinate with the Undersecretary. I assume he's been read-in on all of this, right?"

"Not quite yet. But he will be. You know he's the only one at State who's privy to your little escapades, if we can call them that. But you can be sure we'll keep him in the loop on any upcoming travel so he can cover your ass if need be."

"Thanks," Bill said, glancing at his watch again. "Now, I gotta get back and deal with really important stuff like making sure none of the State Dinner guests bow or genuflect before an African head of state."

CHAPTER FIVE

DuPont Circle—Washington, DC

"Hey, Jess. Ready to go?"

Jess had a condo in the DuPont Circle area. She loved the Victorian-style brownstone built in the early 1900s with its exposed brick wall in the living room, high ceilings, and dark cabinets. She didn't mind being on the top floor, although Ken usually complained about the three flights of stairs whenever he came up to her place.

"C'mon in and sit down for a minute. I just have to send one more email. Then we'll be out of here."

Ken appeared to be scrutinizing Jess's form fitting black slacks and light blue sweater with an approving stare. "You look great tonight. Come to think of it, care to postpone dinner and start with a little dessert?"

"Not right now," Jess said with a dismissive gesture. *And probably not ever again*, she thought as she slid into a chair behind her desk at one end of the room. "This will just take a minute. I want to check on Hal. See how he's feeling."

"Oh? Something wrong?"

"Not sure. He just seemed awfully weak last time I saw him, and he's been coughing a lot. I wish he'd get to a doctor. After all, we keep a medical team in the EOB. He needs to take a break and get a diagnosis. But he's working all the time."

"That applies to you too, my dear," Ken said.

"What? I'm not sick," she replied.

"No, but your hours are brutal. I'm amazed we can grab dinner at all these days. It's been, what? Over a week since you could break away. You really need to take some personal time or you're going to wear yourself out," he said.

She ignored his remark, shut down her laptop, pushed away from the desk and grabbed her purse. "So where are we headed tonight?" she asked, walking toward the door.

Ken opened it for her and said, "I thought we'd go over to The Palm. I made a reservation, if that's okay with you."

"The Palm? Oh, sure. I haven't been there in ages. I remember they have those caricatures of politicians all over the walls."

"Yep," he replied, "Wish I could get mine up there," he muttered.

"What did you say?"

"Oh, nothing. It's just that you're right about the drawings. As for politicians, the real ones do show up there a lot."

"Along with most every lobbyist in town," she observed.

"You're right. But I'm not trying to meet up with anybody but you tonight," he said.

But if he just happens to run into an influential member of Congress, there's no question that he'll figure out a way to stop at his table and glad hand the guy.

They drove around the Circle and headed down Nineteenth Street, then made a U-Turn so they could be on the other side of the street, right in front of the long green awning at the entrance to The Palm. A valet opened Jess's door and helped her out. Sure enough, the place was jammed, and so were the walls. There were drawings of past presidents, vice presidents, well known ambassadors, even a few Hollywood stars who had come to town to push for their pet causes. As she walked past, she mused about how Hollywood types always thought Washington was an exciting place, and Washington types always thought Hollywood was an exciting place. Jess wasn't sure if either group was right.

She had to admit that being *inside* the White House was exciting. What could be more stimulating than being in the same room with the

President of the United States and realizing that he knows your name and often agrees with your ideas and policies? Yes, anyone would say that when it came to her job, she was in a cat-bird seat, and it was at a pretty high altitude.

But when it came to her private life, as she glanced over at Ken, she reflected again that she never felt a high when she was with him. The excitement factor just wasn't there.

When they were seated at a banquette along the side where they had a good view of all the action in the room, Ken grabbed the wine list and quickly ordered a bottle of the 2007 Vieux Telegraphe Chateauneuf-du-Pape La Crau. "I saw that one in a *Wall Street Journal* article about wines that Nelson DeMille buys. I buy his books, so maybe I'll like his wines. That okay with you, babe?"

"Sure. And I like DeMille too. I've read most of his novels. They're clever, even irreverent in places," she replied, reading the menu. *Wish I could meet someone like one of* his *characters.*

He glanced over and studied her expression. "You look kind of down tonight, Jess. What's the matter?"

"Oh, I guess it's the workload," she lied.

"And . . . ?" Ken raised his eyebrows. Then, looking to his left, he saw a heavyset older man sitting with an attractive woman who looked to be in her mid-thirties. "Uh, just a second. I see someone I need to speak to," Ken said pushing himself up from the table. "Back in a minute."

Figures. Happens every time. Jess glanced at the man and realized he was a senator on the Armed Services Committee. She wondered which of Ken's many projects he was going to pitch tonight. Her thoughts wandered to just how she was going to make her own pitch to extricate herself from this relationship. She realized that she didn't really care if he made his rounds to other tables tonight or any other night. In fact, she didn't care much about anything he did anymore. Maybe she should care. It wasn't that he was a bad person. It just wasn't working. Tonight was the night to cut it off. She'd just have to figure out a way to keep it friendly and civil. If she could.

The waiter brought their wine as Ken slid back into the seat next to her. After twirling the liquid in his glass and making a show of sniffing, he tasted it and nodded to the waiter who poured a third of a glass for Jess, then the same for Ken, put the bottle on the side of the table, and quickly slipped away.

Ken turned to her with an apologetic look. "Sorry about that, hon. I've been trying to get in to see that senator for weeks now. Glad I had a chance to make a quick comment."

"Which issue was it this time?" Jessica asked, trying to look interested.

"Well, since he's a key guy on military budgets, I thought he should know about our plan to have the Air Force and the Navy get half of their fuel from renewable resources by the next decade."

"You've got to be kidding," Jess said. "How do you think they could pull that off?"

"Lots of ways, but here's a really clever one. There's new biofuel made from a plant. It's in the mustard family."

"I wonder if that one is also in the Mustard Museum in Wisconsin," Jess muttered to herself.

"What was that?"

"Oh nothing. I just can't imagine that they're going to get enough fuel for their ships and airplanes from a plant," Jess said, shaking her head.

"Well, okay, okay. So maybe that isn't the whole answer. But our people still think that there are a whole lot of other things that the military can do, especially overseas."

"Like what?"

"Like wind."

"So now our troops are supposed to give away their positions in the field by putting up windmills?" She almost started to laugh but stopped when she saw his hurt expression. "Maybe we should change the subject," she said gently.

The waiter sidled up to their table again. "Excuse me, folks, have you decided?"

Jess spoke up first, happy with the interruption. "Yes, I'd like to start with the tomato caprese salad, then the small fillet rare with some leaf spinach."

"No fries for you, miss? Ours are the best in town," the waiter suggested.

"I'm sure they are, but not this time, thank you," she said.

"And for you, sir?"

"Let's see," Ken said, raking his eyes over the long list of entrees. "How are the lobsters tonight?"

"Our specialty, sir."

"Right. Lobster it is, along with some creamed spinach. Oh, and I'll start with the Caesar salad. You can skip the fries for me too. Thanks a lot."

The waiter quickly retreated toward the kitchen with their orders memorized.

Jess took a sip of her wine and decided that as long as they had to finish their dinner, she'd try to make the best of it. "This wine is terrific. One of the better ones you've picked out."

Looking somewhat mollified Ken drank some of his wine too. "Thanks. This is a good vintage."

They went on to talk about books, movies, and the theater. Anything but politics, and that was just fine with Jessica. There was a new show over at Ford's Theater that sounded pretty good, but she had no idea when she'd have a chance to go see it. On the other hand, if this evening ended like she thought it would, she'd probably have her Saturday nights free.

"Say, I was just hearing about that new rock group that'll be coming to town. I think it's next weekend. Want to go?" Ken asked with a hopeful look.

"Which group is that?" Jess asked.

"It's called Toxic Assets."

Jess laughed despite her rather somber mood. "They must have snagged that one right out of the economic meltdown."

"Guess so," Ken agreed.

The waiter brought their salads and once again, Jess felt like she'd been let off the hook. At least conversation-wise. She didn't want to commit to a rock concert or a dinner or anything else with this guy. In fact, when she pondered that thought, she wondered how she had managed to go out with him for the last few months.

They finished their dinner; Ken paid the check and retrieved his car from the valet. On the way back to her condo, he said, "I know that we have different views about things, but *you know* I really care about you. In fact, I happen to think that you're one of the prettiest, no, make that one of the most intriguing women I've been out with." He looked over at the dashboard clock and added, "It's not too late. So do you think I can come up for a night cap . . . or something better?"

Jess was uncomfortable. This wasn't going the way she'd planned. Now he was being nice. Now he wanted to take her home, come up, and make love. She knew that, and she knew that he knew that. She was hardly in the mood, but she wanted to try and let him down easy. She hesitated for several seconds and then said in a low voice, "Ken, that was a very nice dinner. I mean the food was great. The wine was the best, and you've been good to me. It's just that . . ."

"It's just that what?" Ken said, turning right onto Massachusetts Avenue.

"It's just that we keep going out and never really connecting."

"Never connecting? How can you say that?"

"What I mean is a mental connection."

"'A mental connection'?" he mimicked. "Maybe we don't agree on a lot of issues. But tons of people don't agree on a lot of issues. Look at Congress and the White House, for God's sake. Look at how half the people in this town have one set of viewpoints, and the other half want something else. Nothing new about that." he said, his voice rising. "After all, when you try to make some political point, at least I listen."

"Yes, you listen, but 'a man convinced against his will is of the same opinion still.'"

"Well, that's a pithy quote," Ken mumbled.

"Actually, it was a Benjamin Franklin quote," Jess answered. "Look, I just feel like our relationship isn't going anywhere. It's like we're two people playing in a band, but we're never reading the same music. You might say we're meandering to different drummers."

Ken heaved a sigh and pulled the car over in front of her building. "Are you saying you want to call it quits? Now? Tonight?" he said in a frustrated tone.

"I'm sorry. You're a nice guy. You deserve someone who really appreciates you for who you are," she said, echoing a thought she'd had in the past about what she really wanted for herself.

"So that's it, then?" he said in a low tone.

"I think it's for the best. Really," Jess said as she reached for the door. "Don't bother walking me up. I can make it on my own."

And with that she headed for the front door, fished out her key, turned, and waved as he drove away and thought, *That's right. I can make it on my own. And now, I'll have to.*

CHAPTER SIX

The White House

O PRAZER DA COMPANHIA DE
DR. JESSICA TANNER
E SOLICITADA EM UM JANTAR
EM HONRA DO
CONFERENCIA DA ORGANIZACAO DOS ESTADOS AMERICANOS
NO PALACIO DA ALVORADA
25 DE JULHO
OITO HORAS

Jessica stared at the buff-colored oversize invitation sitting on top of a pile of papers on her desk. *What the heck is this*? Then she saw the message clipped underneath. It was a memo from Hal.

> Looks like you'll be filling in for me at the OAS conference in Brasilia. I had their Embassy switch the names and get this over to you. Doctor now says its pneumonia, so can't travel for a while. Sorry to dump it on you, but you may enjoy this one. Take a few extra days to travel around, head to Rio for a break.
> You deserve it.
> —H.

She already had the briefing papers for that meeting of the Organization of American States in Brazil. She had collected them for Hal in the first place. But she hadn't considered that he'd send her as his replacement. She originally thought they would rely on the Secretary of State and his people to fill out their delegation. Hal had been included in order to attend some of the small meetings focusing on financial issues. Now she'd have to handle them. She guessed that J. L. still wanted White House representation so they would all know about the president's interest in lowering tariffs, expanding trade, and a few other initiatives in the hemisphere. She picked up the invitation and tried to make out the Portuguese. It looked like some event at a palace. They could get a quick translation from Google. She set it aside to give to her assistant and turned to the briefing book.

The meeting was less than a week away. She glanced out her tall office window where wind-driven rain was lashing the panes. She could just picture the network and cable news crews scrambling for cover out on the North Lawn, and she wondered what it would be like in Brazil. Probably pretty warm.

She had heard that the capital city of Brasilia was pretty interesting with its modern architecture and all of that. But she had also heard that most of the bureaucrats still hopped on shuttle flights to spend most every weekend on the beaches of Rio de Janeiro, and since she knew there was a two-day weekend break in the OAS schedule, there was no reason she couldn't do the very same thing.

It did seem like a perfect little vacation. She'd take a commercial flight. At her pay grade, they all traveled commercial. She might meet someone. Probably not at the conference itself, but in Rio perhaps. And after her break-up with Ken, she was more than ready for a little adventure. She clicked on her calendar and saw that the next few days were already jam packed. If she was going to carve out some time to go shopping for new clothes for the trip, she'd probably have to go at night. At least most of the decent stores were open until 9:00. Then again, why did she have to buy new clothes to go out of town when no one in Brazil has seen her old ones?

"Connie, could you get me a quick translation for this?" Jessica asked her administrative assistant, who sat at the desk right outside her door. The AAs for Jess and two other members of the council shared space in a reception room there on the second floor of the Executive Office Building, the ornate Empire structure built back in the 1800s to house the Army, Navy, and War Departments as they were then known. The council's suite of offices was right down the hall from some of the Office of Management and Budget staff. Every time Jess got into the elevator or scrambled down the stairs, it seemed that she was surrounded by more economists. At least in Brazil she'd be surrounded by ambassadors and Chiefs of Mission.

"Sure, Jess," Connie said grabbing the invitation. "I saw that one come in and wondered about it myself. Guess you're heading south in a couple of days. Do you know when you want to leave? I'll need to arrange your flights."

"See if you can get a final agenda, and then we'll figure it out. Oh, and double check the hotel where Hal was going to stay and switch the names."

"I'm on it," the young woman said. "Oh, one more thing." Connie poured through a stack of papers from her inbox and pulled out a memo from the State Department. "Looks like you won't be traveling alone. This just came in."

CHAPTER SEVEN

Rio de Janeiro, Brazil

Funk music rhythms blared from boosted sound systems throughout the shanty town known as Rocinha, the South Zone favela on the outskirts of Rio's luxury neighborhood. Dilapidated tin structures painted red, white, brown, and green cascaded down the hillside intertwined with dirt and pock-marked concrete roads. The juxtaposition of fancy high rises and luxurious hotels echoed the national income divide between rich and poor in this South American country. Here, in one of the most crowded areas, home to over 150,000 souls, the constant beat of the recorded drums drowned out some of the gunfire flashing between the military police and members of the Amigos dos Amigos drug trafficking gang. The name, Friends of Friends, seemed odd to outsiders who associated this gang with nothing but terror, greed, addiction, and coercion. Yet, insiders knew that membership meant acceptance, support, and most of all money. Big money.

Children were recruited first as errand boys. The dealers called them avioezinhos, or "little messengers." They knew their way around the huts and alleyways and could skirt the bustling traffic to elude the police whenever they came to raid the place. As teenagers, they became lookouts, or fogueteiros, setting off fireworks to warn of any kind of government or rival gang encroachment on their territory. If they were clever enough, they might work up to a job on the inside of the boca de fumo where most of the drug sales are negotiated. But once in, they could never get out, and today they were fighting for their lives.

All along the roadways, women shielded babies behind flimsy doors as military helicopters buzzed over the masses of thin roofs while dozens of teenagers, clad in shorts and ragged T-shirts piled onto motorcycles and scooters and careened around corners, out of range of the armored cars.

"Do you think we can hold 'em off, boss?" Domingo shouted to their leader as he shoved another round into his weapon and hoisted it up to eye level.

"We've got guns, grenades, car bombs. And we knew when they were coming. Our best people are in place," Pazio called out.

"We knew? How'd we know this time, Paz?"

Pazio liked his nickname because it meant *peace*. Why not be known as the peacemaker even though he spent most of his time figuring out ways to one-up their rival gangs, the Comando Vermelo and the Terceiro Comando. But today, it looked like the government was out in full force to try and rein in his beloved Amigos. At least he had developed allies within their ranks. "Our contact," he shouted over the din. "One of the new police informants we recruited."

"Oh, yeah. So, he gave you the tip off?"

"That's how we knew to round up all our fogueteiros."

"Yeah, you said to text the lookouts, but I wasn't sure how you got the word."

An armored car rattled down an alley right toward their hideout. "We knew when, but seems like they know where," Domingo said, aiming his gun.

"Wait," Pazio said. "Don't fire yet, you'll give away our location. We gotta move." They inched their way past graffiti-stained walls and into a concrete bunker. Running to the back, they lifted a panel in the floor and scrambled down a long ladder. "They may know where some of our crack labs are. Let 'em have those. We'll just replace them. And even if they manage to round up some of our people, we can replace them too," Paz bragged as he hurried down the steep incline.

"That's for sure," Domingo agreed, snagging his T-shirt on a splinter in the ladder. "Damn ladders. Gotta be replaced. Ripped my best shirt on this one."

"Shut up, you fool. With the money I pay you, you can buy all the shirts in the favela."

Outside, gang members on their motorcycles signaled to each other, aiming for secret exits not yet cut off by the military. Despite zigzagging their way through the crowded streets and getting a few shots off at the advancing police, several of the officers fired on the cavalcade, picking off half a dozen riders who crashed into walls and sent residents screaming down the roadway. Not only were the gang members currently outnumbered and out-gunned, but the police were better protected in their charcoal gray uniforms, helmets, and flak jackets with signature blue and white patches on their sleeves.

A half-dozen military police crouched down behind a tank in front of a dilapidated building where windows were boarded up with plastic and planks of wood. "It's one of the crack labs," an officer said. "We have to get inside, but we don't know if their guys are in there or not." He craned his neck, leaning around the side of the vehicle. Nobody fired. He jumped back. "Cover me, just in case," he barked and motioned to four others to follow him. Two raced to the front. Two others went to the back while the men behind the tank kept up an unrelenting barrage of fire over their heads. Once in place, the man in charge blasted through the door and rushed inside.

No one was there. "Must have known we were coming," he muttered as he surveyed the equipment set up on long tables jutting out from the wall. On the other side were shelves stacked with large packages of white powder wrapped in plastic. "Looks like the mother lode," he said as the other officers came through the back door. "Get this stuff out of here. Must be worth millions."

They cleaned out the lab, loading the cocaine along with bags of marijuana onto waiting army trucks as the gunfire quieted down. Another contingent of police rounded up some two dozen young men and marched their handcuffed prisoners through the street to a checkpoint at the edge of the makeshift city.

As things quieted down, people started to come out of their huts and apartments, looking around at the retreating prisoners, the convoys filled with illegal drugs and the police packing up their weapons. A group of children ventured out. When they saw that the fight was over, they ran to the end of the street and climbed over the wall of the house where they knew some of the big drug dealers lived. They jumped in a concrete swimming pool, splashed, and shouted, "Now we can swim here. They're gone."

Mothers and fathers started to cheer, clap, and finally break into song. They had been plagued by the violent gangs for so long, they had almost given up hope. Sounds of the celebration reverberated throughout Rocinha and echoed deep beneath the streets, just as it had after every raid in all the favelas.

"What's that singing?" Domingo called out to Pazio as they crept through a storm drain.

"Sounds like a party," his boss replied. "Gun fight is over. They're leaving now. That's why people are happy."

"Happy because the police are leaving or happy because they staged the raid in the first place?" Domingo asked, crawling at a slow pace toward a juncture where they knew they could climb out on the edge of town.

"Who cares? They're gone, and we're safe. They hit across town last week. Well, you know that. And they'll probably be back in a little while."

"Yeah, but why now?" Domingo asked, pushing aside a pile of refuse in his path.

"Couple of things," Pazio explained. "The Olympics are coming up. They think that tourists won't come unless they stop us and cut down on the crime rate. Fat chance."

"That's not gonna happen," Domingo replied. "You said it yourself. We'll recruit, rebuild, regroup and be back in action in weeks. And next time they try it, we'll be even better prepared. We still have a couple of labs they haven't found yet. Besides, with new informants we'll be ready."

"And not just police. We have another high-level source tipping us off too," Pazio said. "Only trouble is that one costs us a lot, but it's worth it. And with that shipment of guns and grenades we're getting from Nicaragua, we'll be set."

"Right," his lieutenant agreed.

"There will be more raids, though we might even be able to control the timing of some of them. They probably think they have to make a good show of it right now," Pazio said.

"Yeah? Why right now? You said a couple of things. What besides the Olympics?" Domingo asked.

"I hear there's some big conference coming to town. Some high-level government people from the States and other places. But that's gonna be good for us."

"How can that be good?"

"Because the police will be so busy protecting those folks, they won't be able to pay attention to what we're doing. Stay tuned."

CHAPTER EIGHT

Georgetown

"Welcome, ladies, to Kwedar's Special Session," the sous chef said. "What better way to enjoy your Saturday evening? You're not out spending money on fancy entrees at some over-priced restaurant. You're learning to create your very own dinners at a very reasonable price. And at the end of tonight's demonstration, we will all gather to enjoy the delicious meal that our head chef will now demonstrate. So, I present to you Chef Kwedar."

Jessica and Kay settled down on bar stools along with a half dozen other women of varying ages lined up in front of a galley kitchen complete with an eight-burner gas stove, double-wide refrigerators, four ovens, chopping blocks, and a long stainless steel counter. Rows of pots and pans hung from an overhead rack, and a cache of knives, spoons, and ladles lay within easy reach.

"Good evening," the chef said, bowing politely to his new audience. His tall white hat was perched slightly off center, giving the young man a kind of jaunty, casual look. "Now, since this is a new class, we will begin with a very simple coq au vin. It's not very French, as you will see, but I like the name."

As he began to gather onions, celery, parsley and a few other spices, Jess whispered, "Glad you talked me into getting out tonight. I've been so slammed ever since I got word about that OAS meeting in Brazil, I haven't had time for anything, much less eating something decent."

"I know," Kay said, "I want to hear all about that. I'd love to get sent to Brazil all expenses paid. I mean, how great is that?"

"I'm not so sure," Jess said. "When I first saw the memo from Hal with his idea that I take a few days off and go over to Rio and actually have some fun, I thought it could be terrific."

"And?"

"And then I got the second memo about some State Department functionary they're sending to tag along."

"Who's that?"

"Some guy named Bill Black," Jess said, dismissively. "And get this. He's an Assistant Protocol Officer."

"Protocol?" Angela chuckled. "So what's their problem. They don't think you know what fork to use at a state banquet?"

At that moment, Chef Kwedar speared several chicken breasts with a large fork and placed them in a skillet of melted butter and chopped onions. "And, so, ladies, we begin by browning the chicken along with the onions in a small amount of butter, until all are a golden brown."

"Why do they always just serve chicken breasts?" Jess asked in a low voice.

"That's true. You never see dark meat on a menu," Kay said.

"There must be a warehouse somewhere filled with legs and thighs," Jess said. "Oh well, at least whatever he's doing over there smells good."

"Okay, so what else do we know about this Bill Black character?" Kay asked in a whisper, leaning toward her friend.

"I have no idea. I hardly need a keeper or a babysitter, especially some civil servant from the State Department. He's probably a GS-15 with a desk job who just wants a vacation in Brazil too, and he wangles himself a slot in the delegation to take care of place cards or something. I can't believe they fell for it. Then again, they've got so many people over there, they probably don't have a clue what half of them do anyway."

"It does seem kind of odd," Kay said. "I mean sure, the Chief of Protocol goes on the big official trips with the president and the Secretary of State, but why would they send one of their other officers to an OAS conference?"

"I have no idea," Jess replied. "But it looks like we'll be traveling together. Connie said she arranged my itinerary, and this character called to be sure we'd be on the same flight. And here I thought I was going to get away by myself for a while."

"And now we add one cup of chicken consommé, one cup of dry white wine, two stalks of chopped celery, a handful of parsley here in this bowl that we've cut up with our scissors," the chef declared. "We sprinkle the celery and parsley over the mixture, along with a small amount of sea salt, pepper, and a smidgeon of basil. Then we put the lid on, turn the flame down and let this golden mixture simmer for the next forty-five minutes." He then reached for another large saucepan.

"I know you said you could go to Rio," Kay said in a low voice. "You can still do that. I mean, this dude, whoever he is, wouldn't follow you there, would he?"

"I sure hope not," Jess said. She gazed over at the young chef and grinned. "You know, that guy is kind of cute. I wonder if they have anybody like that in Brazil."

"Come to think of it, he does sort of look the part with all that dark hair and those deep brown eyes," Kay said.

"And that's what I'm thinking about. Maybe meeting someone on this trip," Jess said with a slightly dreamy look.

"Could be. It happens in the movies all the time. Well, the Hallmark movies anyway," Kay said. "And that would be quite a contrast to what you told me about your break-up with the Ken-Doll."

"Mm hm," Jess murmured. "I saw that movie, or, rather, I lived that movie, and sure didn't like the ending." They both turned back toward the stove. "I do like the smells over there, though."

"Now along with our chicken dish, we'll be serving our special rice pilaf made with the finest angel hair pasta, broken into tiny pieces along with rice and again, our consommé. We'll be serving this with a salad of

Boston lettuce, arugula, cherry tomatoes, bits of gorgonzola, and a mild balsamic vinaigrette dressing and some crunchy, toasted French bread. We'll top it off with a surprise dessert that I'm sure you ladies will love."

"If it doesn't have *chocolate* in the title, I don't want to waste the calories," Kay said under her breath.

"I'm with you there," Jess said.

"And no matter who's with you in Brazil, just figure out a lot of different ways you can escape from the Black eagle eye."

Jessica smiled at her friend and nodded her approval of that particular suggestion.

CHAPTER NINE

Dulles Airport

"Eleven thousand acres and you'd think they'd have a restaurant. An Olive Garden maybe. And more than one gas station. Is that too much to ask? Can you believe, with all these taxis and people wanting to fill up before they turn in their rental cars, that this station basically has a monopoly? Somebody's gotta be paying off somebody," the driver lamented.

"Hmmmm?" Jessica looked up from the notes she was reading in the back seat of the taxi. She was on her way to Dulles Airport, and he was still mumbling.

"One gas station?" she echoed from the back seat.

"Yeah," he said. "We gotta go over there to fill up, and there's always a line. Big line. And then if we need a receipt—an' we all need a receipt, right?—it says, 'See attendant inside.' So, we gotta leave the car, go inside, and then we gotta wait in another line while all the guys are buyin' lottery tickets. So, everybody's hittin' the horns cause they wanna move up in the line outside. What a mess."

"Yes, I can see that would be a problem," she said, glancing at her watch to check how much time she had before her flight to Brazil.

"And then when I drop you off, you think I could pick up another passenger and get the fare back to DC? No. Why? Because all those gray cabs got a monopoly on that. An' if I stop to get someone, I could lose my medallion. Then there's the whole Uber thing. We're fightin' that too but getting nowhere. Can you believe this place?"

"Huh? I guess not," she said absent-mindedly.

"You guess not?" the cabbie asked, looking at her reflection in the rear-view mirror. "Hey, don't mind me. Just spoutin' off about this particular airport. Now, you take your Reagan National Airport, at least it's not so bad. And Union Station? That's the best. People can come out the side and get a cab. Well, anyway, here's your gate." He leaned down and popped the trunk. "I'll get your bags."

Jess rummaged in her large shoulder bag for her wallet, extracted seventy dollars and got out of the car. She paid the driver, adding a good tip since it sounded like he was having a rough day. Then again, hers had been bad enough, showing up at the White House as usual at dawn, attending the senior staff meeting in Hal's place, clearing a number of presidential remarks on the economy and the new cap gains legislation, sitting in on a planning session with some OMB staff, promising Kay she'd keep in touch, and returning a long list of calls before racing home to do some last minute packing for her overnight flight. She contemplated the idea of sleeping most of the way. Now, there was a pleasant thought.

She raised the handle on the large roller bag and began to drag it inside. It was too big to fit into the overhead bin. She'd have to check it. She usually traveled with a simple carry-on, but this time she needed several outfits. After all, she had to be fairly dressed up for the conference sessions, so she had packed a number of choices including her favorite navy blue suit and silk blouse.

There was an opening cocktail party and a final banquet. She had a black formfitting cocktail dress with a V-neckline and sheer long sleeves for the first reception along with a pair of four-inch strappy heels. She packed an aqua full-length sheath for the big dinner. She took along casual shoes she could wear to walk around the city if she got a few breaks, along with a bathing suit, and completely different combinations for her planned trip to Rio.

She didn't have space in her briefcase for much more than her computer, charger and files, so she had carefully put all of her cosmetics, hairbrushes, toiletries, and a few pieces of inexpensive jewelry in a couple of makeup cases and shoved them along the sides of the big suitcase.

As she stood in the check-in line that snaked around several stanchions and then moved to another line, she knew that her White House Diplomatic Passport would help get her through the entry lines in Brazil, but she still had to go through security here.

She dutifully took off her shoes, stashed her computer, purse and jacket in a bin and proceeded through the magnetometer. It went off. An agent waved her over to the side. "What's the matter?" she asked as she watched her computer and purse move out and roll away from the X-ray machine. She frantically looked over and caught the eye of the young woman who had been standing behind her.

"Could you keep an eye on my stuff?" she implored.

The lady saw Jess's predicament, smiled, and said, "Got it. No problem. Been there myself on my last flight. And look over there. They're even patting down on that little old lady. The one with all the gray hair. You'd think TSA had better things to do, right?"

"Right on," Jess replied. "What do they think she'll do? Hold up the plane with a knitting needle?"

"What's this about a knitting needle?" an agent asked in a gruff tone of voice.

"Nothing," Jess said.

"We don't allow no knitting needles or anything else that's sharp on these flights," he said, motioning to a female guard and pointing at Jessica.

The wand made a buzzing noise when it hit Jessica's wrist. "Oh darn. The watch. I forgot about it."

"Well, you better be more careful next time," the guard admonished.

"Yes, ma'am," Jessica said. She was anxious to get out of the area and reclaim her purse, briefcase, and shoes. She hurried over to the woman standing patiently next to the table, guarding their possessions. "Oh, thank you so much. This is all such a hassle."

"You said it. Makes you wish you could afford Net Jets or one of those, right?"

"In my dreams," Jess said, tossing her purse over her shoulder and grabbing the briefcase. "Well, maybe I'll have a few dreams on the flight tonight."

"On one of the all-nighters, huh?"

"Yes. Brazil."

The woman sighed. "Oh, I went there once. Met the most gorgeous man in Rio."

"You're kidding," Jess exclaimed. "I'm going to Rio too. At least I think I can get there for a weekend."

"Well, keep your eyes open, kiddo. There are a lot of good-looking dudes down there." She turned away and said, "Good luck with that."

Is that what she'd have? Good luck? For the first time all day, Jessica had the beginning of a real smile on her face.

An hour and ten minutes after leaving the talkative cab driver, she was finally leaving the security area and heading for her gate. She found a seat by the windows and was grateful for a bit of time alone. But not really alone. The area began to fill up with families jabbering in Portuguese; dozens of teenagers wearing jeans, T-shirts, and backpacks who looked like they were heading to some sort of camp; and a sprinkling of business types carrying large lattes in one hand and copies of *Barron's*, *Wall Street Journal*, or *Financial Times* in the other.

She reflected that she had been asked to write an article for *The Economist*. On this trip, she was hoping she could gather ideas for a piece in *Cosmopolitan*. In her position, there was no chance she'd be allowed to publish in that one, though.

Finally, her flight was called. She saw that she would be in the first group to board. Figures. She had a seat toward the back of the plane. Even White House aides didn't get first-class treatment on international flights. Not with all the recent budget cuts. She headed down toward the door, smiled at the flight attendant and waited while other passengers stuffed suitcases, duffel bags, coats, even a guitar into the overhead racks. She found her seat and settled in. Now, maybe she could relax and study a bit, or even read the novel she had downloaded to her Kindle.

"How do you do? You must be Dr. Tanner. I'm Bill Black from the State Department," he said, reaching out to shake her hand.

"How do you do?" Jessica thought. *Who says "how do you do" anymore? Oh, right, the protocol guy.* She looked up from her aisle seat in row twenty-four and shook hands with the tall, dark-haired man. He looked to be about six-foot-one with broad shoulders and deep brown eyes. His nose was slightly crooked. It seemed like he might have been in a fight as a child. It gave his face a slightly off-balanced look, and yet the features came together in a somewhat attractive combination. "Oh, did they give you the middle seat? Here, I'll let you in."

"Thank you, Jessica. May I call you Jessica?"

"Uh, sure," she said, shoving her shoulder bag under the seat in front of her and getting up from her aisle seat. "They sure don't give you much room on these fights," she muttered.

"No, unfortunately not," Bill said as he stowed a carry-on bag in the one remaining space in the overhead. "Looks like all of us staff members have to be mindful of the deficits and remain frugal."

"Frugal? Right. Frugal." *Now he's talking like an economist. Might as well try to be nice, though.* "So, Bill, what brings you to an OAS conference?"

He settled back in his seat and turned to face her. "Oh, I do a number of foreign trips to help our embassies with events, ceremonies, seating charts. That sort of thing," he said amiably.

Seating charts, I knew it. "But why did you specifically ask to be on my flight? I'm not exactly the highest-ranking person on this trip, you know. Why aren't you traveling with the Secretary of State?"

"The Secretary left yesterday with a number of assistants. Then when we saw that you were going down today, alone, the Brazil Desk suggested that I go with you. Try to keep an eye on things. Street crime, you know."

"Then you're my, what? Appointed escort or something?" she asked, arching one eyebrow.

"Well, I didn't mean it that way," he said apologetically. "My department simply felt I might be useful to you during your travels."

"I appreciate your concern but once we get there, I'm sure I'll be fine. After all, we're staying at the Royal Tulip Hotel, which is close to Alvorada Palace. I mean, it's not like I'll be in some dangerous inner-city shantytown or something. Besides, I'll be pretty busy. And, as you said, you'll be involved with embassy events." She was trying to set some ground rules for this guy. If he persisted in hanging around, she'd just have to figure out a way to get off on her own. For now, at least she'd try to be civil. "So, Bill, how did you get into a protocol job anyway?"

"Ladies and gentlemen," the flight attendant interrupted, "please take your seats and fasten your seat belts. The captain has informed us that we are ready for take-off, so may I draw your attention to the small screens where you will see our safety video. After we reach cruising altitude, we will begin our beverage service."

"This is going to be a pretty long flight," Bill said when the video was over, "so I guess we should get acquainted. You asked about my position. I suppose it all started when I went to Cornell and got my degree in Hotel Management. I always thought it would be nice to run a Ritz Carlton or a Four Seasons someday. In places like that you have to deal with a lot of foreign visitors. So having real world experience with protocol issues enhances the resume," he said.

As she glanced over and took in his buttoned-up shirt and perfectly pleated slacks, she wondered if he could be another Ken type. She was hoping to meet someone exciting on this trip. Instead, she got some bureaucrat who's working on seating charts. And as he said, it was going to be a long flight. She would just have to make pleasant conversation, if that was possible. "Well then, how do you know about all of the rules? I mean, do they teach that stuff at Cornell?"

"Some of it, of course," he replied. "There are a lot of books we read. The bible of the industry, as we say, is by McCaffree and Innis. It explains that the term 'protocol' is from the Greek word 'protokollen.' You see, 'protos' means 'the first' and 'kolla' means 'glue.' The whole idea, back in history, referred to the piece of paper glued to the front of an important document. That gave it authenticity. Think of the seal of a Notary Public."

"Okay. There was a seal. That doesn't give us rules, though," Jess said, trying to look interested.

"Oh, the rules of protocol developed over many years. For example, John Quincy Adams said that common sense and consideration should be the basis for protocol, and so it was. Now the French and the British courts developed a lot of rules," Bill said, giving her his most studious look.

"Like bowing to royalty and all of that, I guess," Jess remarked.

"And one of our jobs is to make sure that our citizens don't bow when it's not appropriate."

"Guess I shouldn't curtsy then?" Jess quipped.

Bill chuckled, "Not in Brazil."

"You said you had to work on seating charts," Jess said. "How do you figure those out?"

"Now that is extremely important," Bill said solemnly. "The process started at the Congress of Vienna in 1815. They wrote rules so that everyone would know where they should be. For example, if ambassadors or envoys are of the same rank, it then depends on the date and the hour that they presented their credentials. That's what we do today. We keep track of when any ambassador first met with the president."

"But what if one ambassador is from a much more important country to us than another one?" she asked.

"It doesn't matter," Bill replied. "The ambassadors and their countries too, of course, jealously guard their privileges. Now, when it comes to seating senators, for example, that depends on when their states were admitted to the Union. Did you know that Delaware was first, Pennsylvania second and New Jersey third? They all joined within days of each other in 1787, and we still abide by the rules at State Dinners."

"If you're planning a test, I may need flash cards for this tutorial," she said with a lame smile.

"No need. That's my job," he said in a serious tone.

"Okay, but what if the president wants to talk to some particular senator and he's from, uh, California or something?" Jess asked.

"Well, presidents have been known to change a few things, but the White House Social Secretary still tries to maintain proper decorum whenever possible."

How was she going to get through hours and hours with this man if she had to maintain proper decorum or even just listen to it? Was this the most boring person she'd had to deal with lately or what? His idea of something wild is probably renting a car with a manual transmission.

"May I offer you a cocktail? Juice? Coffee?" the flight attendant asked as he stopped his cart next to their seats.

Jess thought she could use a sleeping pill, but she said, "Uh yes, thank you. Not coffee. I'm going to want to get some sleep in a little while. How about some juice? Orange juice with a splash of cranberry if you have it, please?" she requested.

"Certainly. And for you, sir?"

"Just a coke. Regular," Bill said.

Bill listened to the request for juice with a splash of cranberry and figured she was probably the kind of woman who only ate arugula and imported sea bass. He leaned back, sipped his coke, and thumbed through a flight magazine. When he was assigned to this mess in Brasilia, he thought this woman would be his ticket to an easy explanation to Alicia about his getting away. Then the agency had told him that since this woman is an important White House official, he should try to shadow her all over the damn country because she was a perfect kidnapping target. At least, he thought, she was pretty attractive, even if she seemed kind of prickly. He stole another look and told himself that she was actually damned attractive. Nice hair. He had always liked that color. It looked natural too. And he didn't see too many of the light blond types around. He gave an inward laugh when he observed that she'd be a perfect FNC as the guys at the agency called the reporters on the Fox channels: Fox News Clones. But just like those women, this one is smart. He had read her bio about being a top economist. He wondered how long he could keep his cover.

CHAPTER TEN

Rio de Janeiro

The tall, wiry man adjusted his sunglasses and gazed out his balcony to the beach beyond. The blue waters dancing into shore on crested waves beckoned him, much as his mistress tempted him back into the luxurious bedroom. "Not now, Irena. You need to go. I have an important meeting," he commanded as he checked his Patek Philippe platinum wristwatch and calculated how much time he had to coax her out of the apartment and into a waiting limousine.

She appeared in the doorway wearing nothing but a sultry smile. "But, darling, you promised we would spend the afternoon together. And look how beautiful the sea is today. We could lie on the beach, and I could . . ." His shirt was open. She moved in next to him, leaned over and ran her finger down his deeply tanned chest.

He brushed her hand away. "I said, not now!"

"But . . ." she whined.

"Irena. You know the rules. I make the rules, and you follow them. That's rule number one. And when I say I have a meeting and tell you to leave, you leave!"

The young girl tossed her jet black hair back, flashed him a sad smile, and paused by the French doors to the bedroom. "You never said anything about a meeting. I thought we'd have the whole day."

"It just came up. And if you expect me to keep you in, as they say, the style you are accustomed to, you will get your things and get out of here so I can conduct my business."

"When will I see you again?" she pleaded. "It's so wonderful when you can get away and come to Rio to be with me. I love this penthouse you bought. It's like our own special hideaway. And besides, your wife won't be back from Recife for another week. We should have more days and . . . nights together, right?"

He checked the time again, walked to the door, and grabbed her arm. "That's rule number two. You don't talk about her. I told you I'd work out the divorce when the time is right. And rule number three is that *I* make the appointments. And don't you forget it."

"Let go. You're hurting me," she wailed as she wrenched away from his grip.

His face softened. "Sorry, baby, I just have a lot on my mind right now. As I said, I've got a meeting here in just a few minutes. Then we've got preparations for the big conference in Brasilia. Well, you wouldn't know much about that."

"What conference?" she asked, reaching for her silk lingerie that was strewn over a chaise longue in the corner.

"It wouldn't interest you. It's about trade issues. Things like that."

"Will there be any big parties? State dinners? Fun things?"

"Nothing that would include you, my dear. Besides, like I said, it's in the capital, not here in Rio. It's all very official. Now, hurry up. Sago is waiting downstairs to take you home." He turned, walked to the balcony railing, buttoned his shirt, and pulled out his iPhone, quickly dismissing her from his mind.

Irena sauntered into the bathroom, retouched her makeup, pulled a coral cotton dress over her head, and cinched its matching belt tightly around her tiny waist. She slipped on her sandals and grabbed her purse. When she emerged, she took one last look at the curtains billowing around the balcony doors, saw her lover checking for messages, and wondered what could be so important that he would give up an afternoon of lovemaking. She was about to leave but hesitated. Her curiosity got the better of her, and as she heard the buzzer, she quietly stepped into the kitchen, figuring she could leave by the service door and not be seen. Who was taking him away from her on this beautiful, balmy day? She left the kitchen door ajar and listened as he answered the intercom.

"Yes?"

"Pazio."

"Right on time, I see. Take my private elevator up. I'll enter the code."

The drug dealer breezed into the apartment and headed for the bar. He knew where it was. He had been here before. "Mind if I grab a beer?"

"Be my guest," the owner replied. "I see you have a briefcase for me."

"Yeah. Appreciate your help with that last raid. But they arrested a couple dozen of my guys and shut down one of my labs. Cost me millions. I'm not sure I can keep this up if my profits keep evaporating like this."

"You got your tip, not only from me but from others. I know about the others, but in my position, my information is more up to date."

Pazio wrenched off the top of the bottle and took a long pull. "A tip about timing. We didn't know they were bringing tanks, for God's sake. What's with the armored routine?"

"It's all part of our president's plan to clean up the city before the Olympics. We've talked about that. Just like you need your income, we need the revenue from those games. And I need to keep a piece of the stadium contract. Chill out. You'll be back in business in no time if I know you," the man said with a shrug.

Pazio plopped down on one of the long white couches and put his feet up on a heavy glass coffee table, making himself quite at home in the expensive apartment. "Let's get one thing straight. Brazil is the second-largest market for cocaine in the Americas. We're the major transit point for drugs heading for Europe, to say nothing about our supplies moving into the states through Mexico. And without my organization and our agreements with FARC, if they don't go overboard in their negotiations with the stupid Colombian government, the whole thing falls apart along with your hefty payments. As if you didn't know."

"Of course I know. Who do you think did the negotiation with Venezuela to facilitate the FARC connections in the first place? Quietly, of course, just as our negotiations must be kept quiet," the man said emphatically. "If the president or any of his people find out, all *our* deals, all our connections and all your so-called tips are off."

"You think our people would leak this? You have to be crazy! Why would we want to jeopardize our highest-level contact?" Pazio said, his voice rising.

"Keep it down," the man commanded. "I'm only telling you, *and* your people, that this is now a dicey situation. I have a balancing act to do here, and you're going to keep feeding me the commissions or I take my net and go home."

"Go home? With what you've told us so far? That net has too many holes in it. You'd never survive if you screw with us," Pazio said in a menacing tone. Then just as quickly, he looked up and a sinister smile spread across his face. "Now as you just said, let's talk business." He reached for the briefcase. "Here's your payment for the last tip. We need information on the next one, and it better be sooner. That way we can be better prepared."

"I don't want bloodshed next time," the man said.

"How are we supposed to fight back if your guys are shooting at us?"

"Just get out of the way. You'll figure it out."

"Easy for you to say. You're not the one facing the military." Pazio paused a moment and then added, "On the other hand, with enough warning, we can get our key people out and our supplies stashed. Yeah, it could work."

"And for an earlier warning, you will pay ten percent more," the man demanded.

Again, Pazio hesitated, glanced up at the ceiling and then back at his host. "Okay. Once more. But then I have to calculate our losses, how much more we can bring in from Colombia and how much it's going to cost us to open our satellite operations in Peru to get closer to FARC. That takes a lot of reals. So next time we meet, we renegotiate."

"Are you trying to screw with me, Pazio? You know damn well that I could give the order and shut you down completely," he said with exasperation.

"And that would gain you what?" the dealer asked in a quick rejoinder.

This time it was the host who stopped and thought for a long while. "Actually, I have another plan in the works. When I carry it out, you won't have to worry about the future. We'll both be in a better position to make profits."

"Plan? What plan?"

"Just wait. And watch." He paced over to the balcony doors and once again scanned the horizon. "I think we're finished here. You can take the beer with you. Just leave the briefcase."

Irena cautiously closed the kitchen door and slipped out the back exit.

CHAPTER ELEVEN

Aeroporto de Brasilia

Crowds of young students shifting their backpacks and chatting on cell phones collided with bell caps. Several mothers stumbled after young children who had eluded their grasp while the group of businessmen huddled together at the far end of the luggage carousels. Jessica tried to navigate through the throng, but by the time she got to the right area, people were three- and four-deep pushing and reaching for their bags.

She craned her neck while Bill stayed close by her side. "Wait. There's mine," she cried above the din. "Or maybe it isn't. Doesn't look like mine after all," she said with a sigh.

"What color is it?" Bill asked, hanging on to his own roller bag.

"It's black like everybody else's. But it has a red stripe by the handle. I could have sworn . . ." she pushed closer and looked again. "Yes, that's it. See?"

Bill inched forward, stepped in front of two young men, and reached out. "Sorry, guys," he said with a nod as he grabbed the handle. "Got it, Jess."

They moved away from the conveyer and Jessica stared at the suitcase. "It's . . . it's . . . all sunken in. How can it be sunken in?" she exclaimed.

"What do you mean 'sunken in'?" Bill asked, stopping to inspect the bag.

"I usually pack pretty light, but when I thought about all the meetings and then the dinners and going to Rio . . ."

"You're going to Rio?" Bill asked with a note of concern.

She muttered to herself, "Darn it." She hadn't meant to tell him about her plans to sneak away to Rio for a weekend. She certainly didn't need this guy hanging around when all she wanted was to spend time on the beach and perhaps in some of the better clubs. Who knew who she might meet on the way?

"What did you say?"

"Nothing. I just said I packed for a lot of different events, dinners, meetings. I just wasn't sure what I would need down here."

"But you said you were going to Rio," he said, eyeing her curiously.

"Oh, that was just an idea. I know it's a pretty place, but I'll probably be too busy to get away. We've got a pretty full agenda for the meeting." She looked at her luggage once again, motioning to a bank of chairs at the side of the cavernous room. "Can we go over there so I can check this before we go through customs?"

"Sure," Bill said, dragging the large case toward the wall. He hauled it up onto a chair, and Jessica unzipped it.

"You didn't lock it?" Bill asked.

"No. I was in a hurry, and I didn't think about that. I've never had a problem before," she said, peering inside.

"When you travel to other countries, you've got to lock your luggage and take lots of precautions," he said as if he were instructing a schoolgirl.

Okay, Mr. know-it-all world traveler. Do I really need a lecture now? Somebody has obviously broken into my luggage. "Oh no!" she exclaimed, rummaging through the layers of clothing and reaching down the sides. "My makeup cases are gone. All my cosmetics. All my brushes. My . . ."

"What did they look like?" Bill asked, glancing down at the clothing now in complete disarray.

"Look like?" she moaned. "It was all in a pair of nice travel bags. You know, like men have dopp kits. Mine were kind of like those, only bigger."

"That's what they look for," Bill said, raking his fingers through his hair.

"What do you mean? Who looks for cosmetics?" Jess questioned.

"It's not cosmetics, it's jewelry they want. Anything they can fence," Bill explained.

"But I don't have any fancy jewelry. And you can't fence lip gloss!" she said emphatically.

"Look, Jess, this happens all the time down here. Baggage handlers at the major airports only have a few seconds to target certain pieces of luggage, pieces that aren't locked by the way. They open them and grab any sort of leather case, anything enclosed that someone would use to carry special things. Like jewelry, electronics, things like that."

Jessica surveyed the open case, then hurriedly shoved the clothes back in place and zipped it up again. "So now I guess I'll have to file a complaint or something."

"Won't do any good," Bill said. "The airlines get tons of complaints all the time. Oh, you can go fill out a bunch of paperwork, but it won't get you anywhere." He checked his watch. "I think we should get out of here. I've got a lot to do, and I'm sure you do too."

"But what about the stuff they stole?" she asked in a plaintive voice.

He leaned down, took hold of the luggage handle, and pulled it back on the floor. "Go buy new stuff. The hotel probably has a shop with whatever you need. If they don't, there are tons of stores, malls. It's not like we're staying in a jungle."

Now he was talking to her like she was a complete imbecile. Of course she could go shopping. It's just that she wanted her own brands, her own brushes, her own everything. She heaved a sigh as she followed him to the customs inspectors. Would the hotel have what she wanted? She doubted it. Those little shops usually carried toothpaste and aspirin, and their other shops always had overpriced clothing. She was pretty sure they wouldn't have her makeup base or eye shadow. And if she had to go to some mall, she wondered if she could find a store where they had her brands and the clerks spoke English.

And on top of all that, here she was with this guy who had bored her to tears during the flight. Now he was spending his time making her feel like a naïve, stupid tourist. She knew she made a mistake by not locking her luggage, but she was in a hurry and hadn't thought about it at the time. Now she'd just have to figure out a way to replace everything. She really didn't need this, and as she glanced over at Bill, she figured she really didn't need him either. It was no fun having a bureaucrat hanging around all the time. If only she could just hit Control/Alt/Delete and make him disappear. But at least she still had her iPhone and her computer, both of which she had taken on board with her.

When they walked outside, Bill said, "I'm heading to our embassy for a meeting. What about you?"

"I'm going directly to the hotel."

"The Royal Tulip, right?" he asked. "I believe that's where our whole delegation is staying."

"Yes, I know." She turned toward the line of taxis and called over her shoulder, "Have a good one."

"Need help with that luggage?" Bill called out.

"No thanks. It rolls just fine." *And I'll be just fine as soon as I can get away from him.*

CHAPTER TWELVE

American Embassy—Brasilia

"Avenida das Nacoes, Embaixada Americana," he instructed the taxi driver. The man nodded and headed down a wide roadway. Whizzing past the myriad structures, Bill thought that the whole scene would be a great backdrop for a sci-fi movie. Not warm and inviting. More like eerie and supernatural.

The sky was clear, and the morning shone down, acting as a spotlight on a unique stage set. The capital city was amazing. Bill stared at the futuristic designs of the buildings. They looked like upside-down teacups or right side up saucers. Then there was the cathedral in the shape of Christ's crown of thorns and a National Congress that had inverted cupolas on the top. All of these had been built beside long stretches of parkland dotted with trees and ponds right in the center of town.

He had heard that the whole place was the wild idea of a nineteenth-century saint who decided that it would be a great scheme to build a city in the middle of nowhere. It took another century to get this one off the ground. Or get it started *in* the ground. They had chosen a well-known communist architect, Oscar Niemeyer, to create the designs. And what wild designs they were.

It then took another half century to become the bustling city that it is today. Putting it all together and moving the capital had left the government with an incredible debt. But now with the country's oil resources numbering in the hundreds of billions of barrels, Brazil was literally digging its way to becoming the fifth-largest economy. He thought that it just might get there by the time it hosted the Summer Olympics.

On his way to the American Embassy, Bill realized he was quite anxious to meet with Chet and find out if there had been more chatter detected since he left the States. He had kept in close touch on a secure line right up until their plane had taken off, but a number of the leading drug dealers and other shady characters were being monitored 24/7, so he knew there would definitely be an update.

The taxi dropped him at the front of an impressive building. He paid him in American dollars, which the driver was happy to accept. He walked up to the sleek low white structure, the first embassy built when Brazil moved its capital from Rio to Brasilia. Once inside the vast entryway, he checked in, moved though security, received his entry badge, and waited for an escort to take him up to his meeting.

"Mr. Black?" a dark-haired woman of about twenty-five, clad in a red skirt, matching blouse, and extremely high heels walked up to check his ID. "Come with me please."

He took in her outfit and marveled at how women could walk in those shoes all day long. He followed her to the elevator. When she hit the button for their floor, he remarked, "Beautiful day. How's the forecast?"

She replied, "Lovely and warm for the next several days. Usual for this time of year."

"Do you spend all your time in Brasilia, or do you get a chance to see the rest of the country?" he asked, trying to sound friendly, but not too friendly.

"Oh, we try to head over to Rio on weekends whenever we can get away. Brasilia is nice, but Rio has the beaches and the clubs, you know," she said with a half-smile.

He certainly did know, and that reminded him of Jessica's remark about packing for Rio. He wondered if she really meant to slip away from the conference at some point. He had seen the agenda and knew there was a break on Saturday and Sunday with a wrap-up session and press conference resuming on Monday. That was the night of the final banquet as well, hosted by the president and vice president. Jessica and all the other ministers would have to attend that one.

He had her itinerary, but only her flights to and from Brasilia. Would she take off for Rio during the break? He'd just have to keep an eye on her if he could get away himself. He knew that as a senior White House aide, she shouldn't go traipsing around Rio on her own with pickpockets and gangs all over the place. They had talked about that. Or at least some of it. Jess had said she didn't have any fancy jewelry, and that was a good thing because no tourist could walk down a boulevard wearing a gold chain around their neck without the locals taking it as an invitation to rip it off.

"Here we are, Mr. Black," the escort said.

Bill smiled and nodded his thanks. He pushed through the door and saw his contact waiting in a small office. Chet Osborn's official title was Cultural Attaché. But Bill and all the other agents on their team knew he was the Station Chief, a hardened CIA operative who had been assigned to a number of South American embassies during his long career. In his late thirties, he was in great shape and yet had an "everyman" look about him with medium height, medium brown hair, and medium brown eyes. When you were just sort of "medium" you could blend in with all sorts of groups. And with his fluent Spanish and Portuguese, that's exactly what he did. Chet got up from his desk and walked around to give Bill a warm handshake.

"Good to see you again. Sure got my hands full down here. Sit down and I'll get you up to speed on the latest. Oh, want an espresso?" Chet asked.

"No, thanks. Seems like you guys drink that stuff like water down here." He pulled a chair closer to the desk and took a notebook out of his briefcase. He saw that Chet still had that cool demeanor he had noted on his last trip. Cool and calm despite the fact he was the agency's man on the spot in this place. Chet had been in Brasilia the last two years, though he made frequent trips to Rio. He had cultivated a number of good contacts in both cities in their ever-present investigations into drug cartels, terrorist connections, even industrial espionage. He needed a bigger staff and more support, but the embassy only had so many slots, so Chet was glad to see someone who had the credentials and the training to help him out.

"How was your trip down?" Chet asked, thumbing through some papers.

"Basically a non-event, except for my traveling companion," Bill said.

"Yeah? Who was that? One of the economic types headed for the OAS conference?"

"Yep. A top economist from the White House."

"You're traveling with the big boys this time," Chet remarked.

"Not the big boys. The big girl," Bill said.

"Girl? Who was it?"

"Girl? Woman? My guess is late twenties, early thirties. Hard to tell. Supposed to be smart as hell, at least in her field. But I have to say, she was a bit irritating."

"Oh, one of those schoolmarm types, right?" Chet chuckled under his breath.

"No, couldn't say that," Bill said. "In fact, if I didn't know she was a delegate to an economic conference, I'd think she was a candidate in the Miss Universe contest."

Chet jerked his head up. "You lucky SOB! That good?"

"Well, to look at. It's her personality that's a problem."

"But if she's so smart," Chet ventured, "do you think she has any idea what you're doing down here?"

"Definitely not. We talked about protocol and seating charts."

Chet burst out laughing. "I don't know how you pull that off. Question is, how long can you keep it up?"

"I have no idea," Bill said with a shake of his head. "Looks like I'll have to spend more time with her too. When I left State, they said I should try to keep an eye on her because, with her rank and all, she could get in trouble on the streets."

"You got that one right," Chet agreed.

"But I'm here to work with you on this threat, not act like a bodyguard for that woman," he said with a disdainful look.

"I'm sure she'll be busy with all the ministers in town, so I wouldn't worry about it too much," Chet said. "We've got enough on our plate right now." He shoved a memo in front of Bill and pointed to a paragraph. "Look at this intercept we got of a call between Pazio and one of his suppliers."

Bill scanned the transcript. "It's about pay-back for all the raids in Rio." He read further. "Sounds like he's talking about the president," Bill said. "I saw some of these references back at Langley. When did you get this one?"

"About an hour ago," Chet said. "Right now, it's just a lot of chatter. Speculation. Threats. I've been working with palace security. They're trying to get a handle on it too. Beefing up his detail whenever he travels. But the man is all over the place giving speeches, cutting ribbons for new buildings. You name it, he's there. It's impossible to protect him everywhere. Besides, it's not like our Secret Service. Down here you have no clue who to trust anymore."

"Gotcha," Bill said. "What's our next move?"

"I've set up a meeting for the two of us with Palace Security along with a couple of other top staffers. It'll be later this afternoon at three." They went on to discuss the president's schedule for the next few days and whether they felt his security detail could handle it all. They analyzed what contacts they had inside the three major drug rings—Red Command, Third Command, and Friends of Friends—and also who might be trustworthy inside the Palace and who might be on somebody else's payroll.

Bill took notes and thought about the challenge of helping to protect the president of a country like Brazil, a man who was a good friend to the United States, someone who had encouraged a vibrant economy along with the opening of a bunch of trade deals throughout the hemisphere and was building a whole host of new stadiums and roads for the Olympics. He was even talking about special enterprise zones.

At the same time, he was cracking down on the drug gangs, ordering raids on their strongholds, rounding up their suppliers, runners, even their lookouts. He had run on a law-and-order platform along with the usual free enterprise message and was popular as ever. At least with most of the people.

As for crime, the president hadn't yet been able to reduce the murder rate in the major cities, but he was getting the Congress to dole out more money for the police and the military, and they both had beefed up presence, especially near the favelas. The CIA often had word of plots against various heads of state. They couldn't send agents all over the world to deal with the threats. But the relationship with Brazil was a special one, and when Chet had specifically asked for some backup, Bill Black drew the straw.

"When you talk about a threat against the President of Brazil, I keep hearing that he's a good guy and he supposedly has a special relationship with our president," Bill said. "But I get the sense that there's more to it. I mean, more reasons for our involvement here. Anything I should know?"

Chet cleared his throat, leaned back in his chair, and said, "Yeah, there is. Hardly anyone knows this, but back when our President was in college . . ."

"Georgetown, you mean?" Bill asked.

"Right. Undergrad. He was on the Crew."

"I knew that. He rowed. I did too," Bill said.

"Turns out Roberto Mendez was a student there at the same time."

"That just means they knew each other in school, and that both went on to be presidents of countries. All of that is in the bios," Bill said.

"But what is *not* in the bios," Chet explained, "is that one night they were out drinking together. They evidently got pretty smashed. Both were underage. They may have been smoking pot too."

"Bad combo," Bill said, shaking his head.

"You know that better than anyone," Chet said. "Our guys tell me that they took a scull out on the river. It was windy. They never should have been out there."

"Jeez!" Bill said. "What happened?"

"Word is that the boat flipped, and Mendez was the better swimmer. He actually saved our president's life. Or at least we think so."

"Sounds like he's forever in Mendez's debt," Bill said. "No wonder he wants us to get involved with this whole threat scenario."

"You got it," Chet confirmed.

"That sure raises the stakes." Bill looked at his watch. "Are we about done here? Until 3:00 that is?"

"I guess so. But first . . ." Chet looked down, opened his bottom drawer and reached for the weapon. He handed over a Glock. "Here you go. Obviously, you couldn't travel with your own. This should do fine." He then handed Bill some extra clips. "When you go into the Palace or any other facility down here, flash your creds, and they'll let you bypass security. Well, you probably remember that from last time."

"Sure. Got it." Bill stashed the gun and the ammunition in his briefcase. "Thanks for this. Hope I don't need it, though."

"You probably won't. We just like the Boy Scout motto around here," Chet said with a grin.

"Never made Eagle Scout," Bill said, returning the look. "But I did read the Rule Book."

CHAPTER THIRTEEN

Royal Tulip Hotel—Brasilia

Jessica was overwhelmed by the size of the hotel. She'd never seen anything quite like it, surely nothing in Washington or New York. Or even out West. The Royal Tulip Hotel was gigantic, with several low buildings five or six stories high, stretching in graceful arcs along Paranoá Lake. Some of the wings were gray, and others were bright red, which she didn't think she'd seen on a commercial building before. These were sleek, metallic and glass structures that looked more like new age office structures than a fancy hotel complex.

As she strolled through the lobby, she saw red and black tables and lounge chairs, a gray and white stone floor with strategically placed plants that were all so perfectly proportioned they looked fake. She touched one and realized they were real. A shop featured snacks, the ever-present espresso, but alas, no makeup that looked familiar.

After she toured the place, she was going to have to ask someone how to get to the nearest department store or mall. Then she'd have lunch and spend the rest of the afternoon studying her notes for the conference. She had a bit of time since the first session got underway at a cocktail reception that evening.

She found a café with a strange ceiling made of multi-colored panels, brown tables, and silver metal chairs. On another level she found an auditorium, more like an IMAX theater, where it appeared at least five hundred people could watch a program. The ballroom was twice as large.

But the best part of the place was the exquisite pool. She'd never seen such an odd shape. It looked like pieces of a jigsaw puzzle painted in two shades of bright blue with curved edges meandering between patio areas set with yellow and white chaises and white umbrellas. Back inside she wanted to check out the fitness room. She figured they would have all the latest gadgets and machines, and she wasn't disappointed. This room was also huge. About five times bigger than the health club she belonged to back in DC.

The one thing that was not gigantic in this building was her bedroom. It was so simple it was almost monastic with its stark grey walls and simple plain white bed coverings. She doubted that monks had flat screen TV sets though.

When she finished her tour, she wandered back to the lobby and found a pleasant-looking young woman behind the registration desk. "I wonder if you could help me," Jessica began.

"Yes? What may I do for you?" the clerk said in perfect English.

"I had a problem with my luggage when I arrived. Someone stole my makeup cases and all my supplies."

"Oh, I am so sorry. But I have heard of this happening on occasion."

"Yes, well, where could I go to buy some good cosmetics? I mean, are there any stores nearby? And what about a taxi?"

"But of course. Taxis should be waiting just outside the front door to take you anywhere you would like to go. Our concierge usually tells our guests about places to see, but I know about shopping," she said with a smile. She reached under the desk and pulled out a map of the city. She pointed and said, "Now the Patio Brasil is in the central quadrant. It has over two hundred stores and thirty restaurants."

"Wow," Jessica replied. "And I thought Tyson's Corner was big."

"Pardon?"

"Oh, that's just a big shopping mall back in the States," Jess said.

"We have a larger one in the Guara area that has about three hundred fifty shops. But I think you might want to go to Planalto Central. It's closer, and they should have everything you need."

"Hi, how's it going?" Bill said, crossing the lobby to stand next to Jessica.

Oh, great! Him again, she thought. *If I throw a stick, I wonder if he'll fetch it?* "Um, hi. I thought you'd be in meetings or something," she stammered as the clerk moved away to answer the phone.

"Just had one," Bill said. "What are you up to?"

Why couldn't she get rid of this guy? He was showing up like a bad penny, and all she wanted to do was take her own money and go shopping. Alone. "Just getting some ideas about places to shop. For my cosmetics, remember?"

"Oh, sure," he said. "You leaving now?"

"Maybe," she hedged.

"Well, I saw a taxi outside. In fact, there are a bunch of them. Might as well go with you. I want to pick up a few things myself."

What's with this guy? Can't he just go about his job and make out place cards or something? "Oh, I'll just take off on my own, if you don't mind. I doubt if you'd want to look at makeup and things like that." Jess grabbed the map, shifted her shoulder bag, and headed for the door.

He followed her. "No problem. Might as well share a cab," he said.

Now she was feeling smothered. She had an odd memory of the way she felt the last time she went to the dentist. They had taken X-rays and put that heavy lead apron over her. It went all the way up to her neck, but at least they took it off after a few minutes. Now she was probably saddled with this boring guy for an hour or two.

As they pushed through the lobby door and waved to a waiting taxi, she felt a blast of warm air. A nice contrast to the air conditioning inside. She looked over and started scrutinizing Bill again. She had to admit that he wasn't bad looking. In fact, her friends might even call him sort of a hunk. The type who'll spend his downtime here working out in the health club. But there are lots of guys who look decent. She just wished he had a bit of personality. She suddenly remembered a hilarious video she saw on YouTube. It was an ancient clip from the Johnny Carson show where the comedian George Gobel said, "Did you ever get the feeling that the world is a tuxedo and you're a pair of brown shoes?" She glanced down. Sure enough, Bill was wearing brown shoes. The rest of his outfit was okay. Khaki slacks, blue blazer. That's the way Ken had always dressed. It didn't make *him* interesting either.

They sat back in the car, and Jess told the driver to go to Planalto Central. That had sounded like her best bet. And if she could find what she needed, she could get back to her room or maybe take her notes out to the pool and be rid of this guy.

She thought that after her break-up with Ken, she might have an exciting adventure. Some place. Somewhere. She hadn't met any other men in Washington that turned her on. And she certainly hadn't seen anyone the least bit intriguing on this trip. Not yet anyway. In this particular game she was throwing nothing but gutter balls.

A blistering sun reflected off the metal roof of the arch-shaped building where scores of shoppers were hustling in and out. It was massive. Everything in this city seemed to be massive. Jess had no idea where she should start. Bill paid the driver, and they walked inside. "Pretty impressive, huh?" Bill said.

Jess let her eyes wander the expansive walls to a set of posters on the side. She pointed at one and shook her head.

"What?" Bill asked, following her gaze.

"Look over there," Jess said. "They're advertising 'Eco-Hummer Tours through the Amazon.' Isn't that kind of an oxymoron?"

Bill stared at the poster and chuckled. "Yes. I believe they're supposed to be protecting it, not running hummers through it. Did you know that the Amazon produces more than twenty percent of the world's oxygen supply?"

"Well, aren't you just a fount of information?" Jess said, regarding him with a skeptical eye. "I thought your statistics were all gleaned from protocol books."

"Oh, not really," he replied. "I like to bone up on all sorts of interesting data."

Interesting? He sure has a unique definition of it.

"For example," Bill continued in his usual innocent-sounding tone, "Brazil got its name from the nut. Not the other way around."

And who's the nut around here now? Me, I guess, for putting up with this nonsense. Jess checked her watch and said, "I don't really have time to waste right now. I've got to find the right stores. Now that we're both here, why don't you just go do your own shopping? I'm sure I'll see you later."

"I'd just as soon go with you," Bill said. "You never know what kinds of street gangs might be hanging around. Especially in a place with high-end shops."

"I'm sure there's plenty of security around," Jess said as she began to march away. She looked over her shoulder and added, "You don't need to get your worry beads out."

Bill watched her trotting away and noticed a trio of young men turning to eyeball the gorgeous blond walking swiftly down the center hallway. *Sure, guys can't help but stare at a beautiful woman. It's in our DNA. But down here, how do you tell the lookers from the robbers?* He watched as Jess headed into a small shop on the right. He stayed back, kept an eye on the door and waited.

It would make my job a lot easier if she'd loosen up a little bit. Relax or something. Maybe show a little humor. Then again, she's an economist. Guess I've never heard of a humorous economist. Talk about oxymorons.

While he waited, he remembered her saying she wouldn't take long. That means he shouldn't have any trouble getting out of here and making his important meeting at 3:00. He leaned against a wall but was startled when he heard a scream and then a cry, "Ajuda me, ajude me." *Help me, help me.* The three young punks had just shoved a middle-aged woman down on the stone floor. One was pulling her purse away while she struggled to hang on to it. He slapped and shoved her. She scooted back and tried valiantly to fight him off. The second one was pushing her against the wall and reaching for her necklace. The third guy looked like he was standing guard to ward off anyone who might come to her aid.

Bill raced ahead, closing the distance in several strides. "Lert-la ir, voce empurroes." *Let her go, you jerks*, he shouted out in a menacing voice. He had the Glock in his shoulder holster under his jacket, but he wasn't about to brandish it in a crowded mall.

"Ah e? Voce nao pode nos parar. Se perder." *Oh yeah? You can't stop us. Get lost*, one of them yelled back.

When Bill got close, one of the robbers jumped out and took a swipe at his jaw. Bill dodged the blow and swung back, hitting the guy in the nose, just hard enough to knock him off balance and cause some blood to spurt out. Several shoppers stopped in their tracks, transfixed by the fight scene, but none looked like they wanted to get involved.

Bill grabbed the second guy and hauled him to his feet, forcing him to let go of the woman's purse. "Deixe-me ir." *Let me go*, the attacker yelled.

"Nao em sua vida, amigo." *Not on your life, buddy*, Bill yelled back at him. Then he called out to the gathering crowd, "Alguem, de seguranca chamada." *Someone call security.*

At this point, the third one, the lookout, leaped toward Bill, but Bill quickly twirled his body around and with one fierce kick into the guy's legs, the young man crumbled to the ground, grasping his knee and moaning in pain. Now, the second robber came toward Bill with a menacing stare. When he reached out to drive a punch, Bill grabbed the man's arm, wrenched it behind his back and held on to him.

A security guard in a gray uniform ran down the hall, careening through the crowd. Bill had the first hooligan in tow and shoved him toward the guard. The other two were still nursing their wounds, though the one with the bloody nose was trying to get away. Finally, someone in the crowd grabbed his shirt and stopped him. Bill looked at the guard and said, "Sir, eu acho que voce pode lidar com esses." *Sir, I think you can handle these guys now.*

"Hey, obrigado. Bom trabalho." *Hey, thanks. Good work*, the beefy guard exclaimed, digging some handcuffs out of his back pocket and jamming them on the wrists of one of the young men. The second one was still holding his nose when the guard grabbed his hands and cuffed him too. The third was on the ground, holding his leg and moaning. The guard took out his cell phone and called for backup.

Bill went over, crouched down, and peered at the woman. Her brown silk skirt was bunched up around her knees. One of her stockings was torn, and one high-heeled shoe had come off. She was shaking as she leaned against the wall, breathing heavily, clutching a large leather purse to her chest with one hand, fingering a necklace with the other.

"Voce esta bem, minha senhora?" *Are you all right, ma'am?* Bill asked in a soothing voice.

The woman tried to straighten her skirt, took a deep breath, and murmured, "Acho que sim." *I think so.*

Bill very gently took her arm and said, "Aqui, deixe-me ajuda-lo. Voce pode estar?" *Here, let me help you up. Can you stand?* She nodded hesitantly.

He guided her up, reached down again to retrieve her shoe and hand it to her. She quickly put it back on and looked up, staring. "Uh, sim. Mas como posso te agradecer?" *Uh, yes. But how can I thank you?*

Bill shook his head. "Nao se preocupe com isso." *Don't worry about it.*

The woman still looked somewhat stunned. She gazed up at him. "Qual e seu nome? Meu marido vai querer envior-lke uma recompense." *What is your name? My husband will want to send you a reward.*

Bill just gave her a faint smile and adopted his usual public persona, the one that gave him kind of an "aw shucks" manner. "Eu estou apenas visitando. De Washington, DC." *I'm just visiting. From Washington, DC.* He then nodded his head and started to walk away.

Another security guard arrived to help the first officer. They were now hustling all three young men away. "Shame on those men," someone said.

Bill watched the crowd begin to drift off as they continued jabbering and shaking their heads. "Poor woman. Hope she's all right now."

"Looks okay."

"Wonder who that guy was. Sure had some good moves."

"Ought to get a medal or something."

"Three on one. Never seen that before."

"Think I heard him say he was American. Must be a trained fighter or something."

"Can't wait to tell my kids about this one."

Jessica struggled out of the bathing suit in the small dressing room. After finding good substitutes for her cosmetics, she had perused some of the clothes on sale, ambling between the racks. She had taken a light blue sweater and matching linen blazer, the color of her eyes, along with a couple of black bathing suits into the tiny dressing room. She had noticed that the hotel meeting rooms seemed over–air conditioned so the blazer would be a nice addition to her wardrobe, and the bathing suit was nicer than the one she had packed. It would be perfect out by the pool. That is, if she found enough time away from the official sessions to relax a bit. If not in Brasilia, she was sure she could wear it on the beach in Rio.

While trying on the bathing suit, she thought she heard a commotion in the store. It sounded like some of the clerks were shouting or something. As she listened at the dressing room door, she thought she heard a woman yell the word "robbery," but she couldn't be sure. She tugged the suit off and scrambled to put her own blouse and slacks back on before going out into the shop. But it was empty. Everyone was outside the door, pointing and shaking their heads. She left the bathing suit and the blazer on the counter and ran out.

Jess saw the store owner. "What's going on?"

The woman spoke in accented English and replied, "Some guys tried to steal a woman's purse. Three of them. They attacked her. She was on the floor."

"Is she all right? Did they get away?" Jess asked, wide-eyed.

"She's okay, but it was amazing."

"What was amazing?" Jess inquired, scanning the area.

"There was this man who just appeared out of nowhere. He ran over and got into a fight with the men."

"All three of them?"

"That's what it looked like by the time I came out here. He was incredible. Knocked them down, rescued the woman, handed them off to a security guard. It was like something out of a movie or TV show. I don't even think Jack Bauer has all of those moves."

"Where did they all go?" Jess asked.

"Crowd is gone now. We were just talking about it," the store owner said. "Okay everyone," she called out to her clerks. "Looks like it's over. Let's get back to work."

Jess went back inside and over to the counter where she had left the clothes. The owner looked at the pile and said, "Do you want these? Shall I add them to the ticket for the makeup?"

"Yes, please," Jessica said. Now she was rattled. Here she was in the middle of a gigantic mall, trying to do her shopping. What if she had been the one in the hallway instead of that other woman? She could have been the one they attacked. She turned to the clerk writing up her order. "Does that happen a lot around here?"

"What? A robbery like that?"

Jess nodded.

"I guess so. You have to watch where you're going."

Jess offered her credit card, signed the receipt, took the bag filled with cosmetics and new clothes wrapped in tissue paper, and headed out to the massive hallway. She wondered whether Bill had gone back to the hotel. Probably. She had made it rather clear that she had her own errands to do. Now that she thought about it, though, she was kind of sorry he had left her alone.

Maybe he had been right all along about venturing out by herself. Maybe she should have listened and taken his advice. She looked right and left, saw dozens of other shoppers milling around, but how could she be sure that they were just shoppers? What if there were other bad guys in this place? As she pondered that question, she decided she had better get out to the taxi stand and back to the hotel as fast as she could.

As she headed for the main doors, she heard a familiar voice. "Find what you want?" Bill said nonchalantly, falling in step beside her. For the first time, she felt glad to see him.

"Uh, yes. I did. But did you hear about the robbery? It happened right outside the shop. I was inside, and they said some guys tried to mug a woman. Right outside the door."

"Robbery?" Bill said, raising his eyebrows. "Must have missed it. I was over there, trying to pick up an extra shirt."

"I can't believe you didn't hear all the noise," Jess said, pushing through one of the doors.

"Well, I did warn you that these things can happen down here," Bill said, avoiding the question. He hailed a taxi and helped Jess inside. "You head back to the hotel. I've got another off-site meeting. I'll probably see you later at the opening reception. Take care." And with that, he grinned, slammed the door, and motioned to the next cab to pull up.

Now Jess felt a rather confusing sense of relief knowing that on the one hand he was around to protect her and yet, on the other hand, she'd have the rest of the afternoon all to herself. *Good grief. On the one hand, on the other hand. I really do think like an economist.*

She remembered a quote from Oscar Wilde, "Some cause happiness wherever they go; others whenever they go." Was she really happy to see him go? Looking back and seeing Bill slide into the other taxi, she had to admit that it gave her an odd sense of reluctance to watch it pull away.

CHAPTER FOURTEEN

Planalto Palace—Brasilia

The seventeen thousand square foot reflecting pool was home to a collection of Japanese carp swimming around water lilies. The three-hundred ninety thousand square foot building was home to a collection of Brazilian bureaucrats swirling around the president, vice president, and chief of staff. Bill skirted the pool and walked up to the main door of the four-story glass structure known as the Planalto Palace, one that seemed to be balanced on a series of gigantic white stone pegs. Another of Oscar Niemeyer's 1950s creations that Bill thought would fit better in a twenty-second-century city. All of the official structures were so far removed from architecture in the States, the whole scene made him feel like an actor in a sci-fi film.

He showed his credentials to one of the guards known as the Dragons of Independence and was waved through. He passed by the Main Reception Room and Press Office and took the elevator up. He bypassed the second floor with its Supreme Meeting Room, and the third floor where the President of Brazil and his senior advisors had their offices. His destination was a much smaller office on the fourth floor, also home to the chief of staff and the Military Cabinet. Chet was waiting for him in the hall.

"Right on time, I see," Chet said. "Can't always say that about the Brazilians, though. Let's go in and see how long it takes them to gather their troops."

"Speaking of troops," Bill said, taking a place at the long conference table, "I just saw the changing of the guard downstairs. Reminds me of London. Sort of."

"Yeah. Those Dragon types switch around every two hours. They're part of the military. Nobody gets close to this building except on Sundays when they have some public tours. The president's never around then, so we don't have to worry too much about this place. At least I don't think we do," Chet said.

"What about Alvorado Palace, where the president lives? Is it just as secure?"

"Supposed to be. That's where they're having the final dinner for the conference on Monday."

"I know. It's on my schedule," Bill said.

"Glad you could get yourself into that one with your protocol creds. I've got a seat too, using my other title. Most people here don't know the extent of my activities and they have no clue that you're also with the agency," Chet said. "Obviously, we have to keep it that way. They just think we've had experience protecting our principals. At the palace dinner, that's one time where we'll really have to keep an eye on things."

"Why?" Bill asked. "You think some conference delegate is going to take a shot at the president at a banquet?" He shook his head. "Couldn't happen in such a guarded room. The shooter would never get away."

"I realize that," Chet said. "But you never know about the waiters, the staff, the caterers, the janitors. Whoever is behind this deal, if there is a deal, is probably in a position to pay big bucks to an assassin who just might want to take a chance on some kind of clever escape. Some guy who really knows the building."

"As I walked in, I thought about how well our own president is protected inside the White House. Of course, it's tiny compared to these buildings. Only fifty-five thousand square feet. And probably one of the most secure places in the world."

Chet chuckled and said, "Oh yeah? What about Fort Knox?"

Bill tilted his head up toward the ceiling. He thought a moment and asked, "Are you saying you really believe our gold is there? I mean, who's ever seen it?"

"Guess you've got a point there," Chet replied. "Thing is, when it comes to protecting real estate, or a president, whatever, I always consider Murphy's Law: Anything that can go wrong, will go wrong."

"And the point of this meeting is to repeal it?" Bill said with a wry grin.

"Something like that."

The door opened and several members of the president's security detail, along with a few other staff members walked in. Chet and Bill stood up. One of the female staff asked, "Espresso, gentlemen?"

"Of course," Chet said, nodding politely. "You always take their espresso," he whispered to Bill.

After exchanging pleasantries and business cards and taking the first sips of their ultra-strong coffee, Bill began to analyze the players in the room. The President's Chief of Security was a heavyset man of about sixty with salt and pepper hair, large jowls and piercing brown eyes. Bill thought he might have been halfway decent looking about fifty pounds ago.

Next to him, the Vice President's Security Chief introduced himself as Edwardo Rabelo. In contrast to the president's man, this character looked emaciated. Rabelo was so thin his suit coat draped over skinny shoulders resembling a wire hanger. He noticed that the guy kept reaching into his righthand pocket for pills every few minutes, washing them down with large gulps of water from a pitcher that had been set nearby.

Bill snapped to attention when the conversation turned to the word *assassination*. Chet was asking the security detail if they had any new rumors about a plot against the president. The Chief said, "We hear rumors all the time. But yes, I have to admit that this time there are more. We know that heads of state all over the world are threatened. Day and night. Nothing new there. The question is, who is it this time? What are their motives? I mean if it's the drug dealers, we understand how mad they are with the recent raids. Too bad for them. They are our first target, and they are dangerous men. But there could be others."

"What others?" Chet asked.

The chief continued. "Who knows? We monitor phones and computers. You do too. We know that."

Chet didn't respond. Instead, he turned to Bill. "I brought along Bill Black, from our State Department, because as Assistant Chief of Protocol, he attends many high-level meetings and is constantly traveling with our president and Secretary of State. He's worked with our Secret Service, and he has many stories to tell. Stories that are a good reminder to all of us about how these plots can take shape."

That was his cue. Bill leaned forward and said, "Gentlemen, remember back a number of years in Egypt. The assassination of Anwar Sadat?" The others nodded grimly. Bill went on. "There was a reviewing stand and what his security team didn't notice—or maybe they were paid not to notice—was the line painted to separate Sadat from his Vice President Hosni Mubarak. The shooters, Islamic Fundamentalists, as it turned out, only wanted to kill Sadat, not Mubarak.

"The old story in Egypt is that the president always appointed a vice president dumber than he was so there would never be an attempt on the president's life. I mean, no one would want him killed because he would be succeeded by a stupid guy."

Most of the aides gave half smiles and chuckled at that remark. Some of them even glanced over at the vice president's staff member who simply shrugged and poured himself another glass of water.

"After the assassination," Bill continued, "you might recall that the story then went around that Mubarak never appointed anybody as his vice president because he couldn't find anybody dumber than he was." The other men in the room guffawed. Then Bill added, "I think we can all agree that Mubarak turned out to be an extremely intelligent man who simply wanted to rule alone. Still, I think there are lessons we can learn from that little bit of history."

Chet picked up on the conversation. "Here in Brazil, we also have a very bright vice president, so I don't see any connection to that first part of the story," he said with a nod to Rabelo who was once again reaching for his pills. "However, it simply shows the importance of being aware. Aware of small details like a painted line, a chair out of place, a microphone off center, a last-minute change of personnel like a substitute chef or anyone not completely cleared by security. It could be someone rushed into an event at the last minute for some trumped-up reason."

The security chief shifted his bulky frame in the chair and attempted to reassert his authority as chairman of the meeting. "Yes, I hear what you are saying. These are all basic things. We investigate our people. All our people. We train our people. You don't have to tell us to do that."

"Of course not," Chet said with a slight bow of his head.

They continued their discussion, went over the president's schedule for the next several days, estimated the number of additional men they would need on his security team, and talked about their new set of hardened limousines and helicopters with missile defense capability.

Finally, the chief implored Chet and Bill to share any intelligence the American Embassy had picked up. He said he was glad that Bill was in town as it is always good to have extra people available if need be.

"So now I must say that we are appreciative of your concerns," the chief said, "especially for events like this big conference with all the luncheons and dinners coming up. And as I said, we will especially welcome any intel you collect. Is there anything new since our last contact?"

"Just some chatter, as we call it," Chet said. "Conversations have taken place between dealers like Pazio and some of his own informants. We are trying to analyze them, but we have no direct knowledge of a specific plot or specific date at this point. No actionable intelligence." He handed the chief an edited transcript. "We simply want everyone to work together and remain vigilant."

The chief studied the paper and nodded, his double chin creasing in the process. "Yes. This is good. We thank you for sharing this. If there is to be an attempt on our president's life, we must take every possible measure to prevent such a horrible plot." With that he shoved his chair back and, with both hands on the table for leverage, he pushed himself up. It was obvious that the meeting was over.

The chief and the rest of the security staff filed out, followed by the vice president's aide. Chet and Bill were standing together, gathering their notes. When the others had left the room, Chet said in a low voice, "So, what did you think? Can we trust that guy?"

"The security chief?" Bill asked.

"Yeah. That one."

"I think so. He's pretty high profile, though I guess he could be bought. And he's been around for years so why would he take all this time and then all of a sudden try to pull off an operation? Doesn't make any sense."

"Yeah. I agree with you. What about the others?"

"The one guy who seemed rather strange was the head of security for the VP. He looks sick or something."

"You pegged it. He used to look like the human version of Red Bull. Now he's lost a bunch of weight and only drinks water. Doesn't even touch the espresso. I feel sorry for the guy, but we've got much bigger problems to worry about right now."

CHAPTER FIFTEEN

Royal Tulip Hotel—Brasilia

"Update?" Jess was in her hotel room scanning through a few texts and a dozen emails. She clicked on one from Kay who often used the word update when they exchanged stories about their jobs, the non-classified parts anyway.

"Been dealing with a ton of associations demanding meetings. Wonder what the American-Turkish Garment Manufacturers want this time? How was your flight? And the guy? Tell all . . . K."

Jess checked the time and saw that her friend had just sent the message. Maybe she was still online. It was much easier to send an email than a text when she had several things to say. Jess hit "Reply" and typed, "Flight so boring, if I'd had a button, I'd eject. Then figured I wouldn't need Ambien for jet lag. But later, this Bill Black guy helped me out a lot. Don't know what to think. Sometimes he's dominating, then he turns deferential. Go figure. What else is happening there?"

She hit "Send" and scrolled down to answer a few other messages. There was one from Hal. "How's it going? I'm taking a few days off. More tests coming up. Hope Leventhal hits free trade pacts hard. Keep me posted. Hal."

She wondered how soon her boss would recover. He didn't sound worried. Then again, he usually put a good face on things. She hit "Reply," and typed "Welcome reception is tonight. Will try to corner Sec. State and sound him out. Our notes about 'stimulus programs, what works and what doesn't work' ready to go. Got a new title for that part, 'Keynes is Dead—Again.'" She hit "Send," figuring that her last line might at least bring a smile to his face.

She heard the ping of a new email coming in and saw that Kay had answered. "Also dealing with our new petition system. Had over fifty signatures on one asking us to fess up on extraterrestrial creatures, another crowd wants us to legalize raw milk sales. Biggest group (thousands) want backlogged EB2/EB3 folks with 1-140 Approved to file I-485 and Apply EAD and AP."

Jess burst out laughing and quickly replied, "What the heck is that last one?"

The answer came within seconds, "It's all about getting a Green Card. That's the official title. BTW I might like this Bill Black character. Maybe there's more to him than you think. What's he look like?"

Jess thought a moment and quickly wrote back, "Actually good looking in off-beat way. Tall, dark, different."

Kay answered, "Could be best news since Oreos came out with low-fat cookies. Had dinner with a tall dark type last night."

"Really? I want details," Jess typed.

"Great bod, weird job. Says he 'moves golf courses.' Might have something to do with astroturf. Forgot to tell you to look up Estelle Viera, Leventhal's assistant. She's at the conference. Met her last week. She's great."

Jess checked her watch again and saw that she had enough time to swim a few laps in the pool. She sent one more note to Kay. "Thanks for tip about Estelle. Saw her name on the list. I'll find her. Gotta go."

CHAPTER SIXTEEN

Planalto Palace—Brasilia

Vice President Antonio Serra was shooting his cuffs as he casually walked into the president's office. "Mr. President. You wanted to see me?" he asked.

The tall imposing man behind the desk looked up from a pile of papers and motioned for the vice president to sit down. "When we're alone, call me Roberto. I keep telling you that."

Antonio pulled up a leather wing chair and took a seat. "Just being proper, my friend," he said then eyed the stack of memos. "Your assistant should be handling more of that for you."

"Yes, well, there's a lot to review with all of those delegations in town for the conference." He pushed them aside and focused on his second-in-command. "Besides all of them, or maybe because of all of them, we need to take more action against the drug cartels."

The VP sat forward. "We just did that. The big raid came off perfectly as planned. We arrested a dozen men, confiscated millions of reals worth of heroin and marijuana and didn't lose one of our officers. Not one."

"Yes. Yes, I know all that. But you've seen the press. They say it just shows the power, the supply, the obvious ease these men like Pazio and the others have in getting their shipments through. Besides, that was just one favela. Our contacts are telling us that there are many more drugs passing through the others. Places where they are arranging more trans-shipments north. We can't afford to let those shipments out of the country. Not with the delegates in town and especially not with the games coming up. It makes us look like we can't control our own people or our own borders. Think about the fans who will be coming here, fans who will bring an enormous amount of revenue to our cities. They'll come *if* we get our crime rate down, that is." He leaned back, steepled his fingers and added, "I'm not telling you anything you don't already know."

"What do you want me to do this time? Organize another raid?" the vice president asked.

"I've already put the next one in motion. I wanted to give you a heads-up."

This time Antonio stared intently at the president. "If it's the supplies you're worried about, are you also planning to send teams to cut off their connections to FARC?"

"Of course. We've been trying to do that for months now. I don't want to talk too much about it. But our intelligence chief has already sent out a special force to try and intercept the next shipment. We've been getting new information from the American Drug Enforcement people, and it usually checks out," President Mendez said confidently.

"Is there a special assignment for me this time?" Antonio asked.

"Yes, I want you to coordinate the timing of the raid so it is successful but doesn't interfere with the headlines that will come out of this conference. There's a break over the weekend and then the final speeches, exchange of papers, and banquet at my home the following Monday."

"I know, Roberto. Wouldn't miss it for the world," the number two said.

"And in order for the press to highlight the conference and whatever agreements we can sign, the raid must come off sooner. Over the weekend would be best. Most of the delegates will be here, not in Rio. When we know it's successful, we'll have a press briefing, show the prisoners if we have any more of them, and all of that will be out of the way by the time of the final dinner. Got that?"

"But of course. I will see that it's done," the vice president responded. Then as if trying to lighten the mood of the conversation, he said, "By the way, on the subject of the conference, I have the list of attendees. Have you seen their bios and photos?"

"Some of them," the president said, pulling his papers back in front of him. "Why? Is there something I should know about?"

Antonio started to get up and chuckled. "Not really. It's the usual list of Secretaries of State and foreign ministers except for the woman from Washington. She's a last-minute replacement for Harold Carruthers."

"Yes. I was briefed on that. He's sick, I guess. Who's the woman?"

"I read her bio and saw her picture. Quite a beauty, I must say."

The president looked up, a wry smile on his face. "A beautiful American economist? I didn't know they had any up there."

"Just wait. You'll be meeting her tonight."

CHAPTER SEVENTEEN

Royal Tulip Hotel—Brasilia

Shielding her eyes from the bright sunlight, Jess zeroed in on an empty chaise longue off to the side of the glistening pool. There were a lot of what she'd call beautiful people lounging there, sipping tall drinks provided by a bevy of young men clad in white shorts and open neck shirts. She saw that the chairs had little flags hooked to the back. When a flag was turned up, a waiter would rush over to take an order. *Slick system.*

She took the neatly folded towel that was lying on the edge of her chair and spread it out. There was a light canvas bag in her closet that turned out to be a perfect way to carry her workshop notes down to the patio area, but first she just wanted to relax for a while. She reached inside the bag for a tube of sun block, covered her face, arms and legs and realized that the new black bathing suit fit really well and didn't hike up in the back like her old one. She stretched out and told herself not to spend too much time in the sun. After a little while she planned to ask one of the waiters or pool boys or whatever they were called to please raise the umbrella that was perched just behind her.

"Excuse me, are you Jessica Tanner?" a young woman asked.

Jess opened her eyes and sat up. Standing in front of her was a young woman who looked to be in her early twenties with long dark hair the color of mahogany and a pretty, round face with a turned-up nose sporting the largest pair of sunglasses Jess had ever seen. "Uh, yes, I am."

"Sorry to bother you, but I thought that was you. Hi, I'm Estelle Viera from State here for the conference."

Jess grinned and pointed to the chaise next to hers. "Estelle! I was just hearing about you from my friend, Kay Heller back at the White House."

"Right. I met her last week, and then I saw your photo on the attendee list. It's nice to meet you." She plopped down on the nearby lounge and pushed up the little flag. "What a gorgeous day! This is probably the only break I'll have in a while, so I wanted to take advantage of it. My boss is always giving me stuff to do, but he's in a meeting with some Minister from El Salvador, and I was able to slip away."

"You work for the Secretary, right?" Jess asked, leaning back on her elbows.

"Yes. I'm his administrative assistant, though sometimes I wonder if he ever read my job description."

"What do you mean?"

"Well," Estelle leaned over and in a conspiratorial tone said, "Look, I know we just met, and I know he's head of the delegation and all of that, but . . ." she stopped and studied Jess for a moment. "Kay told me about you. Said you were one of her closest friends. I'm new at State, don't know a lot of people so I never know who to talk to or . . . well . . . who to trust, if you know what I mean."

Jess wondered what the girl's problem was, but she seemed rather sweet and sincere. Why not be a sounding board? It seemed like Estelle could use one, though she had no idea why. "What do you mean? Is there a problem here?" Jess asked.

Estelle uttered a sigh. "It's just that Secretary Leventhal brought me along on this trip when I didn't really think I should be going. I mean, he has a lot of other staff here."

"Then why . . ."

"You see, that's just it," Estelle said. "He does have a bit of a reputation. You've probably heard that, right? I mean, I'm not making it up or anything."

"I'm not sure what you mean," Jess said.

"Oh rats! I shouldn't be saying anything. I mean, he's my boss!"

Jess saw that Estelle was rummaging in her own bag for some magazines, and it looked like a rather feeble stalling technique. "Please, don't worry about talking to me," Jess said. "If there's something wrong, why don't you tell me? Maybe I can help."

"Oh, believe me, nobody can help with this one." She leaned over, paused, and then went on. "You see, the Secretary is, well, he's one of those men who really likes women. Nothing wrong with that, of course. Then again, he's married. But word around the building is that he's quite the rogue. When I was getting him coffee the other day, I overheard one of the girls from the European Directorate say that his initials, S. A. L., stand for 'Such A Letch.'"

Jessica laughed despite the serious tone of Estelle's voice. "Oh Lord, does that mean what I think it means? You think he's after you on this trip? He couldn't possibly be that brazen, could he?"

"I don't know," Estelle said. "Let's just say he makes me feel uncomfortable." She paused and went on. "Oh, I know that people say that it's better to be looked over than overlooked. But when it's the married boss who's looking, well, that's something else again. Take this morning. After we all checked in, he called my room and asked me to bring him some papers I had in my case. I go up to his floor and knock on his door, and you'll never believe what happened."

"What?"

"He opens the door, and he's standing there in nothing but a bath towel wrapped around his waist. I'm not the maid with fresh towels, I'm supposed to be his administrative aide. Get the picture?"

"What did you do?"

"He asked me to come in, but I shoved the papers in his hand and said I had to do a quick errand, and I got out of there." She shook her mane of long hair and frowned. "What do I do the next time?"

Jessica eyed the girl and felt a good deal of sympathy. She certainly was pretty. And she looked great in a bright red bikini. She could see why any man might try to take advantage of her. And in the rarefied atmosphere of the DC halls of power, many of the men holding top positions acted like they were entitled not only to a fancy office but more privileges than the average guy.

Jess tried to think of some bit of advice for Estelle, who was in a difficult position. After all, Hal had never propositioned her. He wouldn't dream of such a thing. He was the consummate gentleman. But it sounded like this girl had to deal with a real hustler.

"Estelle," Jessica began. "I see the problem. Believe me, I see a lot of that stuff, even around the White House. Nothing new there. I guess the question is, do you think you can handle it? And do you want to keep your job with Leventhal?"

Estelle leaned back and closed her eyes. It looked like she was deep in thought, and it took her several moments to reply. "You know, when I got this job, I was so excited. I have a degree in International Studies from American University in DC. I always wanted to get a government job, especially in this administration. One of my professors recommended me to the personnel people at State, and after going through HR, I ended up with an interview with the Secretary. I was pretty psyched. It sounded like such a great opportunity. Well, I *thought* it was great. I celebrated when he hired me. But now, after just two months on the job, I'm beginning to wonder if I can survive this whole thing. You know, sometimes I feel like Cinderella running around with one shoe off. But Leventhal sure isn't a Prince Charming, I'll tell you that."

Jess smiled at her description. "Look, you're single, right?"

"Right. With these jobs and the long hours, who has time to find a guy, especially in Washington?"

"How true," Jess agreed. "In fact, as long as we're comparing notes here, I just broke up with someone, and I have to say that I haven't seen too many other guys on the horizon."

Estelle stared at Jessica. "You? I mean you're so well known. I would think that you'd have men calling you all the time."

"Some do, but they're usually money managers of some sort. I keep thinking that it sure would be nice to meet a guy in a different field. Maybe someone just a bit more exciting than the head of the Office of Management and Budget."

Estelle giggled and shook her head. "Yes, I know what you mean. Instead of OMB, you'd like OMG!"

Jess laughed. "Don't I wish. By the way, have you run into a guy in the Protocol Office there at State named Bill Black?"

"Not yet," Estelle said. "We've got something like thirty-thousand employees all over the world. I think there are more than five thousand in DC, and I've only gotten to know the players on the seventh floor." She looked at Jess and added, "So how do you know Bill Black? I saw his name on our delegation list, but he was on a different flight."

"He was on *my* flight," Jess said. "Nice enough. Kind of attractive. Tall and tries to be friendly. But to be honest, all he talked about were seating charts."

Estelle laughed out loud. "Guess I can miss that one."

"Me too. It isn't that I need a life in the fast lane," Jess said. "But it might be nice to get out of the long-term parking lot."

"I like the way you think," Estelle said, picking up a copy of *Glamour* magazine and leafing through it. "I guess we'll have to go get ready for the big reception pretty soon, but the sun sure feels good. It's nice to just kind of veg out for a change." She looked down at a page and showed it to Jessica. "Have you ever noticed that almost every ad you see for a fancy watch has the time as ten minutes after ten?"

Jess glanced over and said, "You know, you're right about that. Maybe they're trying to create a happy face. And I guess that's exactly what we'll have to put on at the party tonight."

"Right," Estelle murmured. "And back on our subject of men, I've been thinking that with so many women around DC, even at the department, why does Leventhal have to pick on me?"

"For one thing, you're right there," Jess replied. "And, he's in charge."

"Not of me he isn't," Estelle objected.

"Maybe you should tell the Secretary that you have a significant other."

"It's not like we talk about our private lives in the office. I mean, he doesn't talk about his wife, so how could I talk about some imaginary boyfriend?"

"Just an idea," Jess said. "Here comes the waiter. Let's get something tall and cool."

"Speaking of tall and cool, now I have an idea," Estelle said. "I heard that some of the delegates might go over to Rio during the break. Are you going?"

"I'd like to," Jess said. "I don't know anyone there, but I could look around and play tourist."

"I've got a cousin who's part owner of a great restaurant. He's single, tall and a nice guy. I'll give you his number if you want to look him up."

"What a great idea," Jess said. "This just might make it all worthwhile. Thanks."

They ordered their drinks, jumped in the pool, swam several laps, and collapsed back on the chaises. By now Jess felt like she'd made a new friend and might be in for a nice adventure over in Rio if this cousin turned out to be available.

She liked Estelle and hoped the woman could figure out a way to handle her boss while still keeping her job. When she thought more about it, she realized that she didn't have those kinds of problems at the White House or with anyone on this trip either. Certainly not with Bill Black. He showed up once in a while, but he hadn't put a move on her. Then again, she wondered what it would be like if he did.

CHAPTER EIGHTEEN

Royal Tulip Hotel—Brasilia

Bill watched as Jessica Tanner walked into the reception clad in a pair of high heels and a black lace dress that practically hugged her body. What was it with women and high heels? Sure, they look great, but he kept wondering how they didn't fall over, especially if they had to walk down a hill or something. As he studied the way she walked, he realized she was having no trouble maneuvering between the little knots of ministers and directors. And the little knots had no trouble unwinding to glance at her as she ambled by.

When he first met her on the plane, he hadn't seen all the curves. But tonight, in that dress, they were front and center. It wasn't that the dress was too revealing. In fact, it was rather conservative. She fit in perfectly with this crowd. It's just that the dress fit perfectly too. As he stared at her accepting a glass of champagne from a waiter in black tie, he couldn't help but be reminded of a new country song he'd heard.

> *I spied a gal who's right real cute, with legs from here to there;*
> *A body that stops traffic, and a head of golden hair.*

Sure was a good description.

He made his way through the throng and stood next to her. "Hi. You look great tonight. Nice dress."

"Oh, hi, Bill. Thanks," she said, taking a sip of the champagne. "As my mom used to say, 'It's nice to hear it while you're living.'"

This woman is always so serious, I wonder how much living she's really done? Then again, I don't really know that much about her. Yet. "By the way, where is your mom? I mean, where are you from?"

"I grew up outside of Chicago. My mom's a piano teacher," Jess replied.

"And your dad?" Bill asked.

"Dad owns a local hardware store. Built the business up by himself. I worked there most summers," she said.

"I guess you got that up-from-the-boot-straps philosophy from home, right?"

"How do you know about my philosophy?" she asked with a quizzical smile. "Have you been reading my policy papers?"

"I've just heard about you, that's all." He scanned the room. "Have to admit I haven't heard much about all these people here tonight, though. Do you know many of them?"

"Besides our delegation, I just know them by reputation. I mean, we've got ministers from all over South and Central America. I was looking over the list earlier and the trouble is, I can't even pronounce most of the names. Can you?"

"A few," Bill said. "I did study some languages at Cornell."

"Oh yes. Cornell." In her peripheral vision, she caught a glimpse of Estelle dressed in a kelly-green silk suit. Her hair was pinned back, and she was looking around like a lost kitten. "Bill, will you excuse me? I see a friend I need to speak to."

"Sure, no problem." Bill watched her head across the room and wondered where she was going. He saw her chatting with a younger woman and figured it was a good time to scan the room and keep his eye out for anything suspicious.

"Hi Estelle, Love your suit. Same color as your eyes."

Estelle looked relieved to find a friendly face. "Thanks. I kind of splurged on this one. Everyone said that people really do dress up in Brazil, and this is just about the only outfit I have that I thought might work tonight. The rest of my clothes are more the kind we wear to work. Skirts, blazers. Well, you know what I mean. About this skirt, though, I found a green and white silk top on sale at TJ Maxx that I'm going to wear to the final banquet. That should work."

"I'm sure it will be perfect," Jess said.

Estelle gazed approvingly at Jessica's dress and remarked, "I'll bet that black lace wasn't on sale. It looks like a designer dress for sure."

"Well, not quite. It's off the rack, but I did get it at a good price."

"And I've seen ads for David Yurman jewelry like that," Estelle said in an inspired tone.

"Shhh. It's a knock-off. I shoved it into my purse at the last minute. Good thing I did too because all my other jewelry, costume pieces, along with all my makeup was stolen out of my luggage at the airport."

"You've gotta be kidding! That's awful. Did you file a claim?" Estelle asked in a worried tone.

"No. I didn't want to take the time. And besides, I heard that they never do much about it anyway. They never find the thieves. It's just par for the course down here. Be sure to watch your wallet if you're walking around town. In fact, I was over at a big mall trying to buy some new makeup and a woman was mugged right outside the shop."

"No!" Estelle exclaimed. "What happened to her? Did you see?"

"Not really. I came out when it was over. Everyone said that some stranger rushed out, knocked down the guys, and then security took them away."

"I wonder who the stranger was? A policeman or something?" Estelle asked, wide-eyed.

"No. Just some guy in the crowd. Everyone said he was amazing. Should have gotten a medal for that one," Jess said.

Bill walked up and extended his hand to Estelle. "Hello, I'm Bill Black from State Protocol."

"Yes, nice to meet you," Estelle said. "I hear you already know Jess."

"Yes, I know Jessica Tanner," Bill said with a grin.

"She's the Deputy Director of the President's Council of Economic Advisors. What other woman has that kind of position? I mean someone young and all that?" Estelle said, her mouth turning up into a smile at her new friend.

"It's just a job," Jess said. "Okay, a nice job. But Bill here is Assistant Chief of Protocol. That's a pretty decent job too, don't you think?"

Estelle looked at Bill appraisingly. She flashed her green eyes and simply said, "Couldn't agree more."

Jess watched the interplay and found herself feeling slightly jealous. What was that all about? Here was a young woman giving Bill Black the eye, something she had every right to do. After all, he did look pretty good in his navy blue pin-striped suit, white shirt, and maroon and blue Hermes tie. At least it looked like an Hermes. Then again, he was a protocol guy. He knew how to dress. He *had* to if he was going to fit the part.

The three of them chatted about the conference, some of the ministers, and what they all thought might be accomplished, if anything, by way of agreements. They all said that if anything was signed by the entire group, it might not amount to much because there wasn't much that they could all agree on anyway and laughed at their mutual assessment. Then Jess recapped by saying that at least it would be an opportunity for the American delegation to make some points about economic recovery and free trade agreements.

Estelle interrupted the conversation when she said, "Uh oh. There's my boss. He's motioning me to come over. Guess I'd better go. Catch you later."

Jessica turned to Bill, "I suppose I should mingle and get to know some of the delegates."

"Good idea," Bill said, and he started to trail after her.

She turned and murmured, "Bill, you're acting like Marine One."

"What do you mean?"

"You're hovering." But she said it with a half-smile.

"You're right. Actually, I see some other folks I should check in with. Enjoy your evening."

As he sauntered away, Jess had that feeling again. The sense that she had just lost something special. Even if it was momentary.

A waiter pushed a cart into the reception room that was covered by a long white cloth topped with a large, covered silver dish. He moved slowly along the side of the room toward the buffet table. President Roberto Mendez was standing next to the table, shaking hands with several ministers who were giving slight bows as they laughed at his comments. They all looked rather obsequious to Bill, but that was the usual scene when any president of a country was in a room glad-handing the guests.

The waiter was coming closer, but at a very slow pace. It looked a bit strange to Bill, so he quickly walked to a place between the cart and the president. The waiter stopped and mumbled, "Desculpe-me, senhor." *Excuse me, sir.*

"Voce esta na equipe hotel regular aqui?" *Are you on the regular hotel staff here?* Bill inquired.

"Nao, eu sou uma substituicao Alguns a chamaram de doente, entao eu tenho uma noite de trabalho. Por que?" *No, I am a replacement. Someone called in sick, and I got a job tonight. Why?* the waiter uttered as he tried to push past. Bill held his ground.

"Eu so vique voce nao tinha uma etiqueta com o nome regulares hotel on." *I just saw that you didn't have a regular hotel name tag on*, Bill said in an authoritative tone, never taking his eyes off the young man.

"Sera que isso importa?" *Does it matter?*

Bill stared at the man, taking his measure. He didn't make eye contact, and he did seem a bit nervous. In fact, his hands were twitching, almost vibrating like a tuning fork. As Bill looked around, he saw

President Mendez was still surrounded. Not an easy target. If he *was* going to be a target tonight. Bill quickly decided he couldn't afford to make a scene. He stepped aside and said, "Acho que nao." *I guess not.* As the waiter guided the cart forward, Bill moved back, keeping himself directly between the table and the president.

CHAPTER NINETEEN

Royal Tulip Hotel—Brasilia

He was coming her way. Secretary Leventhal dressed the part of a distinguished Secretary of State in his gray suit, white shirt, and maroon tie. His wavy salt and pepper hair made him look like a cross between John Kerry and Newt Gingrich. He was a master at working the room. Jessica watched as he wound through the crowd, shaking hands with the Finance Minister of Ecuador, and then a woman Jess knew was from Canada. Jess saw that while he stood in front of the Canadian, he was looking over the woman's shoulder. *Lots of men do that. Always looking for someone more important, more prestigious, or more attractive rather than focusing on the person they're talking to.* She continued to watch him as he quickly excused himself and headed in her direction with Estelle in tow.

"Jessica," the Secretary said with a broad grin, "good to see you here tonight." His eyes took in the lace dress. He smiled approvingly. "You look smashing. Not quite the same scene we have in our meetings in the Cabinet Room."

"Thank you, Mr. Secretary," Jess said evenly. "They do tend to dress up a bit more in this country."

"Yes, well, you certainly keep up with the best of them. Now then, are you ready for the opening session tomorrow? Sorry that Hal had to miss this. We're trying to make some progress on our trade agenda this time."

"I certainly hope so. And yes, I sent over some last-minute suggested edits from the White House. I see that your speech writers incorporated them into your excellent list of points. Looks like we're good to go," Jess said, then added, "I know you'll be persuasive."

He seemed to preen at her praise. "Let's just hope that the delegates are as amenable to my program, I mean *our* program, as you seem to be. Now then, after this little shindig here, why don't you join me for dinner? We could go over any more thoughts you might have."

Jessica saw that Estelle was hanging on to every word of their conversation as she dutifully stood by Leventhal's side. When he talked about dinner with Jess, Estelle had a relieved look on her face. Jess wondered if the Secretary would pressure Estelle to spend the evening with him if Jess turned him down. "Mr. Secretary, I'm not sure how long this reception will last, but it might be a good idea if our whole group got together to go over all of our notes for the other break-out sessions. And that would include you too, Estelle, of course." *There. How's he going to get out of that one?*

The Secretary quickly glanced around the room and said, "Well, I'm not sure if everyone else has made plans, but I'll check and get back to you." Then he made a hasty retreat.

"Thank you," Estelle whispered as she hung back. "That was brilliant."

The buzz in the room seemed to increase as the president's security detail fanned out. Jess saw that a microphone was being checked at the front of the room and various ministers and staffers began to press forward to get a better view. Vice President Serra stepped to the podium first and gave a glowing introduction, "And now, ladies and gentlemen, I present to you the man who is bringing a revitalized economy to our country along with an emphasis on law and order. A man dedicated to your well-being and enjoyment of our city during your stay with us, a man to whom we raise our glasses in a toast tonight."

"Hear. Hear," the crowd said in unison as President Mendez strode forward and mounted the platform. He gave a warm welcome and went on to emphasize his hopes for meaningful agreements to come out of the conference. As he spoke, Jess saw that Bill Black was watching the crowd, not the president. She wondered why.

The waiter had gone back to the kitchen, the president was finishing his remarks, but Bill never stopped scanning the crowd. He saw Chet on the other side of the room giving him a small sign, so he eased himself away from the buffet area and joined the station chief.

"Did you see that waiter?" Bill whispered.

"The one who looked nervous?" Chet asked.

"You've got the eye," Bill said.

"Didn't have a name tag on."

"We're on the same page. I asked him about it, and he said he was a last-minute hire. Said somebody on the staff got sick."

"Heard that one before," Chet said. "What do you think? Anything to be worried about?"

"Not sure. Could have been a dry run."

"Next presidential appearance is at the final banquet. I hear he's leaving the Brazilian presentations to his own finance minister. But he'll do a wrap-up. That one will be at his own palace, and we've talked about how they have a ton of security over there."

"Yes, but the kitchen help may be the same crew. Might show up on Monday too. Can you put a trace on him?" Bill inquired.

"Sure. Already thought about that. I'll get his name from the head chef," Chet said.

"Good move. Anyone else on your radar screen right now?"

"Tons of suspects, but they're not in this crowd. We're got some of our people looking for Pazio and Domingo, among others from the favelas. Trouble is, there are too many of them to track all the time, and they keep switching cell phones. We're just going to have to work with the president's security team from now on through the end of this gig. At least we get a bit of a break over the weekend. I just saw the president's schedule. Looks like he's staying home. No public events. No motorcades, so it'll be a chance for both of us to relax and regroup a bit."

"I wonder if Jessica will head to Rio," Bill muttered.

"Oh, the good-looking one," Chet said, glancing over to see Jess surrounded by the delegation from Peru.

"If you don't need me here," Bill said, "I may shadow her the next two days. We'll see."

"Just keep your cell handy in case anything comes up," Chet said. "I'll spend some time going over the staff lists again and double-check the phone logs. I'm still not convinced there isn't an inside plot of some sort."

"Well, if there is, I doubt if the meager help you and I can offer will be anywhere near enough to stave off a potential disaster!"

CHAPTER TWENTY

The White House

"**M**r. Everly will see you now," the ever-efficient secretary said as she motioned to the spacious corner office of the White House Chief of Staff. Stephen DiZio, Undersecretary of State for International Security pushed the door open to a spacious setting just steps from the Oval Office. Where proximity to the king equals power, this little piece of real estate held the most powerful person next to the president, unless you wanted to count the vice president. And nobody did. "Afternoon, J. L. Got your memo. Glad we could get together for a quick update. I know how busy you are. This won't take long."

"Yes. Thanks for coming over. Sit down," the chief said, shuffling a stack of memos and files to one side of the large mahogany desk. "Just met with the president on that African State Visit. You can't believe the hassles we're going through to accommodate that group. They brought so many people with them that they've taken up an entire floor of the Hay Adams."

The undersecretary pulled up a maroon leather side chair, sat down and opened his leather folder. "Better there than Blair House. Do you remember the stories about when Mobutu Sese Seku came to town a while back?"

J. L. chuckled as he leaned back in his swivel chair. "If memory serves, his staff wasn't paying their bills, even little stuff like parking tickets here and in New York when everybody knew he had billions stashed in some Swiss bank account."

"That was the least of it," Steve said. "I heard that a bunch of his staff complained to our Protocol Office when we didn't provide them with call girls. Evidently, they had much better treatment in France."

The chief of staff shook his head. "Now speaking of your Protocol Office, what do you hear from Bill Black? Anything new on those assassination rumors in Brazil?"

"Just got off a secure call with him. He's met with President Mendez's security people, and he's not sure all of them can be trusted."

"Glad we never have that feeling here. At least we haven't so far. That only seems to happen in thriller novels."

"Right." The undersecretary consulted his notes. "I believe his quote was, 'Being on a security detail doesn't make you an honest agent any more than standing in a garage makes you a car.'"

J. L. guffawed at the comment. "Always liked that guy. I think he's one of our best coverts. How in hell he keeps up that protocol charade is beyond me."

"I often wonder about that myself. Anyway, he says he's working with our station chief to check out various employees, kitchen help. That sort of thing. But he's also concerned about the palace staff. Lots of corruption and pay-offs going on down there. Nothing new about that."

J. L. nodded. "But any actionable intelligence at this point?"

"Not quite. They're also trying to keep tabs on the biggest drug dealer in Rio right now. Pazio. Intercepting his calls when they can, tracing emails, GPS trying to track his whereabouts, getting as much as possible, but he sure moves around a lot. You've heard of him?"

"Of course. If they figure out where he is, why don't they just arrest the bastard?" the chief of staff asked.

"DEA says they're trying to nail his whole supply chain, connections with FARC, the top boys, that sort of thing. They want to take down all of them. So right now, he's just under surveillance."

"I have to say that if someone, somehow figures out a way to take out President Mendez, we are all in big trouble," J. L. said. "Something happens to him, and we're stuck with that vice president, Antonio Serra."

"Yes, not exactly a poster boy for economic reform," Steve agreed.

"What's our next move? We can't keep Black down there indefinitely."

"That's for sure. OAS conference is over next Monday, and if we don't wind this thing up by then, we may have to figure out some other ruse to keep him in Brasilia."

"That's your bailiwick," J. L. said. "I'm sure you can handle Alicia. She's got, what? A staff of sixty over there? How can she complain about just one guy?"

"If there's a way to complain, she'll figure it out," Steve said. "But I didn't come here to talk about staffing problems. I just wanted you to know that Bill's working with our embassy people, doing all he can. I, for one, am glad we were able to get him detailed to State for a while."

"And, besides the whole Mendez situation, he's got an additional assignment from us and the agency," J. L. said.

Steve glanced up. "You mean the bodyguard role?"

"Well, yes. About Hal, it now looks like pneumonia. Not sure how long he'll be out, but he's on a boatload of antibiotics so he should be able to kick this thing pretty soon. Anyway, with Hal out of the picture, you know we had to send his deputy, Jessica Tanner, down there to handle one of the smaller sessions and give our input."

"Yes, bright woman."

"Not only bright, but attractive as hell. Prime target for street gangs. You've seen the crime stats."

"Sure, but we've got a number of people from State Security down there too. She should be okay."

"Maybe. Maybe not. That's why Bill's been asked to keep an eye on her. When he has the time, that is."

"Yes, I heard about that. Let's just hope she sticks to the hotel and doesn't want to venture out."

"Well, that's just the thing," J. L. said. "When I talked to Hal last night to check on him, he told me that when he sent Jessica down there, he told her to take some time off and go over to Rio for some R&R since she's been working such long hours filling in for him."

"So now, one of our best operatives has been given orders to be in two places at once, protect a White House official and prevent the assassination of a foreign head of state," Steve said, shaking his head.

The chief of staff leaned forward and asked, "Whoever said the spy game was easy?"

CHAPTER TWENTY-ONE

Conference Center—Brasilia

"I'd like to wind up this session on fiscal policy with a quote from John F. Kennedy's State of the Union address over half a century ago," Jessica said to a number of delegates who were giving her their rapt attention. "Kennedy's words still ring true today. 'To achieve greater gains, one step is essential—the enactment of a substantial reduction and revision in federal income taxes . . . in every tax bracket. It will encourage initiative and risk-taking, induce more investment, production, and help provide millions of new jobs.' And, I might add, history has shown that any initial deficit is quickly made up by economic growth. With more people working and businesses doing better, tax receipts often have doubled."

Bill had snagged a seat near the door and felt like he was back in college listening to one of his professors trying to explain arcane principles to a reluctant student body. But this time, he realized nobody was reluctant to listen, and everybody seemed happy to look at her. She did look good in a light blue blazer and dark skirt. They could see that underneath the head table where she and three other speakers were seated, her long great-looking legs were discretely crossed. Not bad, he thought, as she was winding up her remarks.

"As I said at the outset when it comes to economic policy, seeing what works and what doesn't work, Keynes is dead. Again! Now, thank you for listening. I look forward to more of our informal sessions this afternoon."

She moved away from the microphone and gave the delegates one of her winning smiles as they applauded her performance. Bill quickly pushed through the crowd that was now taking advantage of a break in the program. He headed toward the front of the room and grabbed Jessica's arm as she was about to slip out a side door.

"Hey, Jess, great remarks. You were the best speaker on that panel. By far."

"Really?" She glanced up at him with wide-set eyes. "I'm just glad that one is over. You don't think it was too dry and boring, do you? Or would you tell me even if it were true?"

"No. I mean yes," Bill said. "What I mean is, I thought it was a good presentation. You had the charts, the stats. The numbers don't lie, and these guys were really paying attention. More to you than the others."

Jessica flushed at the compliment. "Thanks. That's nice of you. But what are you doing here? I mean, I thought you'd be working on banquet details, or something."

"Those are done. More or less. I just thought I'd catch your act, that's all." He looked around and saw that most of the delegates were headed out to the lobby where a coffee service was set up. He didn't want coffee. He just wanted to talk to her for some reason—she was beginning to fascinate him, more so than he thought she would. He turned back toward her. "I guess you have to go to all the other afternoon panels, right?"

She sighed. "Yes, afraid so. But after that I'm glad we have a weekend break."

"What are you going to do?"

"Actually, I just made a reservation to fly over to Rio tonight. Estelle has a cousin who runs a restaurant in Rio. He's going to show me around during the day. He works nights," she said.

"I was considering heading out myself. Want some company?" he asked in a casual tone of voice.

"Are you asking because you want to come with me or because you've been told to protect me?"

"Maybe a little of both," he admitted. "When are you leaving?"

"They have a lot of flights between Brasilia and Rio. I'm on the 6:30."

"I'll think about that. But first I have to tie up a few loose ends here." He checked his watch and added, "Where are you staying?"

"At the Copacabana Palace," Jess said.

Bill whistled. "Pretty fancy. I didn't know government employees stayed in places like that."

"Well, I got a reasonable rate. It's just a small single room. That hotel is right across the street from the beach, so I figured I'd go for it. It's my only chance to get away and see the city."

"The city is great. But again, remember there's a lot of crime down here. You've got to be careful."

"I know. But as I said, I've got a good contact there, and I'm sure he'll look after me," Jess said. "Everything should be fine."

Bill stared at her for a moment, hoping to God that was true.

CHAPTER TWENTY-TWO

Rio de Janeiro

Jessica was checking in with the desk clerk at the elegant Copacabana Palace just across a wide boulevard from the famous beach of the same name.

"Yes, I have your reservation right here, Ms. Tanner. Credit card, please?"

Jess fished in her purse and produced the card. "I have a single room, right?"

The young woman eyed Bill standing just behind Jess, checked the reservation form again and replied, "Yes, a single on the sixth floor. Number 602. It's our more economic offering. Just a shower in the bathroom. But it does have an ocean view. Will that be acceptable?"

"Sure," Jess replied, signing a form, and handing it back.

"One key or two?" the clerk asked, again glancing over at Bill.

"Just one, please," Jess replied. She took her key and moved to one side.

Bill stepped up to the desk. "I made a last-minute reservation just a few hours ago. Name's William Black."

The clerk checked her computer again. "Yes, sir. You have one of our last remaining rooms. It's on the tenth floor. No view, I'm afraid. Will that be suitable?"

"No problem. Just glad it's available."

The young woman went on to explain that the fitness center is located in the Tower Wing next to the spa; the poolside restaurant, Pergula, serves all day, including a breakfast buffet; and the Copacabana Beach has a section just for hotel guests where security guards keep watch.

"Security guards on a beach?" murmured Jessica, turning to stare at Bill with a quizzical look.

"You bet," Bill said. He went through the signing process, offered his own credit card, and the two of them headed for the elevators. Bill said, "After you check in, want to catch a late dinner? No one eats early around here anyway. What do you think?"

Jess eyed him and thought about their trip so far. He had been rather gracious on the plane, kept up a decent conversation, although he did spend a rather long time talking about proper gifts. She had asked him about buying something for Estelle's cousin who was going to show her around tomorrow afternoon. She probably shouldn't have opened that line of questioning because Bill gave her more protocol procedures than she ever needed on that subject.

At least she learned that in Brazil she shouldn't give any sort of personal gift like perfume or a tie. Maybe she could find a good novel for the cousin. Bill had also launched into a list of things you never give anyone overseas, not that she was anticipating any more foreign trips for a while. But she had dutifully listened as he explained that you don't give anything to do with owls in an Arab country and nothing made of pigskin. She got the pig thing, but she had no idea what the problem was with owls and didn't want to ask.

She also learned not to give picture frames to Hindus or a clock to anybody from China or Thailand because clocks might refer to how long someone was going to live, like your life was ticking away or something. She looked over and saw that Bill was checking his watch, obviously waiting for her to make up her mind.

"Sure. Dinner would be good. I do want to get settled into my room, check email, and change clothes. Why don't we meet here at the desk in about half an hour?" she suggested.

"Good plan," he said, punching the button for the elevator.

Once inside her door, Jess glanced around. Though the room wasn't very large, she was delighted to see the restful neutral colors, white upholstered headboard, and silky duvet on the queen-size bed. She had a momentary flashback to the first time she had been in Ken's apartment. He had explained that since he only had a queen-size bed, they might have to use the spoon position to sleep. Then he quipped, "So do you want to spoon or fork?" She didn't think it was all that funny and had decided against sleeping with him at all.

Jess hit a mental refresh button and excised the man from her mind's eye. She put her roller bag on a luggage rack, hung up her clothes and decided to take a quick shower before their dinner date.

Was it a date? No, just dinner with a conference colleague. Of course, that's all it was. Still, it would be nice to go somewhere with Bill rather than trek around town alone, especially at night. Maybe she could steer the conversation to current events, books, or movies to get a reprieve from the whole protocol routine.

She walked into the sleek bathroom, turned on the shower and noticed that there wasn't much pressure. She turned off the water, stepped in, and began to unscrew the shower head. Her dad had taught her so many tricks when she had spent all those summers working in his hardware store, and this was one of the easier ones. Sure enough, she spotted the small restrictor, stepped out, grabbed a nail file from her purse, and reached up again to pry it loose. She replaced the shower head and turned on the faucet. Bingo. Worked perfectly.

Jess inhaled the scented soap, reveled in the warm gushing water, and dried off with a luxurious Egyptian white cotton bath towel. She used some of her new cosmetics, brushed out her hair, and pulled out a simple white linen dress and pair of matching sandal heels. Checking her image in a mirror, she muttered, "Not sure if I'm ready for a close-up, but that's the best I can do right now."

She looked over at the digital clock by the bed and saw that she had another few minutes before she should head downstairs. She sat down at a small desk in the corner, connected her laptop and started to check her email. She knew she had to keep her computer with her and check for any updates from the White House. As she scrolled through, she clicked on a few and saw one from Kay about a date with yet another new man she'd met at a party with some reporters. She said the guy writes about sheep farmers in Patagonia. *I think Bill Black might be more interesting than that one,* she mused.

Besides the usual scheduling items, she saw another email from her AA with news that Congress had just issued its report on dog and cat fur protection. Her assistant loved gathering these tidbits of what she called "Administrivia." Jess laughed to herself, turned off the machine, grabbed a small white evening bag and headed to the lobby.

"You look great," Bill said, walking over to greet her. "I guess I said the same thing the other night."

"Thanks. Again," Jess said. "You're not so bad yourself," she added appraising his black slacks and striped cotton shirt. She glanced around the lobby where a dozen people were milling about. "Maybe I should have brought something more colorful," she said. "Everyone around here is wearing red or orange or blue or yellow. It's kind of like staring at a roll of Lifesavers."

Bill chuckled and said, "I have to admit that when I first met you, I thought . . ."

"You thought what?"

He paused for a moment and said, "To be honest, I thought you were, let's see, what's a good word? Taciturn maybe?"

"Taciturn? I've been called a lot of things, but I've never heard that one," she said, trying to adopt a somewhat hurtful expression.

He put his arm around her shoulder and said, "I had a hard time getting much out of you on our first plane trip. But the more we're together, I think I'm seeing you in a completely new light. To adopt your color analogies, it's as if a stagehand switched the gels over a spotlight from one that's dark to a warmer tone. Something like that."

She gazed up at him and grinned. "You certainly are the descriptive one. I guess I'll just take all of that as a compliment."

"I meant it that way," Bill said and led her toward the door. "Anyway, I've been checking with the concierge. I asked him to make a reservation for us at a great steakhouse. It's called Porcao. Hope that's okay with you." She nodded. As they walked outside, he said, "We'll grab a taxi. It's not a good idea to walk around this town at night."

Was this just a new warmer tone? Jess wondered. *Or did he have more in mind than just dinner?*

CHAPTER TWENTY-THREE

Rio de Janeiro

"Check out that view," Jessica exclaimed, staring out the window at the back of the restaurant. "That has to be the Christ Statue on top of Sugar Loaf Mountain. Maybe we'll go up there tomorrow."

"We?" Bill asked, pulling out her chair and taking a seat across from her in the crowded restaurant.

"Remember I said I had a contact who was going to show me around? Estelle put me in touch. You met her at the reception last night."

"Oh yes, the pretty girl who works for Leventhal."

Jess had a quick reaction to his description. She felt another twinge of jealousy and reminded herself that this man could compliment anyone he wanted to. After all, this is just dinner with a conference colleague. Nothing more. She had been telling herself that all during the cab ride to this place. But when they pulled up in front of the tall red brick building and Bill took her arm to lead her inside, she had felt a warm tingle. A kind of electric tether of some sort. She had glanced over at him and realized that he really was a nice-looking guy who was being especially attentive tonight. Then again, maybe those manners were just something he learned at hotel school or in his State Department office.

"You say you're meeting Estelle's cousin? What's his name?" Bill asked.

"Name's Rodriguez. He owns part of a restaurant here in Rio. He's picking me up tomorrow morning and said he'd take me up to Corcovado

Mountain. It's that one over there with the statue. He said there's some sort of a tram to get us up there."

"You're going to spend all day with this guy?" Bill asked.

"Most of the day. He has to be at the restaurant at night."

Bill thought about her day with this Brazilian and concluded she should be safe with a local. He sure as hell hoped so. He continued to gaze at Jessica while she studied the menu.

"I hear the barbeque is pretty good here," Bill ventured. "And one of the famous things they have down here is Feijoada."

"What's that?"

"It's kind of a stew with beans and pork."

"It's all in Portuguese," Jess said.

"I speak a bit of that," Bill said. "Let's see, we could try Cordeiro, those are lamb chops, or Camarones, marinated prawns. One of my favorites is the Picanha. That's marinated prime sirloin. But if you're on a health kick, there's always Couve refogada. Braised kale."

Jess laughed and said, "Forget healthy. I'm here to enjoy this little vacation, and I have to say, it's pretty handy to have you as my translator."

Bill was not only a pretty good translator, but he hoped he was a pretty good protector. After all, that was his assignment. Whatever he was, he was enjoying this time with her and hoping to get to know her better.

"So have you decided?"

"I'll take your advice and go for the barbeque."

Bill checked the wine list and selected a Pizzato Merlot, and they both gave their orders to the waiter.

"You certainly know your way around. Have you spent a lot of time here in Rio?"

How much could he tell her? I can't exactly tell her that I was here last year and got into a boatload of trouble on a drug raid. I can't get into any of that. Even if she does work at the White House, I don't have permission to read her in on my work. Trouble is, she's so damn smart, I wonder how long I can keep this up.

Bill figured he'd keep it light and general. "I've been here before. Great country, nice people, especially good music. We could take in a couple of clubs after dinner if you're up for it."

"Sounds like fun, but let's see how long our dinner takes. You know it's been a long day with that opening session, the break-out groups, and workshops."

"I know," Bill agreed. "We'll see how it goes. Here comes the wine. See if you like this one." He motioned for the waiter to pour her a taste first.

Jess tasted it. "Mm. I like it. Not too heavy."

Bill nodded to the waiter, who filled both their glasses and hurried away. "Now then, a toast to a beautiful lady in a beautiful city," he said, touching his glass to hers and looking into her eyes.

As Jess sipped her wine, it occurred to her that she had a chameleon here. Bill had now turned from being Mr. Boring to Mr. Charming. It was kind of like a Potemkin Village. That's what the National Security Council staff called the houses the North Koreans had built just across the DMZ. They had tried to create a whole façade of nice homes and even bused in children to play in the yards to give the impression of a wonderful life there in that dreary country. Bill wasn't dreary, but he did seem to have some sort of façade with all that conversation about ambassadors and place cards. Then again, he told her about studying hotel management and learning languages so he could manage a Ritz Carlton someday. It was just that—

"So, tell me more about yourself," Bill interrupted her reverie. "When did you decide you wanted to be an economist?"

Jess looked over at him, paused for a moment, and started to smile. "I wasn't much of a jock in college. I spent a lot of time in the library. I guess it was when I realized I had a love affair with the indoors."

Bill burst out laughing. "Sounds like you weren't the camping out type when you were a kid."

"Not really. I didn't even like Girl Scout camp."

"No wonder you like the Copacabana Palace," Bill said with a grin.

"I figure it took mankind about thirty-five thousand years to develop a good hotel room, and I see no need to go back into the jungle."

Bill laughed again. "They do have the Amazon jungle down here, you know."

"Never mind. I'll stick to the cities, if you don't mind."

When the waiter brought their dinner, they kept up an amiable conversation. Jess steered it to books and movies and found out they both liked mysteries and thrillers in print, but she explained that she preferred comedies when it came to films since she wasn't big on special effects, explosions, aliens, or vampires.

"Would you like movies about technology?" Bill asked. "I saw a review about a new one where a scientist has a different take on mini-bytes and terra-bytes."

"Sounds like 'The Breakfast of Champions,'" Jess quipped. "I'll pass on that one. But I'll take another bit of that great merlot. Good choice."

Bill reached over and filled her glass half full, then topped his off as well. "What about dessert?"

"My dinner was fabulous, but I guess I could handle a small one."

"I think I saw something terrific on the menu if you're into chocolate," Bill said.

"Are you kidding? I'm a choc-a-holic," Jess confessed.

"Then let me get the waiter over here." When the man reappeared, Bill said, "May we have two orders of your double espresso Brazil nut cake?"

"Certainly, sir."

CHAPTER TWENTY-FOUR

Rio de Janeiro

Pazio and his lieutenant sat on barstools in their new warehouse situated in the favela just a short drive from the hotel and other glitzy playgrounds of the rich and famous. They had built it after the police and federal agents had made a major raid that destroyed their previous hideout. The new one was underground with access through a network of tunnels and was fully equipped with the latest laboratory equipment, WiFi, and air-conditioning units to keep their cocaine and other illegal drugs at a proper temperature.

"You'll never guess who's staying at the Copacabana Palace with a pretty lady," he said, clicking off his cell phone.

"Who's that, boss?" Domingo asked.

Pazio looked over and answered, "Our old friend Bill Black."

Domingo jumped up. "You mean that animal who killed your brother?"

"One and the same. At least we're pretty sure it's him. Last year when our guys saw him take a shot at the truck? They heard someone shout his name, got a good look, and never forgot."

"How do you know it's the same guy? It's been a long time."

"Our man who saw him back then was making a delivery tonight to a client in the hotel when he spotted Black with a very pretty woman in the hotel lobby. He's emailing me some pictures he took. Said it looked like they had just come back from a hot date and were heading upstairs."

"I don't know. It's been a long time since anybody's seen that character."

"You're right," Pazio said. "Way too long between visits, I'd say."

"What do you mean? Why would you want another visit? Last time he was in town, he helped the police take down that whole shipment coming across the river. Cost us millions. We don't need any more of those operations. We've got enough to handle with the attacks in the favelas. You know that."

"I'm not talking about him taking us. I'm talking about us taking him."

Domingo started mumbling and pacing around the room. "I know we promised to take him out someday. Our guys said they called him a 'dead man.' And he will be if *I* ever get my hands on him."

"I think I would like to have that job all to myself," Pazio grumbled. "I need to make that guy suffer. I'll have to work on a plan."

"What are we gonna do, boss?"

"We'll figure out a way to stake out the hotel and shadow this character, this Bill Black. We'll take him off the street, bring him back here, and I'll inflict the pain slow but deadly. You watch me."

"What if he's with the girl?"

"When it comes to revenge for what he did, I'm not about to worry about collateral damage."

CHAPTER TWENTY-FIVE

Copacabana Palace—Rio de Janeiro

Jessica eyed the expansive breakfast buffet set up on the patio near the pool. It sure beat the food trucks lined up along Farragut Square a block from the White House that had names like the Far East Taco Grill, Sate Indonesian, Crab Café, and the Real Barbeque. Now that she thought about it, her barbeque dinner last night with Bill was one of the best she'd had in ages. Much better than food truck fare. The rest of the evening was pretty good too.

When they got back to the hotel, she had tripped on the curb. Bill made a comment about how she shouldn't be walking around in those sandal heels. Then he swiftly picked her up in his arms and carried her into the lobby. She told him she was okay, and he finally put her down quite gingerly. For a moment it did feel nice being lifted so effortlessly as if he were carrying her across a threshold, although that was a pretty far-fetched idea. She grabbed a plate and started to examine some of the dishes on the long white table. The fruit platter was glorious with stacks of papaya, mango, guava, a bright red fruit cut in quarters filled with tiny seeds, and a whole mound of purple berries that were much larger than blueberries. She had no idea what they were, but she took a spoonful along with the red fruit.

"Did you know that a pomegranate has 662 seeds?"

Jess whirled around and shook her head. With a wide grin she said, "And I need to know this because . . . ?"

"Oh, you never know when someone might ask," Bill said, picking up a plate and reaching for the berries."

"I suppose you know what those are too," Jess asked, pointing to the mound.

"Sure thing. They're called Acai. They grow on palm trees in the Amazon. But I know you don't want to go there," he said.

Jess moved along the buffet table and lifted the lid on a sterling silver casserole holding a stack of pancakes. "I wonder if these are like the ones we have back home. Maybe not. They're kind of thick. My dad used to say that thick pancakes are like flannel blankets. You need a half bottle of maple syrup to soak them up."

Bill glanced over, chuckled, and said, "Those are probably tapioca pancakes. People down here eat a fairly light breakfast. Fruit, toast, coffee. Lunch is the big meal. But I see that the hotel puts out quite a spread for all the international types that stay here."

"Fruit and toast. That's what I usually have anyway," Jess said. "It's just fun to check it all out. The most important part of my breakfast, though, is coffee."

"It's down at the end there. They have samovars, and I see that they're making a fresh pot over on the side. Should be nice and hot."

While Jess waited for the coffee to brew, another idea percolated as well. She wondered if Bill would be up for another dinner? Rodriguez said he had to be at work by around six today to get ready for his dinner crowd. At least his partner would be covering the midday groups. If I talk about last night, maybe Bill will talk about tonight. "Say, I wanted to thank you again for last night. The dinner was great. That chocolate cake was to die for, and then you played the Sir Galahad role when you carried me inside the hotel."

"I was just worried you had sprained your ankle or something. I've never figured out how you women walk in those shoes."

"I just sort of tripped on the curb. I was fine. Really."

Bill took his plate and motioned to a nearby table under an umbrella. "Let's sit over here. You can tell me all about your plans for the day."

She began by saying that the cousin would be picking her up around ten, so she figured she had plenty of time to finish breakfast, swim some laps and get her act together. "What are you doing today?"

Bill paused and took a bite of fruit.

"You're staring off into space," Jess said. "Something bothering you?"

"Huh? Oh, when I think about the State Department, sometimes I wonder if I could trade it in for the job that's behind door number 2." *Or door number 602, in fact.*

"And what would that other job be?" Jessica asked.

"I couldn't tell you at this point. I'll have to come up with something. By the way, how long do you think you'll be sightseeing with the cousin today? Any idea?" He thought that if she gets back from spending the day with some Brazilian macho-type, maybe they could do the dinner thing again. There was a lot to do between now and then, though. There's a conference call coming up with the embassy that he'd take on the secure line over at the Rio Consulate. He needed some updates on the final banquet, and anything new on the kitchen staff, the security team, or anyone they may not be able to trust. *What about Pazio and his boys? Could they have a plant inside the Palace? And have we learned anything new about their top suppliers? Sometimes HQ makes me feel like a juggler with all these balls in the air, but since they expect me to keep an eye on Jessica while all of the rest of this is going on, I might as well make sure she's not alone tonight. And that's not such a bad assignment.*

"He did say he had to go to work later," Jess said. "I'll probably be back here around dinner time. Why?"

"I know we're both flying back to Brasilia tomorrow, but if you're free tonight there's a great champagne bar about a block away and some other clubs I could show you. How about I ring your room around seven, and we'll take it from there?" Bill said. "I mean, if you're up for it. I do have to check in with my team today, so if there are any problems or delays, I'll leave word."

"Let's just exchange numbers. That's easier," Jess said.

Bill pulled out his phone, saw that he had a dozen messages marked urgent, but he ignored them. They both keyed in numbers, and as he watched her enjoying the fruit and toast, he wondered if he would enjoy this night even more than the last.

CHAPTER TWENTY-SIX

Rio de Janeiro

Pazio slammed down his phone and bellowed to Domingo. "Contact the gang. Round up the messengers."

"What's going on?" his lieutenant asked as he nailed down another crate and shoved it against the warehouse wall.

"Just got a tip. A high-level tip. There might be another raid overnight. We won't know about the timing for a while, but if it's just before dawn like the last ones, we only have a matter of hours to get ready. We've got to get the trucks over here, get some help to load these crates and get 'em all out of here. We'll leave that other stuff. We need the drugs, not the tools."

"I thought we were supposed to follow that Bill Black character later tonight," Domingo said.

Pazio checked his watch. "Let me figure this out. If there is a raid, that probably means Black's in on the action. We can't take him there. We'll have to wait until it's over. We deal with the raid first and then try to pick him off at some point in the morning when he leaves the hotel. Think about it. The raid goes down. He's there giving orders or whatever the hell he does. Then he goes back to the hotel, especially if he's got that broad with him. He gets some shuteye . . ."

"Or another kind of action," Domingo ventured with a leering grin.

"Forget the speculation, focus on the mission. First thing in the morning, you take one of the boys and stake out the hotel. When he comes out, you take him, and you bring him to me. We'll see what happens tonight. The police may not even find our new hideouts or the tunnel. If they don't, you'll bring him here. It'll be perfect," Pazio said. "No one hears gunshots this far underground."

Pazio grabbed his cell again and brought up a series of photos. "Now. Pay attention. Here are the pictures our messenger sent of Black and the chick last night."

"Great bod," Domingo said, staring at one of Bill carrying Jessica into the hotel lobby. "I wonder what's the matter with her."

"Nothing," Pazio said. "Flick to the next one."

"He sets her down, and they walk to the elevator. Maybe he was just clowning around."

"From what we heard about his reputation, I don't think he's much of a clown," Pazio said. "In fact, he's downright dangerous. Just study their faces. I'll email you the photos so you can have them handy when you watch the hotel."

"You want me to grab him in front of the Copacabana? You've gotta be joking."

"Of course not, you fool," Pazio blurted. "You just follow him. Wait until you're in a good spot *away* from the hotel, get Black into your car. Then, like I said, bring him back to me. I want to handle him personally."

CHAPTER TWENTY-SEVEN

Rio de Janeiro

"So how was your date with the cousin, Rodriguez? What was he like?" Bill asked, meeting Jessica in the hotel lobby. He wasn't sure if he wanted to hear the answer. The fact that she had been squired around town by some hot-shot Brazilian had been bothering Bill all day, even while he was in planning sessions and on conference calls. He hadn't felt this way about a woman in, what? Years? He'd dated a number of females, a few pretty attractive ones. DC was full of them. None had lasted very long, though. With his travel schedule and agency assignments, he hadn't managed to maintain any kind of decent long-term relationship.

When it came to finding a date, it wasn't just looks, although that always seemed to be the first thing he or any other guy noticed. There had to be more to it. Sense of humor was high on his list, along with smarts. When he first met Jess, he knew she was smart, but the humor bit had eluded him until he got to know her better. Now she was . . . what was she? A momentary attraction? Or possibly something more? As he was trying to sort out his conflicting reactions, she answered his question.

"Rodriguez? What was he like? Let's see," Jessica paused and grinned. "He sort of had that 'shaken, not stirred' look, if you know what I mean."

Oh great. Now I'm competing with another agent type, Bill thought.

"We had a nice time," she continued. "He was a perfect tour guide, and he turned out to be pretty funny too. When he picked me up, the sun was awfully bright, so we stopped at a stall where they sold hats. He told me where Panama hats are made. I thought it was pretty obvious. But no. He said they're from Ecuador."

"Never picked up that bit of trivia," Bill murmured.

"Then when I was trying them on," she continued, "he said that we were going to play 'No Photos.'"

"What's 'No Photos'?" Bill asked.

"While we were shopping, he would stand just in front of me and say to people milling around, 'No photos. No photos.' And he kept doing it, so finally people started staring and must have thought he was my bodyguard, and I was some movie star or something because they all started taking pictures of us with their iPhones."

Clever bastard, Bill thought. "So now you're a movie star." He studied the blue silk blouse she was wearing. That together with her gorgeous blue eyes created quite a picture. He added, "Of course, you could be."

"Thanks, but that was never an option in my book."

"Well, now that you've seen the town, how about seeing some clubs?" Bill suggested. "I have a taxi waiting."

They turned and pushed through the heavy glass doors where warm, balmy breezes wafted over from the ocean. They quickly got inside the cab, and Bill asked the driver to take them to the Lapa section of town.

"Where's Lapa?" Jess inquired.

"It's about twenty minutes from here."

"What kind of place is it?"

"Party atmosphere. Let's just say it makes Bourbon Street in New Orleans look muted by comparison."

"Great music, huh?" she asked.

"All kinds. Samba, reggae, rock, funk, techno . . ."

"Techno?"

"Just wait. You'll see."

Jessica stared out the window as the driver left the beach area and drove toward the center of the city. She began to see rows of colonial-style houses. But they weren't homes. They had been converted into restaurants and nightclubs. The taxi finally came to what looked like the center of the action. "What's this?" she asked, pointing to an odd structure.

"That's the Arcos da Lapa. It's an aqueduct they built back in the eighteenth century. Everyone hangs out around there." He leaned forward and told the driver they would get out at the corner. He paid the man, and they joined the throng.

"It's like a great big fair," Jess said, looking around at couples dancing in the street.

"Exactly," Bill said. He took her arm and directed her over to a kiosk where they bought cups of black bean soup. "We can catch some burgers or pizza over there. I realize this isn't like going to a fancy restaurant, but I thought you might get a kick out of it."

"Are you kidding? I love it," Jess said, taking a taste of her soup from the paper cup.

After sampling more dishes and a can of beer, they headed into a club called Fixos Fluxos where a group of musicians was pounding out samba beats.

"What a great sound," Jess said, staring somewhat mesmerized at the bandstand.

"Let's see if we can grab a table." Bill scanned the crowded room and pointed to one toward the back. "C'mon. I think we can snag that one over there." He held a chair for Jess and sat down next to her, so they were both facing the dance floor. "What's your pleasure, my lady?"

Jess looked up at him and smiled. "You sound like an actor on *Masterpiece Theater*."

"And that's a bad thing?" he asked.

"Do they teach good manners in the protocol office?" she asked, though she had to admit that the more time they spent together, the more he didn't really seem like a protocol type. He was more . . . she didn't really know *what* type he was. He knew a fondue fork from the one used for escargot. But what else did he know? He certainly didn't fit any of the stereotypes or characters she worked with at the White House. He was much more adventuresome. Perhaps that was it. After all, he did speak other languages, and he talked about traveling to a lot of places. Maybe she could get him to open up a bit more tonight. Maybe she could delve a little deeper.

When a waitress swung by their table, Jess decided to try a rum drink. Then two.

After another hour, she was feeling quite a buzz. As she watched Bill keeping time with the music, she realized she was having a great time herself. When she turned the conversation around to their families, she began by commenting that her mother, the classical music teacher, would have been amazed at the wild sounds coming from the band.

Later, when she asked Bill to tell her about *his* family, he finally told her the story of his little sister being killed by a teenage driver drunk and high on marijuana. He said the kid evidently had been eating snacks called Pot Tarts and Kit Kats that were laced with it.

Jessica had been shocked and sympathetic when she heard the details. She didn't care for pot, though some of her friends seemed to get hold of their own stashes. The White House position on the whole drug trade was somewhat muddled since there were federal laws against it but state laws permitting it. Or at least some of it. She knew some people developed a craving for the high they got from drugs. Right now, she was feeling her own high from the rum.

Bill ordered another round, and their conversation veered from family to pets. Jess said she once had an adorable black and white cat named Domino. Bill ventured that when he was a kid, he had two German Shepherds.

"What were their names?" she asked.

"We called them Rolex and Timex because they were watch dogs."

Jess burst out laughing. She truly was having a great time with this man. He had turned out to be so much easier to talk to than Ken ever was. As she reflected on past dates with her ex, she remembered that she had often felt they were having parallel conversations. They may have been on the same road, but never used the same vehicle. When it came to Bill Black, at this point, she felt she could go with him just about anywhere.

CHAPTER TWENTY-EIGHT

Copacabana Palace—Rio de Janeiro

The elevator door opened on the sixth floor. Bill took Jessica's hand and led her to Room 602. She reached in her purse for the room key. He took it and leaned over to slide it into the lock. He held the door open and looked down into her eyes. She held his gaze. Then she gestured at the open doorway and said, "You could come in for a while, if you'd like."

He stepped inside, pushed the door closed, and, out of habit, turned to lock it. There was one light on in the room on the night stand next to the bed. He saw that there was only one chair, and it was stationed at the desk where her computer was set up.

Jessica reached down, pulled off her sandals and walked over to the mini-bar. "I think there are a few things in here if you'd like a drink or something," she said, opening the small refrigerator door and peering inside. "We could have another rum drink, a beer, coke, or maybe just some M&Ms. What's your pleasure?"

Bill knew exactly what his pleasure was, but he wasn't about to tell her now. Not yet anyway. He already had plenty to drink, and after Jessica had polished off her third rum drink at the last club, he was amazed she still looked steady on her feet. What did he want? Certainly not anything from the fridge. "I don't need anything else, Jess. I think I've had enough for one night. How about you?"

"I think I went a bit overboard at the last stop we made. In fact, I'll probably have a heck of a headache in the morning, but it was worth it. That club was such fun. Where did you learn to dance like that?" she asked, closing the mini-bar, and sauntering over to perch on the edge of the bed.

"Back in school they had this class in ballroom dancing. My folks made me go. At first, I hated it, but later I guess I got the hang of it," he explained, coming over and sitting down beside her.

"You probably have to dance at some of those formal events in your job, right?"

"My job? Oh, right," Bill said. "The protocol staff sets up the dinners for visiting dignitaries. But we don't dance with them." *And in my real job, the closest thing I ever came to dancing was when I had to leap away from an explosive or shimmy under a fence.*

As for real dancing, he had to admit that holding this woman in his arms, even for a little while, felt awfully good. She seemed to melt against him. Then again, maybe it was the rum melting her resistance. He hoped that wasn't all it was.

Jess stood up. "Excuse me for a minute. I want to freshen up a bit."

"Sure. Mind if I turn on the radio?"

"Go ahead. Might as well continue our music marathon." She slipped into the bathroom and closed the door.

Bill turned on the clock radio and scanned the stations until he found one playing slightly subdued tunes, a rarity in this town. He pulled out his cell and quickly looked for messages. There was a secure text from Chet in Brasilia. It was a follow-up to their conference call. He said the dinner staff checked out, but he still had questions about the security team. *What do we do about that crowd?* Bill wondered.

Another note was from his counterpart in the Rio Consulate. They were waiting for an order about another raid involving a new drug shipment and asking him to stand by. Bill shoved the cell back into his pocket as Jess came out of the bathroom.

She hesitated in the doorway and wondered what to do next. She had told herself that when she came to Brazil it would be great to meet someone exciting. Hal even encouraged her to take this little side trip to Rio to relax and rejuvenate. The trouble was, she wasn't sure how relaxed she was right then. After all those rum drinks, she'd usually be ready for a nap. But as she glanced over toward the bed and saw Bill sitting there, his head cocked to one side, a quizzical expression on his handsome face, she realized she didn't want to go to bed alone.

As Jess moved over to the bed, Bill stood up. He raised one hand and traced a line down her cheek. Was there such a thing as a gentle electric shock? If there is, she certainly felt it. The expectant look on his face told her he wanted her as much as she wanted him. She stepped into his arms as he pulled her toward him.

He tipped her chin up and lowered his mouth to hers. She opened to him as he deepened the kiss. He cradled her head with one hand while circling her waist with the other. She heard a slight moan and wasn't sure if it came from him or from her.

CHAPTER TWENTY-NINE

Rio de Janeiro

"Get those crates on the truck. Hurry up, you idiots," Pazio bellowed. "Line 'em up farther back. No, not that way. Pile them carefully. You can fit more in that one." He turned to Domingo who was giving out his own orders. "Where are the messengers?" Pazio looked at his watch for the third time. "They should have been here by now. I need to tell them where to fan out in the favela and warn the others."

Domingo pulled out his cell to check for messages. "They say they're on the way. Should be any minute now."

"Yeah, well the police could be here any time too," Pazio lamented. "That is, if they've figured out where the tunnel is. Our contact said he wasn't sure which location would be hit and I never told him about this new warehouse. But you never know. They could be tracking me. Tracking you. Even with the new cell phones. Who the hell knows? We gotta get out of here."

"I thought you said we still had some time," his lieutenant countered.

"We have no idea how fast or how far they're gonna go. We've got too many supplies on hand in here. Too many customers waiting. Have to move it all. And I mean *all*," he ordered.

"I got it. I got it," Domingo shouted. He motioned to his men to go back to the lab and get the rest of the crates. "Just get the other stuff. Forget everything else. We got no time to clear out the whole place. Get moving." He turned to see a dozen teenagers on motor bikes careening down the tunnel.

"You sure took your own sweet time," Pazio shouted as the boys dismounted and ran up to him. "Now listen. We might get hit again tonight. Not sure where. Here are maps with your assignments marked in red." He passed them out. "Each of you has at least three stops to make. Now get yourselves organized and warn our members. Now!"

The leader grabbed the maps, handed them out and motioned for the whole group to head back down the tunnel. With a slight wave over his shoulder, he and the rest of the avioezinhos were gone.

After a few more frantic moves, the older men lifted the last crate into place, locked the warehouse, slammed the doors of the two trucks marked with grocery store logos and sped down the tunnel to the open road.

"I just hope they haven't figured out the location of our other safe houses," Domingo said, swerving to avoid a row of garbage cans as the second truck followed close behind.

"Unless we have a rat in the organization, they won't," Pazio declared. "Our own stooge, so to speak, is holding us up for a bundle with this last tip-off. I'd like to off him, he's getting too greedy, but we can't afford that right now."

"Yeah. Better pay him off and lay low for a little while, right, boss?"

Pazio studied the road and checked his watch again. "Once we get this shipment out of town, you see it gets unloaded, tell the guys to scatter, grab some shut-eye, and then you can go watch the Copacabana. Just like we planned."

CHAPTER THIRTY

Copacabana Palace—Rio de Janeiro

Jessica stretched out under the soft white sheets and opened her eyes. Bright sunlight invaded the room. She quickly shut her eyes and rubbed her forehead. She wondered what time it was. After all those rum drinks and then that mind-blowing . . . wait . . . did all of that really happen? It wasn't just a dream? If it was, that had to be the most incredible one she'd ever had. The trouble was that this headache is also one of the most incredible ones she'd ever had.

She turned her head away from the window and opened her eyes again, squinting as she reached across the bed. The other side was empty. She tried to sit up and sank back down again and thought about if she had packed some aspirin. She needed water. But first she needed to know where Bill was.

She waited and listened, but the only sounds she heard were muffled voices out in the hallway and the noise of traffic six stories below. Maybe he got up early, didn't want to wake her and went out for coffee. He wouldn't have wanted to order room service. That would make too much noise. He must have gone out to get it. *Maybe he'll bring some back for me*, she thought. She smiled at the notion and decided she'd better get up and deal with the headache first, then grab a shower and make herself presentable.

She glanced over at the digital clock that read 10:45. *Good grief. Did I sleep that long? Must have been exhausted.* She lay back down and began to relive the previous night's escapades. She remembered the drive to that street fair by the aqueduct, the soup in the paper cups, the samba music, the dancers, and the rum drinks. *Why did I have to have so much to drink? I never do that.* She chastised herself. *But . . . it was worth it.*

She remembered that Estelle had made the funny comment that instead of OMB, she wanted OMG. Last night she had experienced it in spades.

She sat up and stared at the empty pillow. She saw that her skirt, blouse, and lingerie were strewn across the end of the bed, but all of Bill's clothes were gone. *Of course, they're gone because he went out for coffee.*

She stood up, steadied herself and walked slowly into the bathroom. She poked around in her new cosmetic bag and sure enough, she had bought some aspirin along with the makeup, brushes, and toothpaste she had found at the shopping mall in Brasilia. She swallowed two pills with a big glass of cold water and started the shower. When she stepped inside, she once again marveled at the strong spray, figuring that the next person to use this room would also be glad she had removed the restrictor.

After washing and drying her hair, she began to feel marginally better. She applied a bit of makeup base, eye shadow, mascara, a touch of blush, and some lip gloss. She brushed out her hair and checked the closet. She knew she had to fly back to Brasilia that night since the last of the OAS meetings would get underway first thing in the morning. Then the final banquet featuring the Brazilian President's speech would be the big event tomorrow night. The whole delegation would fly back to Washington the next morning. At least she and Bill would have one more day here in Rio.

She looked at the clock again. Now it was 11:30. *Where is he?* She wondered if he got called into some meeting. No, that didn't make any sense. All the State Department people are in Brasilia. He might be making conference calls, though. *Yes, that's it.* He probably went out to make calls about all the last-minute preparations for the banquet, and he couldn't do that from the room if she were sleeping. He was the perfect gentleman.

Jess went over to the closet and selected a casual off-white shirt, long beige skirt, and an alligator belt with matching alligator flats. She rolled up the sleeves and decided to call room service for some much-needed caffeine. Since Bill hadn't returned with coffee, he must have been tied up with calls, so she might as well handle her own breakfast. She picked up the phone by the bed, placed her order, and went over to the desk to check her email.

She first logged on to her secure account and saw that there were a few of the usual listings of the president's schedule and an update on Hal who was out of the woods and would be back in the office mid-week. She heaved a small sigh of relief when she read that one and scrolled down. Nothing else was so important it couldn't wait a while, so she switched to her personal email.

She saw a note from Ken asking if she was sure she didn't want to have dinner again. *After a night with Bill Black, she couldn't imagine spending another evening with the Ken-Doll.* Of course, she hadn't wanted to spend *any* more time with that man, which is why she broke up with him in the first place. It was just that now the comparison between the two of them was so stark, she knew she could never go back. Not to Ken. Ever.

The next note was from her friend Kay, who wrote, "So how's Rio? Meet any handsome Brazilians down there? Tell all . . . K."

Jess quickly hit Reply and typed, "You'll never believe it. Not a Brazilian. Someone else whose name begins with 'B'—I'll explain as soon as I get back." She signed off.

It was then that she saw the card. Bill's card left next to her purse over to the side of the desk. She grabbed it and saw one word scribbled at the top. "Later."

Later? What does "later" mean? He'll be back later? He'll see me later? When later? I thought he was an expert on protocol. It's hardly proper to spend an incredible night with someone, then walk out and leave a one-word note. He could have said "thank you," or something nice, couldn't he? But "later"?

PROTECTING JESS

Jessica stared at the card with his name, title, and State Department seal embossed in black ink. Would he have left just that one word if he were going out for coffee and doughnuts? No. He would have written something like "back later." And if he had to go make phone calls or go to a meeting, wouldn't he have said "I'll meet you later," then given her a time or told her where to go?

This was baffling. Or was it? She leaned back in the desk chair and thought for a long moment. The more she reflected on their weekend together, the more she thought she was getting to know the man. He had told her about college, his job, his sister, even his dogs. But now that she tried to recall their conversations, he never said if he was married, engaged, or had a girlfriend. A great-looking guy like that must have a woman somewhere.

Maybe he's really married, she thought. *Why didn't I ask? Was I so smitten by the manners, the easy banter, the looks, the build, that I let my guard down when I should have had my antenna up?* She continued to chastise herself for a while, for letting herself get blown away by the rum and romance of it all, and now she wasn't sure it was worth it. *Is this what I really wanted when I told myself I was looking for a little adventure in Brazil? Or did I let myself get emotionally involved while we were so . . . so physically involved?*

As she kept going over the good points and the bad points, she felt as if she were engaged in an inner tennis match but there was no "love" in the score.

She heard a knock on the door. She jumped up. *Maybe it's Bill. Maybe he's come back after all.* With her hopes rising, she ran to the door.

"Room service, madam," the waiter said, wheeling in a small cart covered with a white tablecloth, silverware, several dishes, a basket of rolls and croissants, small plate of butter with a selection of jams and honey along with a large thermos of coffee, cream, sugar, and a single rose in a tiny sterling silver vase. He set it next to the desk, handed her the bill and said, "Will there be anything else?"

She grabbed the bill, signed it, and shook her head. "No, thank you. This looks just fine."

The breakfast looked fine, but she wasn't. Not by a long shot. When the waiter left the room, she pulled her desk chair around to sit at the little breakfast table and poured a cup of steaming espresso. *The coffee may help the last vestiges of my headache, but it's not going to do anything about a heartache*, she thought while buttering a muffin. She kept ruminating about what a fool she'd been to fall for this man. By the time she had finished the last morsel, she was telling herself, *Get a grip. Grow up. You had a fling. You enjoyed it. Now get over it.*

In order to do that, she decided she needed some air. Take a good long walk. That's what she'd do right about now. She unplugged the charger from her iPhone, slipped the cell into the side pocket of her purse, grabbed her room key, and marched out the door.

When she stepped out of the elevator, she went over to the registration desk. She was still mad. Still upset by Bill's disappearance, but she wasn't about to call his room. No. She wouldn't stoop to contacting him first. That was *his* responsibility after his cryptic note. *Not a note. Just a word.*

"Excuse me," she said to the woman behind the desk.

"Yes, may I help you?"

"I wondered if you might have seen Bill Black this morning?" Jess asked, holding her breath.

"Bill Black?" the clerk asked. "I'm not sure I know the gentleman. We have so many guests here, you know." She looked down at her computer and typed in the name. "Oh, here it is. He checked out."

"He checked out?" Jessica exclaimed. "Why? When?"

"Let me see. Yes, it was very early this morning."

"Early? How early?"

"I wasn't on the desk, but it says here he checked out about 3:00 a.m."

"That's it?" Jess said. "No forwarding address or message or anything? I mean, did he leave a message for me?"

"And your name is?" the clerk inquired.

"Jessica Tanner. Room 602."

The woman checked again, then looked around the desk area. She leafed through a few envelopes stacked on the right and leaned down to check a shelf under the desk. "No. Sorry. Nothing here for Jessica Tanner. Is there anything else I can do for you?"

Jess stood there stunned. *How could he just check out? Where would he go at three o'clock in the morning? This doesn't make any sense. He couldn't have been called back to Brasilia to deal with a banquet.* She looked at the clerk and said in a halting voice, "No. Sorry. Thanks for checking." She was about to turn away when she said, "Oh, I thought I'd take a walk, look around a bit. Do you have any suggestions of places I should go this time of day?"

"There are so many lovely things to see, especially our churches. After all it is Sunday, the clerk said. "Though many of the services are over, you could still walk around and see the architecture. Our concierge is right over there. He'll give you directions."

"Oh, yes, the concierge," Jess said. She gave a sigh, crossed the lobby, and chatted with a young man who circled some locations and handed her a map.

CHAPTER THIRTY-ONE

Rio de Janeiro

"We've been staking out this hotel since dawn, boss, and haven't seen that Bill Black character yet. How long do we have to stay here?" Domingo begged, holding his cell phone to his ear while peering out the car window.

"They're probably still up there sleeping in. Or whatever they're doing."

"Yeah, but now it's noon. Wouldn't you think they'd take a break or something?"

"Look, you idiot. This is our one chance to nail my brother's killer. And it's not only that, you know that Black was in on that raid last night at our other warehouse. Our man spotted him with the police and some DEA types who work with the American Consulate. They're all in it together. He must have gotten back late. Makes sense that he's sleeping in. As for last night, at least they didn't find where we stashed our new shipment."

"They didn't find the tunnel or the lab either," Domingo said. "What do I have to do now?"

"You stay there. I told you before. Why do I have to tell you again?" Pazio asked in an exasperated tone. "Like I said, this is our big chance. Besides, we don't know how long he'll be in town or when he might be coming back. It has to be now. Keep your eyes open, and don't bother me again until you've got him in the car."

"Okay, okay. Once we've got him, you still want us to bring him to the lab in the tunnel?"

"I already told you to take him there. You just call and tell me when you're coming, and I'll meet you. Then, as I've said before, I will have the great pleasure of taking care of that bastard myself."

Domingo kept watch and suddenly he punched up Pazio's number again.

"Boss? It's not him, it's her," Domingo announced into his cell.

"You mean Black's girlfriend? She's out of the hotel without him? Is she alone?" Pazio demanded.

"Yeah. Looks like she's just taking a walk or something, kind of looking around, not going to the taxi line."

"I wonder . . . let me think," Pazio said in a halting voice. "Black's not out, but maybe we can force him out. In fact, we can force him to come right to our door."

"How are we gonna do that? I don't see him?" Domingo said.

"Isn't it rather obvious? Follow the girl. Make sure it's her."

"It's her all right. Got sunglasses on, but she's got the same long blond hair, the same great legs from what I can tell. I sure like that bod."

"Stop salivating and start moving," Pazio commanded. "Follow her. When she gets away from the hotel, you pick the spot. Get her in the car. You know how to do that. You've done it enough."

"Then what?"

"Then you bring her to the tunnel and down to the lab. I'll meet you there."

"Then what?" Domingo said.

"What is this, an echo chamber?" Pazio said. "Just do it."

CHAPTER THIRTY-TWO

American Consulate—Rio de Janeiro

"We may get these low-lifes to talk yet," the local station chief said.

"Too bad we didn't get Pazio this time," Bill said. "I know we've been trying to ferret out his contacts, but the time has come to bring him in. If and when we can find him."

"He's slippery," the officer observed. "Trouble is, I hear he can also be somewhat sophisticated since the latest is that he's been able to pay off, or maybe a better term is 'pressure' a whole slew of policemen to look the other way when it comes to the drug raids."

"Not just police," Bill said. "He must have some pretty high-level contacts tipping him off about your schedule. This time his boys had cleared out one place and were just trying to run out of that other one when we got there."

"Right. At least you were able to stop two of them and get them back here for questioning. Appreciate your help on this one. We've been pretty short-handed lately," the chief said. "Here we're trying to coordinate with our Drug Enforcement people to stop shipments going to the States . . ."

"And at the same time, the government wants our help to stop them before the Olympics," Bill added.

"And yet FARC keeps shipping, and Pazio and his boys keep receiving, refining, and re-shipping." The chief turned toward the one-way window and stared into the interrogation room. "Think we'll get anything actionable about Pazio's hideout this time? Or better yet, the names of their suppliers?"

"If we get lucky." His cell phone buzzed. "Excuse me, have to take this." Bill stepped out of the room and punched up the call. "Black here. What's the latest?"

"We need you back here ASAP," Chet Osborn said.

"In Brasilia? Now?"

"As soon as you can get your ass back. We've got some leads on the assassination plot."

"But we're trying to wrap up last night's raid."

"Yes, I heard they roused you out of the sack in the middle of the night to help out. How much did you get this time?" Chet asked.

"Just a small stash. Didn't get the kingpin, but we did pick up a couple of his seconds. They're grilling them now."

"Let the Consulate staff and DEA handle that. Forget the airlines, I've already dispatched a jet for you. Should be landing in about thirty minutes. Get over to the airport right away."

"There was something I wanted to do before I left," Bill objected.

"Whatever it is, it'll have to wait. The president's life is in danger. That's why they sent you down here. The fact that you took that side trip to Rio means you could help out on a local raid. But here we're talking about a national emergency. Get your ass in gear. I'll send a car to meet your plane as soon as you land."

"All right," Bill said, reluctantly. "I sure could use a bit of shut-eye, though."

"Grab it on the plane," Chet suggested.

"It's a short flight. Takes less than two hours," Bill said.

"Two hours is better than nothing. I'll see you at the President's Palace. I'm setting up a meeting with the security staff. We'll meet just as soon as you get here."

Bill explained the situation to the Rio chief, grabbed his bag and headed out to a staff car that would take him to the airport. He checked his watch. Noon. He'd been up all night, but what a night it was.

He couldn't remember when he had ever felt that way about a woman. Jess was incredible. He hated to leave her. But when she fell asleep and he had checked for texts and saw the urgent one about a raid, he had no choice but to slip out. He really wanted to stay. She looked so gorgeous sprawled out on the bed with all that long blond hair spread across the pillow. It was all he could do to get his clothes, dress in the bathroom, and leave the card. He probably should have written something better than just the word "later," but he thought he could help with the raid and get back to her. No such luck.

Now he really wanted to go back to the hotel and see her before hightailing it to Brasilia, but there was no time. He decided he would call her cell on the way to the airport and try to dream up some logical explanation for why he cut out on her and had to head back to the capital.

CHAPTER THIRTY-THREE

Copacabana Palace—Rio de Janeiro

Jessica slung her alligator bag over her shoulder and started down the boulevard in front of the hotel. She was glad she had brought her sunglasses since the noon rays were reflecting off the sidewalks, creating a hot, shimmering effect. She was sorry she had forgotten the hat Rodriguez bought for her. Around the corner, she saw that she could walk on the shady side of the street. That helped quite a bit as hot, gusty winds ruffled her hair along with her cotton skirt.

She peered into shop windows, closed for the day. At least she could study some of the local art displayed in the many galleries along the way. She spied a dress shop down an alley and decided to see if it might be open.

As she sauntered in that direction, she noticed two men walking the same way. That seemed odd. When she stole a glance at them, they didn't seem like the type to be checking out galleries and certainly not dress shops. She hurried her pace in an effort to get to the next corner and try to lose them.

As Jess turned, she felt one of them grab her arm while the other clamped his hand over her mouth. They were holding her too tight for her to wrench away. She tried to scream, but the sound came out as a muffled squeal. She kicked one of the men in the leg and twisted her body, but they were too strong for her, and they held on and dragged her toward a car idling at the curb.

In broad daylight on a side street near a major hotel, Jess couldn't believe what was happening. She kept struggling, praying that someone would come along and help her. But no one did. The men hustled her over to a dark SUV. One of them opened the door, while the other one, with his hand still firmly planted over her mouth, shoved her inside and got in next to her. The first man jumped in the driver's seat and gunned the engine.

The man in back finally let go to fasten her seat belt. Jessica struggled and cried out, "Who are you? What do you want?" She was terrified, and they wouldn't answer her. She started to reach for the door handle, but he grabbed her wrists and in a deft move, pulled a roll of duct tape from his pocket, and tore off a long piece with his teeth and taped her hands together. With another piece, he started to plaster it across her mouth. She shook violently. "No. No," she cried out.

"Shut up, and you won't get hurt," the man ordered. Next, he slid a bandana out of his shirt pocket and used it as a blindfold. Jessica was shaking and squirming, but the seat belt was tight. She couldn't move, couldn't cry out, and now couldn't see. He must have pulled out his phone because she heard him hit some keys and then, after a moment, he simply said, "Got her. On our way."

Got her? Got who? Jess wondered. Were they looking for her or just any woman on the street?

She reminded herself that they said they wouldn't hurt her, so she tried to figure out what they were after. She could still feel her shoulder bag next to her, not that there was a lot in there. She did have her credit cards and cell phone, which she regretted she couldn't get to right at that moment.

Jess had a frantic thought about the warning Bill had given her about street crime. After that, she had googled "Street crime in Rio" and remembered reading about so-called Express Kidnappings where gangs would target a well-dressed woman, throw her in a car and force her to go to an ATM and take out as much money as she could. Then they would simply toss her back onto the street. She remembered the name for this gambit: Sequestro Relampago. *Could that be what's happening? I pray that's all it is.*

The man next to her smelled like sweat and tobacco. She tried to inch away from him, but realized she was trapped where she was. He had spoken to her in English. She didn't know about the other one, and she only knew a couple of words in Portuguese she had picked up from Bill. She tried to make a sound.

"See what she's trying to say," the driver said. "Nobody can hear her in the car anyway."

The other man tore the duct tape off her mouth. Jess blurted out, "Sequestro Relampago?"

The driver chuckled. "The lady here thinks this is a simple street snatch."

"Yeah," the other man said. "She'll soon find out."

What will she find out? If they don't want money, what do they want? She wasn't wearing any fancy jewelry, and she didn't have anything with her that was valuable except maybe her watch, though it didn't cost all that much.

She couldn't see anything, but she heard the street noises. As the car made several turns, she began to hear bits of rock music. *We must be getting near one of those shanty areas with all the wooden shacks and tin roofs. I can hear children shouting and some dogs barking. Dear God, where are they taking me?*

Her mind was reeling. Her heart was pounding. Nothing so scary had ever happened to her. As she thought about past experiences, her life and job in DC, she realized she had always felt safe. After all, she worked in the most protected eighteen acres on the planet. And while none of those "protectors" could help her now, still . . . she was always known as someone who was calm. Cool and collected as Hal always said. She sensed that even in the current situation, she had to stay calm if she possibly could.

Think! Just figure out what they want, try to give it to them if I can and then find out how to get away. Then again, why didn't I listen when Bill warned me not to go out on the streets alone? I just thought a walk in the middle of the day would be fine. I never thought . . . in fact, I wasn't thinking about much of anything except for Bill. Where is he?

She wondered how long her midday nightmare would last, and her mind began to turn toward more dire thoughts, like rape and murder. She tried to slow her breathing, but it was no use. She was still shaking when the car came to a stop.

CHAPTER THIRTY-FOUR

Rio de Janeiro

Finally, Bill had a few minutes to himself. He sat back in the staff car and scrolled through the latest texts and emails. He didn't have a message from Jessica. He thought she might try to call him when he didn't come back. He paused for almost a minute, once again thinking about their night together and how he had to slip out. Maybe she was upset because he didn't leave more of a note. Again, he thought about protecting his cover. What was he supposed to say? 'Have to go after some bad guys who are sending millions of dollars' worth of drugs into the United States to destroy lives, including my own sister's?' Hardly the job of a protocol officer.

He still hadn't decided what he *could* tell her once he had a chance to explain. Now, in addition to leaving in the middle of the night, he was leaving in the middle of the day to go back to Brasilia, which meant she would be in Rio by herself until her return flight tonight. He didn't like the idea of her being in that city alone, and he had no idea if that Rodriguez character was around to entertain her. She hadn't said anything about specific plans today and obviously counted on being with him before they both would head back to Brasilia for the big OAS banquet tomorrow. Earlier he had thought about their last day in Rio together and how they could lie on the beach . . . or lie in bed for that matter. Now, he'd just have to lie to her on the phone.

He stared at his cell and decided this might be his only chance to reach her for a while. He'd be on the jet to Brasilia in a few minutes, then in more security meetings, going over possible suspects again, and Lord knows what else the rest of the day. He wanted to hear her voice, wanted to gauge her reaction to his disappearance, wanted to tell her how great last night was. Maybe he could keep it short, just let her know he had been called away, apologize for his absence, and tell her they'd catch up at the Palace dinner tomorrow. That should work.

He punched in her number. It rang once, twice, three times. Then it went to voicemail. That seemed odd. Jess usually kept her cell handy. Maybe she had gone down to the hotel's restaurant where it was probably noisy and didn't hear it. He didn't want to leave a message. That was lame. He needed to talk to her. He clicked off, vowing to try again as soon as the plane landed in Brasilia.

CHAPTER THIRTY-FIVE

"That was my phone," Jessica declared. "Let me answer it."

"Do you think we're that stupid?" the driver asked. "You think we'd let you talk to someone? Tell somebody you're in a car with men you don't know? How dumb do you think we are?"

"But, if I don't answer, my friends will try to find me," she said, wondering if that could possibly be true. One person who might be calling was Bill, and even if she somehow got a message to him, how in the world would he be able to track these guys? Was it Bill? She desperately wanted to know. She needed to find out where he was. She thought for a moment, saw the man next to her eyeing her legs and prayed that's all this was. She needed to get out of there.

Jess wondered again if they would demand a ransom because they thought she was some kind of high-value target. If that's what they wanted, who would they contact? They wouldn't be dumb enough to try and contact the White House even if they knew she worked there. She had left her passport in her hotel room, and she didn't have her White House business cards with her either. Just a few credit cards. And they were welcome to those. No, she figured they wouldn't know where she worked. They wouldn't contact the Americans or the Rio Consulate or anyone else in authority. If they did, it would mean a whole army of people—Americans and Brazilians—would be out looking for her.

What was it that they wanted? She hoped to God that they weren't some sort of diabolical snuff film producers. She had heard about such things, but not recently. She shuddered. Then the car stopped, and she heard the driver say, "Gotta open the gate. Stay there." A moment later, they drove a bit farther and her fears heightened when the man in back got out and yanked her out of the car. Then he tore off the blindfold. She saw the driver leaning in to grab her shoulder bag.

Jess quickly started taking stock of her surroundings. They were at the end of a long tunnel lit by a few lanterns on crude walls. The man with the worse body odor pulled her toward a metal door that had a deadbolt and another lock on the outside. The driver took a key out of his pocket, undid the lock, pushed back the dead bolt, opened the door, and switched on a row of fluorescent ceiling lights. The other man hustled her inside. As he marched her across the room, the driver slammed the door shut and locked it. *Why would they have locks on both sides of the door?* she wondered.

After scanning the area, she thought it looked like a warehouse or laboratory of some sort. She caught the pungent odor of marijuana and then she thought she smelled solvents and acetone. They must be drug dealers, she thought as she gazed around the large windowless room. There were tables with piles of plastic bags, scales, tarps, crates, boxes, hammers, pry bars, staple guns, and other assorted bits of hardware. She didn't see any bags filled with white powder or any other identifiable substance. It looked more like a place where they might refine it and then pack it up.

Maybe they had shipped out what they had and were waiting for the next haul. *Yes, that must be it.* But why bother with her? She wasn't a DEA agent. She was an economist, and the only thing she would be good for might be to analyze the profit and loss from their operation.

She quickly dismissed such inane thoughts when the two men dragged her across the floor and made her sit down in a chair near what seemed to be a staging table, a place where they probably packed up the crates. "What am I doing here?" she demanded. "What do you want with me? Why won't you tell me?"

The man who had been in the back seat reached in his pocket and once again took out his fat roll of duct tape. "You talk too much," he said, tearing off a long strip and smacking it across her mouth. He tore off several more strips. He taped her ankles against the front legs of the chair and pulled the tape off her hands to separate them. At that point, she wanted to struggle again, but with two men in the room who probably had guns, she knew it was no use. Her captor used one piece to secure her right hand to one of the arms of the chair and repeated the process, taping her other hand to the left arm. "There. That ought to hold you for a while until the boss gets here."

Jessica stared wide-eyed at the men as they sauntered into a back room. She heard a refrigerator door open and the clink of bottles or glasses. Her mouth was so dry, she wanted to beg for water. But she couldn't talk, couldn't scream, couldn't do anything but wait. Wait for what?

She heard a key turning the lock. The main door swung open, and a well-dressed man walked in. At least he was better dressed than the other two kidnappers. He looked over at Jessica, gave her a sidelong smirk and said, "Welcome to my world." He slowly walked up to her chair, lifted a strand of her blond hair, saw beads of perspiration on her forehead and said, "I guess we should turn down the air conditioning."

Jessica sat completely still. What else could she do?

"The pictures were right. You're not bad looking," Pazio said, flipping more hair off her forehead. "I wonder if you're Brazilian or American or a guest from another country?" he said, heading to the back room. "We'll figure that out later, won't we?" He joined the others and shut the door.

"What do we know?" Pazio said as he reached into the fridge and took out a beer. He sat down at a small table and looked at the items strewn on top. "I see you got her purse. Who is she? Local or what?"

Domingo held up a driver's license. "Her name's Jessica Tanner. Lives in Washington, DC. Don't know what she does or any of that. Maybe she a model of some kind."

"Could be," Pazio said. "What else?"

"Found her cell phone in a side pocket. There might be a lot of stuff on this little baby. I was just going to check it," Domingo said.

"We don't have her passcode," Pazio lamented as he reached for it. "Oh, wait a minute. It hasn't asked for one yet. There's a recent call."

"That must be the call I heard when we were driving over here," Domingo said.

Pazio fiddled with the phone and exclaimed, "Bingo. That call was from our dear friend, Bill Black," he said sarcastically. "Now we've got his number." He glanced over at his henchmen. "You didn't hurt her, did you?" Pazio demanded, narrowing his eyes.

"No, boss," the other man said. "We just taped her up so she couldn't make a lot of noise. The broad kept asking questions, but we didn't lay a hand on her."

"I wouldn't mind laying a hand on that one, though," Domingo said with a leer.

"Forget it. This is business. *My* business," Pazio said. "First thing we do is use the little camera app to take a photo. Always comes in handy."

CHAPTER THIRTY-SIX

Brasilia

The pilot executed a smooth landing, touching down and taxiing to the private terminal. Bill unhooked his seat belt, gathered up his things, and walked forward.

"Nice flight. Thanks for making good time," he said to the two men in the cockpit.

"Any time. Enjoyed having you on board. There's a car waiting over there," the pilot said, pointing out the windshield to a black sedan. Chet Osborn stood next to it.

Bill hurried down the stairs and over to the car. "What have we got?" he asked, tossing his bag in the back as he jumped into the passenger seat.

"Got a strategy session set up with a few of the same players we met with the first go-around," Chet said. "President's Chief of Security, his Chief of Staff, the VP's guy, and a few other agents. The president has been home all weekend, working on his speech, spending time with his family, or whatever presidents do down here, so at least his people could work on the threat assessment, the set-up for his speech at the banquet and re-check the magnetometers, scanners, and screeners they'll have at the entrances."

"You think some of those machines could be faulty or that someone could sneak in a weapon?" Bill said.

"Not sure. Something that's been bothering me is the new plastic guns that are out there."

"Yeah, the ones you can make on a 3D printer. Last one I saw was called the Liberator."

"Right on," Chet said. "They're trying to outlaw them in the States, of course, but I hear that the CAD blueprints for those things have been downloaded about a million times. And they can pass right through an X-ray machine."

"Kind of expensive to make, though," Bill said. "A long shot, I'd say. But for this meeting, what's the latest on surveillance? Phones, computers?"

"That's just the thing. We've been trying to track Pazio, his Friends of Friends gang as well as the other two major players. We're using Stingray," Chet said. "That tool that mimics a cell phone tower so it can connect and spot a location. That's another thing some groups in the states object to. Anyway, the dealers keep changing cells all the time. We've managed to get hold of a few conversations before they switch, and that's led us to believe there's definitely some plot against the president is in the works."

"It would make sense that he'd want to get rid of Mendez in retaliation for his crackdown on all the drug dealing," Bill speculated.

"The trouble is, we haven't been able to nail down the other end of his conversations. Whoever he talks to probably has a throwaway phone too."

"Let's say he's got someone on the inside, a high-level staffer, a security guard, someone who's got access that he's paying big bucks to kill the president," Bill speculated.

"Besides the idea of a possible assassination, maybe the insider is also the tipster," Chet added. "How else would Pazio and his gang always know to slip out before the raids? You saw that yourself last night."

Bill gave a sigh. "Exactly. We thought for sure we'd get him when we hit that one warehouse outside of town last night. But he was nowhere. The drugs were nowhere. He *must* have had a tip from on high. At least we rounded up two of his helpers. They're grilling them at the Consulate, but I doubt if those two have been clued in about the whole operation. They looked like low-level labor to me."

"How many people knew about the Rio raid?" Chet asked.

"Not sure. In order to mount one of those, they need a ton of police, some armor, backup along with an order from the president's office."

"Somebody is getting paid off and paid big time," Chet said.

"Have you been able to trace bank accounts of some of the Palace players?" Bill asked.

"Kind of hard to do down here. Most of the politicians have off-shore accounts. Caymans mostly. With so much corruption, who can keep track?"

"Gotcha," Bill said.

"Okay, we're here," Chet said, flashing his creds to a guard at the entry gate of the Presidential Palace. "We've got to get inside right away. Meeting starts in a few minutes."

Bill checked his watch. He wanted to call Jessica again, see how she was, what she was doing. But he needed some quiet time to have the conversation. Not here. Not with Chet and the others around. He'd have to try her later. She must have at least seen his "missed call" and, even though he hadn't left a message, it would have to hold her over for a while.

CHAPTER THIRTY-SEVEN

Rocinha—Rio de Janeiro

Jessica strained at the bindings. The duct tape was strong and even if she somehow managed to get it loose, she'd never get out of here with those three goons in the back room. They had guns. She had nothing. She tried to listen to their conversation and could hear snatches of it because the door was flimsy. The problem was, they were speaking in Portuguese.

She tried to make out a few words. Some of them sounded similar to English, but she couldn't be sure. She heard a couple of names. Pazio. Domingo. She made a mental note of them. Then she heard the word *photo*. Okay, they were going to take her picture. What would they do with it? Who would they send it to? And whoever it was, would they pay some sort of ransom in exchange for her release?

She slowed her breathing and tried to analyze the situation as she sat there desperately trying to figure out what to do next, or if she could do anything at all. It occurred to her that her friends and especially the younger staffers she knew always seemed to want instant answers for everything. They were constantly checking their texts, Facebook postings, and Twitter accounts as if they didn't dare miss any momentary development. She called it the 'Tyranny of Now.'" And right now, she couldn't do a darn thing but sit here. She had to think longer term.

Maybe things would change since that head man had arrived. He didn't look like a terrorist or a weirdo. He looked like a savvy criminal, more like a business type involved in illicit dealings. The other guys seemed a lot more dangerous, though, with their piercing gazes, almost undressing her with their eyes. She hoped their boss kept them and their appetites under control.

The backroom door opened. The three men stepped out. The leader was holding up a cell phone. Was it hers? Hard to tell, but it might be. He walked over to her, turned the chair so she sat in more direct light and said, "You're probably used to having people take your picture, right?"

Jessica shook her head. As the other two advanced toward her, she stared at them with a sense of foreboding.

"Now that's a good look on you," the boss said. "We'd like you to appear scared. It'll help us immensely." With that comment she heard several camera clicks.

CHAPTER THIRTY-EIGHT

Planalto Palace—Brasilia

"What did you make of the security chief's suggestion?" Chet asked as he and Bill walked out of the meeting at the Presidential Palace.

"You mean about how they all will be armed at the banquet?" Bill said.

"Yeah. I figure the president's closest security detail would always have their weapons with them anyway, just like our Secret Service. I just wasn't sure about the other guys in the room."

"I'm with you there. We'll just have to keep a close eye on the president and, of course, we'll have our Glocks."

"Sure," Chet said. "And who knows, maybe all of these rumors are just that. Rumors, not an actual plan. Could be that the president's enemies are just kicking around their wish list."

"At least his security guys do seem pretty well prepared if that wish list ever becomes a reality," Bill said.

They walked down the hall and headed toward the elevators. "Better head back to my office," Chet suggested. "We still have a ton of work to do screening the guest list, double checking the catering staff, and the president himself has asked to meet with us later tonight."

"The president wants a meeting?" Bill asked, raising his eyebrows. "That sounds like a command performance. We'd better have our act together." He felt his cell vibrate and fished it out of his pocket. "Had the ringer off for the meeting, but I see I've got a call from Alicia herself," Bill said.

"You mean the pushy broad who's your boss at State?" Chet said with a grin. "Well, not your real boss, but at least the one you have to answer to once in a while. See what she wants. I'll wait."

Bill answered the call. "Hello, Alicia, what's up?"

"Glad I caught you. We have a problem, and you have to handle it," Alicia said.

"What is it? I'm pretty busy down here," Bill said.

"The Argentine Ambassador wasn't on the list of delegates to your OAS meeting there because he had some sort of personal issue. But we just got word that he's better, and he's going to come after all. He's flying down tonight. He will be attending the final session and the banquet."

"So?"

"So, since he is Argentina's Ambassador to the United States, I want *you* to make sure that he is treated properly."

"I'm not the host here, Alicia. The Brazilians are in charge of most of the details for this little confab you know," Bill said, shaking his head.

"Of course, I know that," Alicia said. "But you know how the Argentines are."

"What do you mean?"

"Some of them can be a bit arrogant. They feel like they're greatly superior to the Brazilians."

"I know a lot of them want to think they're descended from the European aristocracy, if that's what you're talking about," Bill said.

"That's exactly what I'm talking about," Alicia said.

"I still don't see what you expect me to do about it."

"I expect you to make sure that he's seated properly," Alicia said in an imperious tone.

"I submitted our suggested seating charts, but the president's people have the final say. That's the way it always is," Bill countered.

"Just try to make sure they don't seat him next to a woman. I hate to admit it, but they can be rather chauvinistic," Alicia said.

"I'll see what I can do," Bill said. Checking his watch, he added, "Look, I've got a pretty full schedule down here, is that all?"

"For now, yes. And after the final session tomorrow, I expect you back here first thing the next day," Alicia said.

"Why? Is there another event on the schedule I don't know about?"

"We're trying to get Zaire to pay their parking tickets. It's been going on for years. The Russians also refuse to pay, and it's becoming a bit of a diplomatic hassle. I need you to handle these things," she said. "Now, go deal with the Argentine situation, and then get back here." She clicked off.

"What's her problem this time?" Chet asked.

"Alicia wants me to figure out how to make the Argentine Ambassador happy," Bill said, "as if we didn't have enough on our plate."

"He'll probably want steak on *his* plate," Chet said with a grin. "You know they act like the English, flirt like the Italians, drive like the Germans, but eat like Texans."

Bill burst out laughing. "Yeah. Guess I should make sure the guy has a steak knife at his place."

"Just what we need," Chet said. "Another weapon at the banquet."

CHAPTER THIRTY-NINE

Rio de Janeiro

Pazio checked the photos. "These came out pretty well," he said, showing the device to Domingo. "Now I need to decide where to take her, where to make the trade. I'm thinking this might not be the best place. Let's go back and figure it out."

He was speaking in English. They seemed to switch back and forth between English and Portuguese. *Maybe they speak English when they want me to hear certain things. This time it sounds like they actually want me to know their plans. Maybe that boss wants me to know he's going to trade me, not kill me so I'll relax and co-operate. Well, thank God for small favors,* she ruminated.

The three men retreated to the back room once again and closed the door. Jessica sat there trying to collect her thoughts. *They took my picture. Who are they going to send it to? she asked herself again. If they ask for a ransom, they could be arrested. Didn't I read somewhere that kidnappers make that mistake all the time? They arrange for the money to be dropped somewhere, and then when they go to pick it up, they're captured. Yes, that's how it's going to be. Dear Lord, let it be just like that.*

She thought about everything the head man had said when he took the pictures. He said they were going to move her. Why would they move her? As she looked around the cavernous room it certainly seemed like a secure hiding place. Then she thought about the second thing he said about making a trade. Maybe they want to make sure that no one on the outside discovers this laboratory, so they have to go to some other location to hand her off. That must be it.

She racked her brain considering all the angles. Since she had surmised that they were engaged in the business of drug dealing, they must know all the local officials. They probably bribe a lot of them. She had heard about that too. Brazil was notorious for harboring corrupt politicians and police. These men wouldn't be contacting any of the locals, though.

If it's money they want, they must be thinking about contacting someone in the States. *They don't know my family. They don't know I work at the White House. So where would they send the pictures?* As she tried to process the puzzle, she heard a few more snatches of conversation from the back room.

First, there was the word *mova*. That made sense. But when would they move her? Then she heard the phrase, "Vamas a aigums alimentos." What did that mean? She had heard the Spanish term *vamos* so that must be it. They were going to go somewhere. Would they take her with them? What about the other words? She focused on the last word, *alimentos*.

The more she thought about it, the more she was sure it had something to do with food. She had heard a term like that when she and Bill had been over in that Lapa section of town. There were food stalls all over the place. *Maybe they're all going out to get some food. I wonder if they'll give me something to eat. At this point I couldn't eat a thing, although I'd sure like a drink of water . . . I can barely breathe when I think about how I'm trapped here with a bunch of criminals.* She sat there and tried to pick up more of their conversation, but the only other word she could make out was one she had heard before: *photo*.

CHAPTER FORTY

Planalto Palace—Brasilia

Bill and Chet went down in the elevator and out the front door. As they headed for their car, Bill said, "Guess I better send a note to the Social Secretary about the Argentinian."

"I have no idea how you keep up this crazy front," Chet said, unlocking the car and getting in.

Bill sat in the passenger seat and pulled out his cell again. He saw that he had several texts. He hit the Message icon and glanced at the list. "Here's one from Jessica. Finally."

"The beauty from the White House?" Chet asked, steering toward the exit.

"Sure thing. We, uh, were both in Rio," Bill said.

"Together?" Chet asked with a glint in his eye.

"Well, yes," Bill said.

"Lucky you."

"Exactly. Except that I had to hightail it out of there when I got that message about the raid, and I never got a chance to tell her where I was going."

"You couldn't tell her much of anything anyway," Chet said. "You haven't blown your cover, have you?"

"Nope. Can't do that," Bill said. "I'm glad she decided to send me a text. Let's see what she has to say." He glanced down and saw a photo. He enlarged it and shouted, "Oh my God!"

"What? What's the matter?" Chet said.

"Pull over. It's a picture of Jessica. She's tied up. Jesus. You have to see this."

Chet hit the brake, parked on the side of the road and grabbed the phone. "My God! She's been kidnapped all right. Why? What do they want with her?" He handed it back.

"I'm sure they want me, not her," Bill said in a shaking voice. "Let me read the message below the picture."

Bill stared at the cryptic words and read them out loud. "A year ago we said you were a dead man. Better you than her. We'll let you know where and when we will make the trade. Our message will be from a different cell. Stay tuned." Bill's face turned ashen.

"Good God!" Chet said. "Who's it from?"

"Got to be Pazio," Bill said. "How the hell did he get her? She was staying at the Copacabana Palace." He ran his fingers through his hair and took a deep breath. "They must have been watching the hotel. But how did they know we were there?"

"When you went on that raid, do you think some of his boys spotted you? Could they have recognized you from that take-down last year? Wait, that doesn't track. You didn't go back to the hotel. So how . . . ?"

"Unless someone saw us earlier. Together. We did go out Friday and Saturday night," Bill said. "We were in cabs mostly, but we weren't exactly hiding. Someone could have spotted us around the hotel. That means they saw her, and after I left in the middle of the night, she must have gone out later and they grabbed her." He ran a hand through his hair in complete frustration. I can't believe I've gotten her into something like this."

"Okay. Okay, calm down," Chet said. "We've been in worse situations."

"Us? Yes," Bill said. "Her? No."

"They said they wanted you not her, so let's think about that. Pazio is still steamed about his brother. He wants revenge. And when he talks about making a trade, we'll have our people there to get her out and take them down," Chet said.

"But they want me, not any of our other agents," Bill said. "She's in Rio. I've got to get back there."

Chet reached over and put a hand on Bill's arm. "Wait. Slow down. First, you're meeting with the president tonight. Second, you can't fly back to Rio and think you're going to take Pazio's gang down all by yourself. We have to arrange backup. We'll get our agents at the consulate on top of this."

"I can't just leave her there," Bill said. "If I don't show up, they might kill her."

"No, they won't," Chet countered. "They get rid of her, they lose their leverage."

"Christ! This is all my fault. Getting involved with Jessica, taking her out in public, figuring we could just go have a good time, not considering that Pazio and his boys have tentacles everywhere in that town, what the hell was I thinking?" Bill leaned down and put his head in his hands.

"Look, buddy, I said we've been in tough situations before. This one is going to take some planning, some analysis, some help. Let's head back to the embassy and get the rest of our crew together so we can figure this damn thing out."

"And in the meantime," Bill said, "Jessica is sitting there, trussed up and terrified."

CHAPTER FORTY-ONE

Rocinha—Rio de Janeiro

"**N**ow, here's what we're going to do," Pazio said, turning to Domingo who was driving the SUV down the tunnel. "First, we'll go get something to eat."

"I'm starving, boss," Domingo said. "You wanna go to the barbeque place we like or get something quick in the favela?"

"Let's go to a decent restaurant," Pazio said. "I didn't get breakfast. I'm thinking Posh Pasta in the South Zone. No, better yet, since it's Sunday, let's go to Gero. They've got great bread on the weekends. Drive over to Rua Anibal de Mendonca in Ipanema."

"You got it," his lieutenant replied. "Then what?"

"Then drop me off at the first warehouse the police hit last night. They'll never think about coming back there for anything since they more or less cleaned it out. I can work there for a while. I've got calls to make. Remember, tomorrow night is the big event. I have to be sure it's all on track."

"While you make calls, what about us?" Domingo said.

"You go back and keep an eye on the woman," Pazio said. "I'll let you know when I've sent another message to Bill Black and heard back from him. I knew I couldn't keep using her phone because it would eventually ask for the passcode and she sure as hell wasn't going to give it to us, and I wasn't about to hurt her to get it. I told Black I would be contacting him from a different phone. I'll just use one of the new many throwaways since I made a note of his number."

"Good thinking. But that Black guy's gotta be pretty wired about seeing the picture and our having his woman," Domingo said.

"Obviously," Pazio said. "I'm letting him stew a bit, but when I tell him where to meet me to retrieve the lady, I'm damn sure he'll answer."

"Yeah. If that broad was mine, I'd wanna help her too," Domingo said. "Come to think of it, that broad *will* be ours for a while. I wouldn't mind having a little fun with her. Sure is a beaut."

Pazio turned and stared at his driver. "I told you before, keep your hands off her. She's not the target. Bill Black is. I have a good reason to deal with Black. He killed my brother. I've got no beef with the woman. She goes free. You got that?"

"I got that. But if we take her to the warehouse and she goes free, what's to keep her from going to the feds, her feds, whatever feds, and showing them our locations?"

"How stupid can you get?" Pazio said with a dismissive shake of his hand. "When you go get her at the lab, you blindfold her just like before. You put her in the car. You bring her to me at the warehouse. Then later, after I get my hands on Black, you keep her blindfolded, and you dump her back near her hotel. She'll never know where she was, so she could never give us away even if she knew who to call. Now, do you understand?"

Domingo stared straight ahead at the road, made a few turns, and mumbled, "I guess."

CHAPTER FORTY-TWO

They were gone. Jessica was alone for the first time in hours. They had left the duct tape over her mouth, but she was pretty sure she could deal with that. Twisting her body, she leaned over to where her right hand was taped to the arm of the chair, trying to move her fingers. She pulled and yanked and was able to get her thumb and forefinger out about an inch. She leaned way down. With her two fingers, she grabbed an edge of the tape on her cheek. Her nails dug into it. She pulled the tape and forced her head back at the same time. The duct tape came away from her mouth, and she took a deep breath.

I could sure use some water. Can't think about that now. I have to concentrate. Let's see if I can bite the other tape off my hands.

She hunched over again and tried to pull it away on the right side, but the ends were taped under the chair arm, and all she could do was lift up the edges a tiny bit more.

Jess began scanning the room, the shelves, and the equipment on the staging table. Over at the end, she saw a can. It looked familiar. She started to inch her chair along the floor, slowly pushing the chair legs with her feet. She felt it scrape on the cement little by little. It was slow going, but she didn't want to tip over. She had to stay steady. As she got near the end, she looked closer. It was a blue can with a yellow and blue label. WD-40. They had tons of those in her dad's hardware store. She knew it was a silicone spray. And silicone spray could loosen an adhesive.

She wiggled and pushed until the chair was right next to the table's edge then stretched forward and clamped her teeth over the top of the can where a little red spray straw was connected. She slowly turned her head, leaned down and managed to shove the end of the straw underneath the edge of the tape covering her right hand. Steadying the can against her chest, she pushed down on the top with her nose. She heard a small sound as a bit of the WD-40 was shot under the duct tape. She stopped and tried to move her hand. The tape was slightly loosened. She repeated the process over and over until she felt the adhesive give way and she pulled her hand free.

"Yes!" she cried out to the empty room as she quickly pulled the tape off her left hand and then started working on her ankles. She had no idea how much time she had before the men came back. She only knew she'd better work fast.

With the can placed back on the table, she got up and raced to the back room where she found a glass, filled it with water from a grimy sink and took a big gulp. She also saw a bathroom, quickly used it, and rushed back. Then she saw a microwave and small refrigerator, but she didn't have time to look for anything else to eat or drink. She had work to do.

She saw her purse with its contents spilled out on a small table. Her driver's license, wallet, money, and credit cards were all there.

They took my cell phone, but why didn't they take the money?

She quickly stuffed everything in her bag, turned and hurried back out to the front entrance area and tried to open the door.

Just as I figured, bolted from the outside.

She looked around again. No windows.

Now what? I can't just stand here. When they come back, they'll tie me up again. There has to be something in here I can use.

Once again, she inspected the crates and the shelves. There were hammers and nails. She might be able to use a hammer, but not if there were two or three of them. Besides, they were bigger than she was. That was a non-starter. The plastic bags wouldn't help. The scales wouldn't be much use either. Then she saw something else. As she reached for it, she thought, *Could this be a great weapon or what?*

CHAPTER FORTY-THREE

American Embassy—Brasilia

Bill was frantic. He and Chet had gathered their embassy team in a secure room and were examining the photo of Jessica. A pitcher of ice water and set of glasses sat at a sideboard, but no one reached for them. They were all focused on a large photo.

"Can't tell anything from the background. All I can see is a table, some tools, boxes, and scales. White walls. No windows. Could be underground somewhere. They must have her stashed in one of the staging areas, but which one?" Bill asked. "We've *got* to find her."

"Does anything there look like the places you hit last night in those raids?" Chet asked.

"I don't think so. We were in two warehouses. This looks more like a lab." Bill turned to another agent. "What do you think? You spend a lot of time in Rio. Ever seen this place?"

The special agent looked at the picture they had enlarged and printed out. "Can't say I have. Pazio and his minions keep building new hideouts. No one has been able to keep up with him. He has plenty of cash to build whatever he wants, wherever he wants. And think about it. They may not even be in Rio. Maybe he's got her holed up somewhere else."

"Right. At this point, we have no idea," Chet said. "What about tracing the location of the cell phone he used."

"Jessica's phone," Bill interjected.

"We've tried that. Can't get a true fix. It moves around," the agent said. "Now if he were to call you instead of texting you, and if you could keep him on the line, then of course we could get a location right away and then move in."

"He's not dumb, and he's not calling," Bill said as he studied his own cell sitting on the conference table in front of him. "I just have to keep watching for a follow-up message about where and when I'm supposed to meet him and exchange myself for Jessica."

"Which you are not going to do," Chet said. "You know we've alerted Rio. They're standing by, and they'll be ready to move in as soon as you get the next text. We've talked about this. Besides, it would take way too long for you to get on a plane and get to Rio in time to make a switch."

"I can't just sit here and hope for the best," Bill said, raising his voice.

"You've got to sit tight," Chet said. "Look, you're a pro. I'm afraid you're letting your personal life get in the way of your professional life here."

"You bet I am. Jessica Tanner not only means something to me. She means something to the President of the United States, for God's sake. This is not just some street crime. This is a very big deal, and I can't let anything happen to her," Bill said emphatically. He grabbed his cell and started to get up. "I'm flying to Rio. That's the most likely place. I *have* to see this through."

The other agents exchanged a look and pointed to the picture again. "Bill, wait. We're with you on this. We know what's at stake. We're just trying to figure out the best way to get her free."

"But," Chet interrupted, "we're also trying to figure out how to keep *you* from getting shot by the leading drug dealer in Brazil. Got that?"

Bill was near the door when he turned around. "I just got a new text." He looked down and touched the screen. "It's not from Jess's phone. Looks like Pazio's using a throwaway cell. A burner."

"What's it say?" Chet asked.

Bill read the text aloud.

You were there last night. She will be there today. You come ALONE in two hours, or the lady pays the price.

"That sounds like they've moved her to one of the warehouses we hit. I know where they are. The Rio team can meet my plane. We'll figure it out and go from there. Now, how soon can I get a jet?"

"You can't get there in two hours even if we ordered it now," Chet said. "And that is if we thought it was a good idea in the first place. Which we don't."

"I can answer him," Bill said. "I'll say I'm on my way. He knows how long it takes to fly from Brasilia to Rio. He's waited a whole year to kill me. I'm sure he'll wait another couple of hours."

CHAPTER FORTY-FOUR

Rocinha—Rio de Janeiro

"I'm glad we took a break for lunch before we have to go back and babysit that woman again," Domingo said. "I wonder if we should be bringing her some food?"

"Nah. She's thin, probably doesn't eat much anyway," the other man replied.

"C'mon," Pazio said, slapping some bills on the table and standing up. "Let's get on with it."

They headed back to the car, drove down the road and dropped Pazio off at the other warehouse so he could make his calls. Then the two men drove back toward the lab to get the woman. Domingo slowed down as they approached the gate to the tunnel. "Go open it," he ordered the other guy. "We're gonna get the chick and come right out. You can leave it ajar for a few minutes. It shouldn't take us long. Gotta get her over to that other warehouse so Pazio can make the switch. Do you think Black will show up?"

"He better or Pazio will be pretty pissed off."

The other man unlocked the gate and got back in the car, and they drove down toward the lab. Domingo pulled the SUV to a stop in front of the entrance. He pushed the dead bolt back and opened the door. His partner followed a few steps behind.

"What the hell?" Domingo yelled as he surveyed the room and saw the empty chair next to the table. He walked through the door and started to shout as Jessica, standing just to one side armed with a Craftsman nail gun that was about eight inches high and four inches across. She fired, propelling long nails into his chest with the help of an air compressor she had attached to the bottom of the handle. Domingo fell to the floor screaming and cursing.

The other man rushed in and stood transfixed on the threshold of old wood by the door. He looked at Jessica aghast. He was about to draw his gun and lunge toward her when this time she aimed the barrel of the nail gun at his feet and squeezed the trigger. *Bam, bam, bam.* She fired three sets of two-inch nails into his shoes, effectively pinning him to the floor. He tried to move, to lash out, but he was stuck. He too started to wail in pain as the nails were embedded through his shoes, right into his toes. Instead of getting the gun out of his pocket, he was kneeling down, grabbing his feet, and Jessica pumped two more nails into his back.

She slung her purse over her shoulder, ran outside, and threw the dead bolt into place, still hearing the cries and moans of the two men on the other side. She saw the SUV parked there and glanced in.

They took the keys. No time to try and start it. Their boss might come back.

She turned and raced down the tunnel.

CHAPTER FORTY-FIVE

Brasilia

Bill paced around the private airport, checking his watch, waiting for the government jet that would take him to Rio and a meeting with Pazio. It was getting late. He had to wait for a plane to return from another trip, refuel, and be ready for his own flight. Two hours had passed since he sent his own text saying he was on his way but would be delayed due to air traffic. He hoped and prayed that Jessica was all right, though he knew she must be scared out of her mind.

He wondered if she knew Pazio intended to trade her life for his. Once he hooked up with the agents in Rio and checked out the warehouse where the drug lord had her stashed, he figured they'd come up with some sort of rescue plan. On the other hand, he also knew Pazio was one devious and calculating character, and that he'd undoubtedly have his own team in place, making sure that they got their hands on what they really wanted. What they wanted, Bill knew, was him, but all he could think about right now was Jessica's safety.

He could see two images in his mind's eye. The first was the beautiful woman with light blue eyes, her long blond hair spread out on the pillow, her arms reaching for him in a state of passion. He had wanted her, and he remembered how it felt when he finally made love to her. She was awesome.

The other image was of this same woman in a chair, her eyes furtive, her hair askew and her arms tied down. He had to find her, free her, tell her how sorry and devastated he was that he got her into this mess. Would he have a chance to talk to her and explain? Would they try to take him first and talk about setting her free later? He pondered these questions when a clerk at the desk called his name.

"Mr. Black? Your Citation Ten is being refueled right now. The pilot will be in shortly to escort you out. The tail number is 462 Fox Lima."

Bill looked out the window and saw the pilot emerge from 462FL and walk in his direction. He looked at his watch again. It would be another three hours or so before they could take off, land in Rio, and drive to the right warehouse. Once he was in the area, he planned to send another text to Pazio. They had not been able to locate the guy's cell location. Bill was sure he was moving around a lot and would probably be using another phone pretty soon. He'd estimate his arrival time and ask for proof of life. He had to be sure she was okay.

His phone rang. *What now?* He looked at the screen and muttered an oath. *Not again. Can't she leave me alone?* He took the call. "Yes, Alicia. Another problem?"

"I just wanted to make sure you were dealing properly with the Argentine diplomat. I understand he's on a flight to Brasilia right now. Are you going to meet his plane?"

"I'm afraid I can't do that. I'm sure staff from his own embassy will be there."

"Yes, well, be sure to check the details on that. We have some touchy relations with that country now, and I want him to feel especially well treated."

"I'll see what I can do," Bill said, holding back his exasperation. "I'm quite busy right now. I'll have to talk to you later." He clicked off. *"Touchy relations"? Here I am trying to deal with one of the most powerful criminals in the country, praying that a top White House official is well treated and not being manhandled or worse. How the hell can I be concerned with pampering a diplomat while I'm trying to save the life of Jessica Tanner?*

"Mr. Black?" the pilot said, extending his hand. "We're ready to roll."

CHAPTER FORTY-SIX

Rocinha—Rio de Janeiro

Jessica reached the end of the tunnel, pushed through the gate, and ran out into the street. Where was she? What if that boss came back? She had to get as far away from here as fast as she could. She looked around and was appalled by the sight. Metal lean-tos, cardboard shacks, garbage cans, dirt roads, mangy dogs wandering about, a group of children kicking a frayed soccer ball next to a makeshift clothesline. She wondered if those little boys would get a chance to see any of the Olympics that would be held just a short distance away but doubted it. She was in the middle of the worst slum she'd ever seen.

Jess couldn't imagine that such poverty, such squalor could co-exist with the beautiful hotels, restaurants, and beaches that had to be just a few miles away. In a country with such an abundance of natural resources, vibrant companies, a thriving tourist trade, how could they not figure out ways to lift up this sorry section of humanity? There were problems like this all over South America. All over the world, in fact. At least there had been reports that the current Brazilian President had plans to invest in reasonable housing projects.

But now wasn't the time to think about changing the world. Right now she had to change her direction. Jessica dashed down a side street but had no idea where she was going. She had to get back to her hotel. Someplace safe. Searching for a shop, a restaurant, someplace where she might be able to make a phone call and order a taxi, but there was nothing.

Jess kept running, zigzagging across potholes and ditches, jumping over broken sewer pipes, and watching out for gangs. *It would be just my luck to run into another bunch of street thugs. They'd probably take one look at this alligator purse and think it was valuable when it's really a knock-off.* She clutched the shoulder bag closer and kept running.

Turning a corner, she saw a young girl getting on a rusty motorbike. She ran up to the teenager and said in a hurried voice, "Copacabana Palace?"

The girl looked at her quizzically. Then she stared at Jessica's clothes and her purse. She paused for a few seconds, glanced at her bike, and finally said, "Dollars?"

"Dollars? Yes, dollars. Dollars for you," Jessica said anxiously. "I'm Jessica. Your name?"

The teenager looked like she understood. She said, "Christina."

Jess pointed to the scooter and said, "Vamos Copacabana Palace?"

Christina hesitated, then nodded and motioned for Jessica to get on the bike behind her. She didn't have a helmet. Jessica couldn't have cared less. Running into this girl was a godsend, a fast way to escape this whole dreadful episode. She just hoped the girl knew where she was going.

As Christina turned on the scooter, Jessica shouted, "Thank you. Uh . . . Gracia." The girl seemed to get it. She gunned the little motor, and they took off heading east.

CHAPTER FORTY-SEVEN

"What do you mean she's not there?" Pazio bellowed into the phone. "Where is she?" he demanded.

"We don't know," Domingo coughed.

"How can you not know?"

Domingo tried to take a breath, but the nails were still embedded in his chest. He didn't think they'd kill him, but he was bleeding, and they hurt like hell. "We got back here, and she was out of the chair and . . ."

"Out of the chair?" Pazio screamed. "You mean you didn't tie her up right, and she got herself loose? I always figured you two jerks didn't have all your oars in the water. What kind of total idiots are you?"

"I don't know how she did it. I had taped her real good. I know I did. But somehow, she got the tape off," Domingo said, spitting out the words.

"Even if she got the tape off, she was locked in. There were two of you and one of her," Pazio said. "Are you telling me that a woman, a skinny broad overpowered both of you at once?"

"Not like that, boss," Domingo said as he crouched on the floor holding his cell phone in one hand, while pressing his other hand to his chest to stop the blood.

"Then like what?" Pazio demanded.

"She used one of our nail guns. She shot us. Got me in the chest and even nailed my guy here to the floor."

"What?" Pazio blurted. "She nailed him to the floor? How the hell did she do that?"

"She pointed the gun at his feet and shot the nails through his shoes. He's trying to pull them up with some pliers, but he's crying it hurts so much."

"I can't believe you guys. Letting her get the best of you. She obviously used your own tools and took you down. I should hire her. She's way smarter than the two of you," Pazio said.

"Can you come get us, boss?" Domingo said, with a hitch in his voice.

"Come get you? Why would I come get you? You've got your SUV."

"She used the dead bolt. We're locked in."

"Now I *know* she's smart. I can't come get you. I'll send one of the other boys."

"I think we need to see a doctor."

"We'll see about that. You two come to this warehouse. There's a good first-aid kit and a bunch of painkillers here. You can use those. Now, I've got to see what I can do without the girl."

"Is Bill Black coming?" Domingo asked.

"Yes. He's on his way. Had to fly over from Brasilia. Taking a long time. I'll have to figure out a way to stall him so he doesn't find out about the woman." He paused a moment and added, "We didn't tell her we contacted him. You didn't use his name ever, did you?"

"No. Honest, boss. We didn't," Domingo said.

"If she's out on the street somewhere and Black is on a plane from Brasilia, she wouldn't be able to contact him even if she had an idea he was involved. And maybe she doesn't know that."

"You're right," Domingo said. "She probably thought it was a straight ransom deal, and she doesn't know who you sent the pictures to."

"Right," Pazio said. "I've got to keep Bill Black thinking that we're still going to make a trade. First thing I'm going to do is move out of here. He'll be heading to this warehouse, but I'll get out the back way and decide on a better meeting place. With you idiots out of the action, I'll have to get some of our other members to help me out. This is going to take some planning. Now, as for you two, I'll send somebody over. I just never thought that while Black is coming to rescue the woman, I have to end up rescuing you." With that, he ended the call.

CHAPTER FORTY-EIGHT

The teenager maneuvered the scooter over rutted lanes, down alleyways and finally out onto a concrete pavement. Jessica felt salt air. After being cooped up the entire day in that dank lab, surrounded by smelly barbarians, now sensing a fresh ocean breeze was wonderful. They must be getting close to the beach. She held on tight as Christina swerved around a corner and turned left onto a wide boulevard. Jessica looked ahead and saw lanes of traffic, restaurants, hotels, and off to the right, she saw the beach.

Thank God we're out of there, she thought. *I wonder if those goons or their boss will come after me again since they know where I'm staying?* She thought about that but knew that if she could just get inside the hotel, she'd be safe. She looked down at her watch and was surprised they hadn't taken it. She saw that it was just after 7:00. Shadows were beginning to move in. Street lights had come on. She never thought she'd appreciate street lights and the smell of salt water as much as she did right now.

The girl drove the scooter up to the front of the Copacabana Palace and hit the brake. The doorman looked askance at the scruffy teen and was about to shoo her away when he caught a glimpse of Jessica in back. He rushed over. "Can I help you, miss? Are you all right?"

"At this very moment, I'm just fine. Better than ever," Jessica said with a smile. She unzipped her shoulder bag and dug out her wallet. She first pulled out a twenty-dollar bill. Christina stared at it wide-eyed. Then, without touching the money, but pointing at it, she said, "Tudo para mim?"

Jessica turned to the doorman. "What did she say?"

"She said, 'all for me?'" he replied.

Jessica looked at the girl wearing a ripped T-shirt, shorts, and tennis shoes with a hole on one side. She looked in her wallet. She didn't have much cash since she usually relied on credit cards. But this girl just might have saved her life. She took out all the other twenties she had, leaving herself a few bills for tips she might need until she checked out later that night.

Jessica said to the doorman, "Tell her thank you. Tell her I was lost. She helped me, and I am most grateful."

The doorman addressed the girl, nodded toward Jessica, and translated.

Jess asked the doorman another question. "Could you get her address for me?"

The doorman shook his head. "I'm sure you would not want to go there."

"No," Jess said. "I'm checking out of the hotel later tonight. But this girl did a lot for me, and I'd like to keep in touch. Maybe help her in some way. So please ask for her address, and also ask what her family does. Do they have jobs?"

The doorman glanced at Christina who looked like she was trying to understand what they were talking about. Then he looked back at Jessica and said, "That's very nice of you. I'll try."

Once again, he spoke to Christina, asking the questions as he translated.

Christina reeled off some numbers along with several other phrases.

"What did she say?" Jess asked.

"I have her address," the doorman said.

Jess pulled a pen and slip of paper out of her purse and the doorman wrote it down. "What about her family?"

"She said her father worked for a while as a laborer clearing the area for one of the new stadiums for the Olympics. But his job is over now, and he can't find work. Her mother takes in laundry when she can get it. It's very difficult in Rocinha," he explained.

"Rocinha?" Jess repeated.

"The favela where she lives."

"So near and yet so far," Jess said. Then she turned to Christina and thrust $120 into her hand.

The girl hesitated but Jessica insisted. Then Jess held out her arms. Christina rushed forward into a warm embrace. Jess had arms around the girl and gave her a warm hug. Christina's eyes were filled with tears, but she was smiling. Jessica held her for a moment, then let her go. Christina pocketed the money, got back on her scooter, and with a broad wave, drove out the driveway and turned right.

Jessica waved back and thanked the doorman. As she headed toward the elevators, she too wiped a tear from her eyes.

CHAPTER FORTY-NINE

Copacabana Palace—Rio de Janeiro

As Jess rode up to her room in the elevator, she thought about the awful men back at that lab, and she wondered again who they sent her photo to. It didn't matter now, though. She had outsmarted them, and she was free.

Once inside, she thought about calling Bill, but figured he was at the Presidential Palace getting ready for the big banquet tomorrow evening. He must have been called back to handle some ridiculous dust-up. She was still miffed by his exit from this very room and the way he left only that card behind. But it all paled in comparison to her kidnapping and escape today. Right now, she needed a bath to get rid of the stench of drugs from the lab and the sweat from those goons.

Jess tossed her purse on the desk in the corner, tore off her clothes, vowing to get them cleaned as soon as she got back to Washington, and sauntered into the marble bathroom. She opened the faucets and saw a small bottle of bath salts. She poured them into the churning water, pinned up her hair, and climbed into the tub.

She lay back and began to feel her muscles relax. She had been so tense, so scared, so wrought up with adrenaline at its peak that by contrast, this was pure luxury. Just like savoring the twinkling street lamps and warm breeze from the beach, she closed her eyes and relished the sense of freedom.

As she lay there soaking and savoring the subtle fragrance of the bath salts, she thought about Bill again. Was he actually called back to the conference? Would she see him there tomorrow? He had to be there, at least at the banquet. He'd probably be checking all the seating arrangements. But should she be the one to search for him? No, she thought, it should be him looking for her.

I wonder if he was the one who called my cell today. I'll never know since those guys have my cell. I suppose I could try the hotel phone, but I don't remember his number. Or I could try his room at the Royal Tulip Hotel. No. After last night, I really want to see his face, see how he reacts, find out what excuse he might have for running out on me.

She needed to stop feeling sorry for herself and look ahead. After all, she got away and was all right now. That was a lot to be thankful for.

There was another hour or so before she'd have to pack up her things and head to the airport for her flight back to Brasilia. She was scheduled to make remarks tomorrow at one of the early workshops, and she'd be a backup for the Secretary of State who would be plugging the president's South American trade policy. More trade would mean more jobs, and that's what Christina's family and all the families in the favelas needed now. She could certainly push hard for that one, having seen the awful shanties and extreme poverty in this city.

As the temperature of the water cooled, she climbed out of the tub, toweled off, dressed in a pair of slacks and simple blouse, and realized she was ravenous. Those awful men hadn't offered her as much as a cracker. She called room service, and they assured her they could deliver a club sandwich very quickly.

While she waited for her supper, she packed up the rest of her clothes and turned on her computer to check her email. As she scrolled through the list, she glanced at an urgent update from Hal. It was a set of revised statistics for tomorrow's workshop. She'd print those out when she got to Brasilia.

Then she saw an email from Kay Heller. She hit "Reply." She wanted to tell Kay about her horrific ordeal. She had to tell someone. She also wanted to get her friend's take on the whole episode of Bill's disappearing act. She decided it would be better to wait until she got back to DC and explain it all in person. By then she was sure she'd have some answers. She cancelled the Reply.

She sat back in the desk chair and thought again about her day, the men, the tunnel, the lab. She wondered if she could tell the authorities where it was so they could go in and arrest that crowd. She had Christina's address, and even though she had run some distance before meeting the girl, maybe she could give the police a rough idea of the location. Within several blocks anyway. She did want to report the whole ugly affair, but she wasn't certain who to call.

If she were in trouble in the States, she would call GETS, the Government Emergency Telecommunications Service. When she had joined the senior staff at the White House, she had been given a GETS card. That number isn't what she should be calling now though. Not in Rio. Here she could call the consulate but with all that had happened, they would undoubtedly want to interview her in person, and her time was running short before her flight. She decided it would be just as effective to wait until she got back to Brasilia and make a formal report.

Yes, that's what she would do. She would get hold of the station chief at the US Embassy and arrange to meet with him during a break in the conference schedule. That's when she could give him a complete report including descriptions of the men, her best guess as to the location of their laboratory, at least within a radius of the hotel perhaps and anything else that might be helpful. Besides, the tunnel and that lab would still be there tomorrow. Once she alerted the proper authorities and gave them all the details, they would put a plan together to find it and arrest those thugs.

There was a knock on the door. "Room service." She had a fleeting thought the bad guys, those thugs, might have returned and were impersonating the hotel waiter. But that only happens in movies, she thought, so she shook her head and answered the door. She asked the waiter to put the tray on the desk, signed the check, and sat down to enjoy the sandwich along with a glass of Sauvignon Blanc.

As she took her first sip, she thought some more about how she had been dragged off the street, secreted away in a dungeon-type room at the end of a dusty tunnel, taped to a chair for hours and hours and finally found a way to literally nail her captors. After the initial terror and stress, seeing those guys so shocked and then shackled by her nail gun, she had to smile to herself. It would make a pretty good scene in a movie after all, that is, if she could ever find time to write the script.

CHAPTER FIFTY

En route to Rio de Janeiro

"I should be there in another hour or so," Bill said, cradling the secure jet phone against his shoulder. "How's it going on your end? Got those warehouses staked out?"

"Sure do," the Special Agent said. "We've got teams covering both of them. No one has spotted Pazio, but two of his guys were dropped at one of them."

"Which two?" Bill asked.

"It was kind of weird. We think one was Domingo, his main lieutenant. But he was doubled over, could hardly walk, and our man on the scope said it looked like he might be bleeding."

"That's strange. I wonder if they got in some sort of fight with one of the other gangs," Bill ventured. "What about the other guy?"

"He was in even worse shape. He was using some contraption as a cane. He was limping. So, you're probably right. Must have been a real brawl of some sort. Anyway, we've got that place surrounded."

"No sign of Jessica, though, right?" Bill said.

"Nothing yet."

"When I get to the airport, I'm going to try and send another message to Pazio. I might even call the cell number he's using. If he actually answers, I can try to keep him on the line long enough for you to trace him. Then again, he's probably wise to that idea."

"Probably. At least send the text. We're sending a car for you. The driver will bring you here to the consulate. We have a team waiting to strategize," the agent said.

"Thanks," Bill replied. "See you soon."

"Temperature okay for you back here?" One of the pilots asked, making his way down the narrow beige carpeted aisle to the lavatory at the back of the cabin.

"Sure thing," Bill said. He reached to the right of his leather seat, pulled up a dark brown wooden table with a sleek polyurethane finish and started to make some notes on a small tablet. He wanted to talk to the Rio agents about what they learned, if anything, during the interrogation of the two drug dealers they picked up last night. Did they know about any more labs or safe houses? Were they privy to Pazio's current home address in Rio or any houses he used? With all of his money, surely the kingpin had fancy real estate in a bunch of places. Even more important, would they reveal the names of their major suppliers or FARC contacts? He knew the agents had been trying to get answers to these questions for ages, and they would keep trying.

He sat back and thought some more about the woman who had made such an impression on him in such a short time. Beautiful? Yes. Smart? Obviously. Prickly? At first. Sense of humor? Definitely. Sexy? Out of sight. The future? Who the hell knows? He had to concentrate on the here and now, and that meant freeing this very special woman, one who had come to mean so much to him in such a short period of time.

CHAPTER FIFTY-ONE

Royal Tulip Hotel—Brasilia

It was close to midnight by the time Jessica's flight from Rio landed in Brasilia, she found a taxi and got back to the conference hotel. Even though it was late by her standards, the place was alive with guests coming and going, congregating in the lobby, and chatting amiably. She heard strains of samba music emanating from the Old Barr, a popular spot decorated like an English pub.

She left her bag with the desk clerk and wandered down the hall. She was curious to see if any members of their delegation might be having a late drink. Though she had pulled off her wild escape many hours ago, she was still a bit keyed up and didn't want to turn in just yet. Besides, what she really wanted to know was whether Bill might be in there.

She stood at the door and surveyed the crowded room. She saw several ministers she recognized from the opening reception. The Canadian delegate was having a drink with a woman Jess thought was from Costa Rica, a large group of men from Colombia were clustered on several tall stools at the bar, and over in the corner she spotted Estelle sitting with another young staffer that Jess didn't know. She went over to their table.

"Hi Estelle. How are things going?" Jess asked.

"Oh, Jessica, great to see you," Estelle replied with a radiant smile. "Say hello to Mia. She's with the Mexican delegation. She has a job like mine. We're comparing notes. Come join us."

Jess shook hands with Mia and slid into an empty chair. "Nice to meet you. I see that everyone stays up late around here, even on a Sunday," Jess said.

"It's that way everywhere you go in Brazil. Real night owls down here," Estelle said. "Did you just get back from Rio? I want to hear all about your weekend. Did Rodriguez take you out? Did you have a great time? What did you think of the city? Where did you go?"

"Slow down," Jessica said with a tentative smile. "Let me order a drink, and we'll chat." She had that same sense again that she really wanted to tell someone about her horrific ordeal, but this certainly wasn't the time or the place. She didn't want to upset Estelle, and she had just met Mia. She raised her hand when a waiter passed by.

"What can I get for you?" he asked.

"Just some juice. How about grapefruit with a splash of cranberry," Jess said.

"Coming right up," he said and turned to the other two women. "And can I get you two something else?"

"Sure," Estelle said. "One more Mai Tai for each of us."

He nodded and scurried away.

"By the way," Jess said, "have you seen Bill Black tonight?"

"No. I thought he went to Rio for the weekend. Weren't you with him?" Estelle said.

"Yes, we were there together. For a while, anyway," Jess said somewhat wistfully. "He, uh, had to leave, and I just wondered . . ."

"Tell me about Rodriguez," Estelle pressed. "Did you like him?"

"He was a great host," Jess said. "He took me all over the city, even up to see the Christ statue. Fabulous views from that mountain." As she said it, she remembered how she had tried to conjure up that image while she was strapped to the chair saying a prayer that she could somehow get away from those awful men. She suddenly realized that her prayers had been answered when she was able to use the tools they had left behind. She recalled that her dad often said that luck happens when opportunity meets preparation. In that dank, dingy lab, she was presented with both.

"You look kind of distracted," Estelle said. "You must be tired going back and forth from Rio and all of that."

"Oh, it's not that hard," Mia interjected. "I hear that most of the government workers here do the same thing whenever they have a free weekend. I would have gone there myself, but I had to work on some papers for my minister for one of the final sessions."

"I did too," Estelle said.

"And did everything turn out okay for you this weekend?" Jess asked Estelle, wondering if Leventhal had made another move on her.

Estelle exchanged a look with Jess and said, "Let's just say there have been a few challenges, but I've been hanging out with Mia whenever I can."

"I will say that in contrast to some of the men around here, Rodriguez was a perfect gentleman. Handsome too." She turned to Mia. "Are you staying here beyond the conference?"

Mia said, "Actually I'm going to take a couple of vacation days, and I'd like to get over to Rio myself."

"If you do, be sure to meet Rodriguez," Jess suggested.

Estelle interrupted. "That's a great idea. I think you two would really hit it off. I'll arrange it." She laughed and added, "I should work for Match.com."

Jess finished her drink, signed the bill, and added her room number at the bottom. She pointed to the check. "Now that's where I'm heading. I'd better get some sleep. I'm scheduled for that first workshop tomorrow."

"Oh, right," Estelle said. "I'll be there too since the Secretary will be making opening remarks."

Jess got up, smiled, and said, "Nice to meet you, Mia. See you all in the morning."

When she left the bar, Jess retrieved her roller bag from the clerk and remembered she needed to print out Hal's stats for the first meeting tomorrow. She stopped in the business suite, logged on to the computer, pulled up the information, printed it out, and walked to the elevators.

Back in her room, she unpacked her bag, brushed her teeth, and stretched out on the cool sheets, making a mental note to meet with the station chief at the embassy during one of the scheduled conference breaks. Jess certainly wanted to report the kidnapping to the right people and knew that he would figure out the best way to get the local police to search and arrest those men. She'd tell him she figured out they were drug dealers, but she hadn't figured out just what they wanted when they grabbed her off the street. They must have been planning a ransom exchange of some sort. Then again, she knew these types of crimes happened a lot in Brazil, so maybe they wouldn't be able to find the dealers or do anything about it, just like they never did anything about stolen luggage.

As she was drifting off to sleep, she had a fleeting thought about a line from *Gone with the Wind*. Wasn't it Scarlett O'Hara who said, "I don't want to think about that today, I'll think about that tomorrow"?

CHAPTER FIFTY-TWO

American Consulate—Rio de Janeiro

"**A**re we set to track this call?" Bill asked, walking into his second meeting of the day at the Rio Consulate. He glanced over at one of the agents and said, "I've been on so many planes the last forty-eight hours, I'm beginning to feel like a flight attendant."

"I hear you. We're pretty well organized now," one of the agents replied. A small group was arrayed around equipment in one of the SCIFs, a Secret Compartmented Information Facility in the thirteen-story American Consulate General building on Avenida Presidente Wilson in downtown Rio. The modern stainless steel and glass structure had been constructed in 1952, but today it was equipped with the best technology and secure lines in town. At least they thought it was.

It was originally built as the American Embassy. When Brazil's capital was moved to Brasilia, they turned it into the Consulate where people lined up for visas, immigration information, and a myriad of other requests. But not on a Sunday, except for a selection of special agents working with DEA and other offices dealing with industrial espionage, cybercrime, and especially terrorism. They all worked 24/7.

Though it was after midnight, lights shown brightly as an assistant poured coffee and put a tray of sandwiches and cookies on a conference table in the center. The men and women in this room were used to working odd hours. Several had been involved in last night's drug raid. Others had been questioning the two dealers they grabbed at the last warehouse. Two were computer analysts pouring over data streams.

"I'm going to try Pazio's cell now. Let's see if he answers," Bill said, punching in the numbers as others listened in.

"Keep him on as long as you can," one reminded him.

"I'll try," Bill said, listening to the first ring, then three more before voicemail kicked in. When the beep tone came, Bill simply said, "I'm in Rio. Where are you?" Then he ended the call. "Damn," Bill said.

"He didn't want to be traced," an analyst said.

"Obviously," Bill replied, running his hand through his hair in frustration.

A moment later he heard the twang of a text message. He keyed it up. "It's from Pazio. He says, 'I won't take your call. I'm not that stupid. You wait for my order where to meet.'"

"That must mean he's looking for another place to hand her off," an agent said. "You know we've got two warehouses under surveillance. We've talked about how his two henchmen are in one of them, but we don't know if Pazio is in there with them or in the other one."

"Or if he took her out earlier, looking for a better place where our people couldn't hide in the shadows," Bill said. "I'm getting back to him." Bill typed in a return text. "I want proof she's okay." Then he waited. Everyone waited.

An agonizing two minutes went by. Then five. A moment later, Bill saw an answer. "You want proof? Here she is." Pazio had attached a photo. When Bill enlarged it, he saw that it was a close-up of her face, her blue eyes open wide, a piece of duct tape still stretched across her mouth." He held it up.

"Wait a minute," the Chief of Mission said. "He could have taken that at the same time he took the first one he sent you. What we want to know is how she is now."

"You're right," Bill said. "What's next?"

"Answer him. Demand the meeting site," another agent suggested. "Keep him connecting so he doesn't keep turning off that cell."

Bill punched in another message:

Don't screw with me. Tell me where she is and HOW she is.

Another long wait. Finally, a return:

I set the time and place. Stay tuned.

"This could go on all night," Bill said, leaning back in his chair. "Any advice here?"

"Still trying to get a fix on the cell phone he's using," one computer analyst said. "We're doing all we can to measure power levels and antenna patterns to see how his phone is communicating with certain base stations. Sometimes we can tell what sector he's in, but getting a precise location is tough."

"It's hard to triangulate," the other analyst said. "He could be in one of the favelas where the coverage is spotty. Some of the tower equipment has been cannibalized. It's not like we're in the States or Europe. You'd think that a major city in Brazil had all the latest telecommunications gear. And it works in the good areas for tourists and business. But in the shanties? Good luck."

When no further messages came from Pazio, the group got plates of sandwiches and chips, gathered at a conference table, and went over their notes and tips again. They had contacted a host of informants, but no one had seen Pazio with a beautiful blond American. As the night stretched on, Bill became more agitated, more worried, more determined to get Jess out of the man's clutches.

"Whenever they decide to make the trade, I'm going in. No matter what it takes," Bill said.

"I don't like this. Any of it," the station chief said. "She's not the target. They're not going to hurt her. She's the only leverage they have to get their hands on you. But we can't let you go in alone, for God's sake. That's just not happening. We'll have a whole team with you."

"He'll say I have to come alone. You know that's how it'll go down," Bill said. "Besides, I can take care of myself."

"No way," another agent said. "As soon as we get the drop-off site, we'll get our team together."

CHAPTER FIFTY-THREE

Royal Tulip Hotel—Brasilia

J essica opened her eyes and looked at the clock on the bedside table. 8:40 a.m. "Oh no! Why didn't I set an alarm? I'm going to be late. The first session starts in twenty minutes. How could I have slept so long? I never do that," she muttered. She jumped out of bed and ran into the bathroom. She took a quick shower, dabbed on some makeup, and brushed out her hair before opening the closet and selecting a navy skirt, matching blazer, and white silk blouse.

She hustled over to the desk and glanced at her computer. *No time to check email or texts. I don't have my cell, so I'll have to come back up here and do it later.* She took her briefcase full of notes along with her purse and raced down the hall toward the elevators. She looked at her watch. 8:58 a.m. By the time she found the meeting room, Secretary Leventhal was at the microphone greeting the delegates. She slipped in the door and slowly walked up the side to the front row where she saw a sign that read Reserved, Dr. Tanner placed on a chair.

The Secretary gave her a cursory nod and began to outline the latest US proposal for a free trade agreement encompassing the Americas. It was a reprise of one President Reagan had proposed way back in the '80s. While certain aspects of that one had achieved a modicum of success, in subsequent years various factions and unions had demanded more protection and many of the deals had been gutted.

As she watched him giving his pitch, Jess had to admit that he was making a valiant effort and good case for the creation of jobs, new industries, and the sharing of technology. She had a flashback to the image of little Christina with the ripped T-shirt and ragged tennis shoes, Christina with a dad who couldn't find work, Christina who had undoubtedly saved her life. Just reviewing that exchange, Jess made a promise to herself that when she got back to Washington, she'd figure out something, some way to help that family. Other than sending more dollars, she had no clue what else she could do. Maybe she'd ask Hal. A good mentor might have a good idea.

When the Secretary finished his remarks, he called on Jess. She had Hal's notes handy when she went up to the microphone to recite them. After a long period of Q&A, she once again checked her watch and saw that it was almost 10:30. The delegates were getting restless. Time for a coffee break.

Several people came forward to follow up on the trade issue. She tried to be polite, but she really needed caffeine. She also wanted to get to a phone to call the embassy and see if she could track down the station chief to tell him about the kidnapping. She had meant to do that first thing this morning, but when she overslept, it had to slide. Now she wanted to slip away to the business suite to make her call. She first grabbed a cup of coffee and then headed down the hall.

She looked up the number, dialed and identified herself as a member of the Senior White House staff. She was immediately put through to the ambassador's office. "Good morning, Miss Tanner. How may I help you?" an efficient-sounding young man asked.

"I'm here at the OAS meeting . . ." Jess said.

"Yes, I know. We saw your name on the attendee list. I hope you are enjoying Brasilia."

"Brasilia has been fine," she said. "But I need to talk to our station chief."

"The station chief?" the assistant said. "May I ask why? Is there something I can help you with?"

"I'm afraid I need him. What's his name?" Jess said.

The young man hesitated. "You are the Deputy to the Chairman of the President's Council of Economic Advisors. Is that correct?"

"Yes, but what does that have . . ."

"What I mean is, you do not work on national security issues," the man said.

"I'm not calling about a national security issue. I'm talking about an incident in Rio. No, not an incident, a kidnapping," Jess said. "Can you please put me through?"

"A kidnapping? Who has been kidnapped?"

"I was," she said. "I need to make a report."

"Wait a minute. You said you were kidnapped, but then how can you be here? How—"

"It's way too complicated to explain right now. I just need to talk to the station chief. Please connect me."

"All right. In this instance, let me see what I can do. Hold, please."

Jessica checked the time and saw that she should be back in the meeting when it reconvened in a few minutes. Now that she had the embassy on the line, she decided that this was more important than the next session. She wasn't expected to make any remarks there and she really wanted to meet with one of the agents.

The young man finally got back on the line. "Miss Tanner, Chet Osborn is the man you should be speaking with. Right now, he's on a conference call. May I suggest you come here to the embassy? I will see that his staff arranges for you to meet with him as soon as he is free. Would that be convenient?"

"Yes. I'll be there as quickly as a taxi can get me there. Thanks."

CHAPTER FIFTY-FOUR

Barra da Tijuca, Brazil

"Now here's the plan," Pazio said to two of his men standing in the hotel suite of the Promenade Casa Del Mar. The contemporary brown high-rise was situated across a wide boulevard from a beach stretching for miles in the West Zone just outside of downtown Rio. The rooms weren't as fancy as the penthouse where he often met his highest-level contact, but for his purposes, it would do just fine. "I reserved this room for one day because *this* is the day we finally get our revenge for the death of my brother." The two men nodded solemnly.

"You both were there a year ago when the DEA intercepted our shipment. You saw this Bill Black character. You know what he did."

"You got that right, boss," one remarked. "We got a good look at him too."

"I know," Pazio said. "And you, Guillermo, are the one who sent me those photos of him and the girl at the Copacabana the other night. That was good work, and that's why I need you here. To be my lookout. You'll be downstairs watching the entrance to the hotel. As soon as you spot him, call me. Here's the number."

Guillermo programmed it into his phone. "Got it. No problem. I'd know that dude anywhere."

Pazio turned to the other man. "And Juan, you'll be stationed at the elevators on this floor. As soon as Black comes out, you'll grab him and bring him to me."

"Will do."

"It took a while to round up both of you, but with Domingo and his number two in such bad shape, I figured I'd rather work with you anyway."

"Yeah, can you believe that a girl took down two of our guys using a nail gun? When you told us about that, we couldn't believe it," Guillermo chortled.

"I'm going to reorganize the network and see that those two imbeciles are never put in charge of anything important again."

"Maybe have them manage the avioezinhos," Juan suggested. "They should be able to deal with a bunch of little messengers."

"That's about all I'll let them deal with after that screwup," Pazio said. "Now, since we lost the girl, I had to keep Black on the hook so that he'll come to get her."

"When I saw the way he looked at her in the Palace lobby," Guillermo said, "you can be sure he'll come after her. I got a question, though. Once he gets here and you dispose of him, how are you going to get away? Black works with a bunch of other agents. He's not about to come here alone."

"I've been telling him to come alone or the girl's dead," Pazio said. "But, even if he's got backup out there, one reason I picked this place is I've been here before. I've scoped it out, and I know how to get away through the basement. I'm not worried about that. All I care about is pulling the trigger on that bastard."

Pazio stared at his new cell and continued. "Now that we're set up, I'm going to text Black where to meet me and rescue the girl," he said with a glint in his eye. In the last text I sent, I told him I'd be in the West Zone, so he can't be too far away. I'll tell him to be here in an hour. That'll give us enough time to go downstairs and get some breakfast. After all, when you rent a suite, breakfast is free."

• • •

Bill stared at his cell. "Here, another text from Pazio. Finally," Bill said to the three other agents in the staff car. "He says to head to Avenida Sernambetiba 5740. Sixth floor of the Promenade Casa Del Mar in one hour."

"I know that area," the Rio Station Chief said. "Pretty ritzy place for a kidnapping trade. Nothing but fancy apartment buildings, hotels, and beaches. Some people call it the Miami of Rio."

"Don't forget the companies over there. Shell, Nokia, along with the new stadiums. Place will really be booming during the Olympics," another agent said. "I wonder why he picked that place?"

"I have no idea," Bill said. "Maybe he thinks it's better to be in a crowded area for his getaway rather than in some remote section. Anyway, get going. With this traffic, we have to make time. I just pray Jessica is still okay with that maniac shuttling her all over town."

"Remember, we talked about that," the first agent said. "He's got no reason to manhandle her. She's just his ticket to manhandle you."

"I still don't like this," Chet Osborn said, his voice booming through Bill's cell phone speaker as he was monitoring the ongoing situation. "I'm glad you've kept me on the line, though. I want a play-by-play of everything you see or don't see. I wish to hell I was there with you."

"We've got it covered," an agent replied.

"I'm staying on the phone while this goes down. Besides making sure that Bill survives this whole episode, it's our one chance to take down Pazio," Chet said. "Keep this line open."

"Doing just that," Bill said.

They drove through a lot of traffic, passed people heading to the beach along with others going to work at a myriad of tall office buildings. He glanced at his watch and saw that the meeting with Pazio was in ten minutes.

The driver pulled into the parking lot of the hotel and found a spot. Bill and the three agents got out and surveyed the area. "I'll follow Bill when he goes inside. I'll be a few steps behind in case they're watching," the Rio Station Chief said. "You keep covering the entrance," he said to one of the agents. "And you head out back. Both of you keep an eye out in case this doesn't go down right and Pazio tries to get away. Our local backup should be on the way. Pretty soon the police squad will have the whole place surrounded."

"We're heading in," Bill said to Chet who was still on the line. "Looks like several tourists are around, lots more across the street on the beach. As for the hotel, we're now in the lobby, and I see the door to the stairs over to the right. I'm going to take the stairs to the sixth floor."

"He's probably got his people up there, Bill," Chet said.

"If he does, I can handle them," Bill said.

"We can't be sure about that," Chet said. "I still think we should send the whole team up there first. You stay back."

"Can't happen that way," Bill said. "You know Pazio has Jessica. If he doesn't see me alone, he told us before that she'd pay the price." Bill opened the stairway door. With his Glock clutched in his hand, he headed up.

• • •

"He's on his way, boss," Guillermo said. "He's on the phone but looks like he's alone. You'll have him in just a few minutes."

"Good work," Pazio said, reaching over to turn on the TV set. "I've got a silencer on my gun right now, but I'm turning up the volume on a program here, just to cover any sounds the guy might make when I plug him."

CHAPTER FIFTY-FIVE

American Embassy—Brasilia

"You can wait right here, Miss Tanner," a secretary said. "Mr. Osborn should be with you shortly. He's still on a long conference call. May I get you an espresso? Water?"

"No thank you," Jessica said with a nervous smile. "Just had my morning quota."

"Of course," the woman said. "Now, just to be sure I understand the nature of your visit, the ambassador's assistant said you are on the White House staff, here for the OAS conference. May I ask what this is all about? He was in a hurry to leave for a meeting when he called over to say you were on your way."

Jessica looked at her watch. "Actually, I don't have a lot of time, and it is important."

"If you could tell me the subject, perhaps I could slip a note to Mr. Osborn. I don't usually interrupt, but since you're here from Washington . . ."

"That would be terrific. I do have to get back to the conference. Could you please tell him it's regarding a terrible incident in Rio that happened yesterday?"

"A terrible incident?" the secretary asked with a note of concern.

"Yes, I was kidnapped and held by some drug dealers. I want to make a report," Jess said.

"My word!" the woman exclaimed. "You say you were kidnapped? But did they take your money and let you go? That does happen a lot here in Brazil, especially in the big cities."

"It wasn't like that. I need to explain it to Mr. Osborn, so if you could just . . ."

"Yes, of course. I'll get a note to him right away. And you said your name was Tanner?"

"Yes. Jessica Tanner. And thank you."

• • •

"Now where are you?" Chet said into the phone.

"I'm on the fifth floor," Bill said. "One more flight to go."

The secretary opened Chet's office door and tried to hand him a note. He started to wave her away, but she walked up to his chair and thrust the note in front of him. He was still listening to his call, but he finally glanced down.

"What the hell?" he stammered. "She's here? Here in the office? But how? Why?"

"What are you saying?" Bill said into his cell.

"Bill, you're not going to believe this. Stop. Stop right where you are and get the hell out of there," Chet demanded.

"Why? What's going on?" Bill demanded.

"It's Jessica."

"What about Jessica?"

"She's here," Chet said, a note of triumph in his voice. "Can you believe it? My secretary said she's right outside in our reception room waiting to tell me about a kidnapping in Rio."

"But how could she possibly be *there*?"

"I'm about to find out. She must have escaped somehow, though I can't imagine how a man like Pazio let her out of his sight. But it seems that she's here and safe, which means that Pazio has obviously been stringing you along to lure you into his little trap."

Bill sighed heavily. "That's incredible." He was stunned, and he fell silent for just a moment before he continued, "I still want to take Pazio, though."

"No, you don't. Not you," Chet ordered. "As I said, you get out of there. Let the other agents and the local police go in and arrest Pazio and anyone else they can find."

"Look, Chet," Bill said, "I've been Pazio's target for more than a year. And he's been our target, one we've been trying to track for all that time. I need to be on hand for the takedown."

"Oh, for Christ's sake. We can't lose you now," Chet argued.

"I don't want to lose any of our agents," Bill countered. "We'll handle it. Now, send an agent to the seventh floor and have him walk down the stairs," he said, aiming his order to the Rio Station Chief. "We'll meet on the sixth and he can handle any lookout while I go to handle Pazio."

The chief came on the line and said, "Our backup is almost here. I'm sending an agent up as Bill instructed."

"I still don't like it," Chet said, "but I'll have to trust you. I know you're one of the best. I'm staying on the line."

CHAPTER FIFTY-SIX

Bill waited until he heard that the Rio agent had reached the seventh floor. They coordinated their timing, and both arrived at the sixth-floor stairway door at the same time.

"As soon as I open this door and we see the lookout, I'll take him and you head to Pazio's room," the agent said.

"Right," Bill confirmed. He gingerly turned the knob and peered down the hall. Sure enough, there was one of Pazio's men standing at the elevator with his gun drawn. "That's the lookout," Bill whispered.

The agent nodded, stepped into the hall, took aim, and fired. At the same time, Bill rushed to Pazio's room and saw the kingpin open it with his gun drawn, obviously curious about the shot.

It was now or never. Bill shouted, "Hands up!" Would he try to take Bill out as he had promised, or could they stop him once and for all? Bill felt his heart rate speed up as perspiration damped the back of his neck.

The second agent raced forward, also aiming his gun at Pazio, who stared at the two of them wide-eyed, evidently trying to decide his next move.

"Your time's up," Bill said in an ominous tone of voice. "Put the gun down." When Pazio didn't move, Bill said, "Hear those sirens? Backup has arrived. This place is surrounded. Even if you tried to take us both out, which you can't, we're taking you in." He saw Pazio hesitate and finally drop his gun.

Bill felt a great wave of relief knowing they finally had this man who had contributed to such suffering and death from his corruption and drug dealing. He hoped that with the ringleader in custody they would be able to learn about his entire operation and shut it down. That would take a while. For now, Bill kept his gun trained on Pazio as he heard the elevator door open.

Several agents and police swarmed onto the floor, grabbed Pazio, cuffed him, and led him away. Bill then held his cell up to his ear. "Hear that?"

"I did," Chet said, exhaling a huge breath. "Great job, you all. Congratulations. This is huge. I can't wait to let the president's security chief know. And Bill, about security, when it's all over there in Rio, we need you back in Brasilia for the big event tonight. We're still checking out some more possible suspects and enhancing the president's security inside and outside the palace. I'm sending the jet for you again. It'll be waiting. Now Jessica is waiting too. I have to hear her story."

CHAPTER FIFTY-SEVEN

Alvorado Palace—Brasilia

Jessica was ushered in to Chet Osborn's office. He stood and extended his hand. "Good morning, Ms. Tanner. Sorry to keep you waiting. I understand you were kidnapped. This is hard to believe. Please sit down and tell me what happened. I want to hear all of it."

Jess took a seat and began to explain how she was in Rio for the weekend and happened to take a walk outside the Copacabana Palace on Sunday morning when two awful men grabbed her off the street, blindfolded her and stashed her in an underground warehouse. She wasn't about to disclose that she had spent Saturday night with Bill Black from the State Department. That was personal. This was perilous.

"So, there you were in a warehouse," Chet said. "How in the world did you get away?"

"When the men went out for food, I managed to use some of their own tools, like WD-40 to loosen the duct tape they had put around my arms and legs as I was sitting on a chair. When I ripped it off, I searched the place. It looked like a staging area for drug shipments, and I found a nail gun. When the men got back, I was standing by the door and shot nails into both of them. I ran out, locked them inside, and ran out of there. I was desperate . . ."

"You physically nailed two men?" Chet asked, emitting a large laugh. "What an incredible scene."

"Right. Anyway, when I got out, I looked around and saw I was in the middle of the worst slum I've ever seen. It's called Rocinha. I found a teenage girl with an old scooter. Her name was Christina. I paid her to take me back to the Copacabana. It was late. I couldn't take time to meet with our Station Chief in Rio, although I'm sure they would want to figure out the location of that drug lab, but I had to make my flight back here last night because I had a presentation at the OAS meeting first thing this morning. That lab isn't going anywhere. I'm here now to tell you all about it so you can try to shut it down. Oh, and I got the address of where that girl with the scooter lives. I'm sure the lab can't be too far from there, if that helps." She rummaged in her purse and showed him the address.

Chet sat back and said, "This is the most extraordinary story of bravery and brilliance. Ms. Tanner, you are amazing."

"Uh, thanks. I'm still wondering why they kidnapped me, though. Oh, and they took my picture and sent it to someone. Do you think they were asking for a ransom?"

"Unfortunately, these crazy kidnappings are happening more and more in Rio as well as in Sao Paulo and a few other places," he said. "Since they must have been following a well-dressed woman, they knew where you were staying, and they might have sent the photos to the Manager of the Copacabana to get him to pay a ransom. After all, they couldn't afford to have their hotel guests harmed by a gang of hooligans."

Jessica thought that sounded a bit strange, but it might have made sense. *After all, this man works on criminal issues all the time, so he must know what goes on.*

Chet invited her to stay for lunch in their executive dining room so they could go over a few more details. Since she didn't have any breakfast, she was glad to accept.

When she got back to the hotel, she caught the last workshop of the day and before getting dressed up for the final banquet. She was looking forward to seeing Estelle and Mia, though after talking to Chet, he had asked her to keep the details of her ordeal quiet for now. But the most important thing she wanted to do at the dinner was to try and find Bill. He had to be there.

CHAPTER FIFTY-EIGHT

As Jessica stepped out of the taxi that had taken her from the Royal Tulip Hotel to the President's Palace at the appointed hour for cocktails and dinner, she hoped she could find Bill so he could explain exactly what had happened to make him leave her Saturday night.

She held her bag open for inspection by the security staff at the front door, walked through the magnetometer, and entered the reception. The room was mobbed. Every minister, ambassador, staffer, and assistant here for the conference had been included on the guest list. Waiters clad in black pants, crisp white jackets, and bow ties circulated through the crowd, holding silver trays of wine and champagne. She saw two full bars set up on either side of the room where gaggles of men had congregated evidently opting for something stronger than champagne.

As she scanned the crowd, she saw Estelle dressed in her green skirt and green and white silk top, looking nervous as she stood next to Secretary Leventhal. When she caught Jessica's eye, she gave a slight nod. Jessica walked over. "Good evening, Mr. Secretary," she said. "I thought the workshops went well today."

"Yes, hello, Jessica. I agree. Of course, the most important meetings take place one-on-one in our suites, as you know. I had an excellent exchange with the foreign ministers of both Peru and Colombia. We just may get their support on the trade agreements along with some new initiatives on curbing FARC and the drug trade. You know they've been trying to negotiate with that terrorist group for years."

Jessica didn't want to think about the drug trade right now, but she had to be polite. "Congratulations, sir. I know that Hal and the president will be looking forward to reading your summary report. Then again, you'll probably be meeting with the president in person."

"Yes, I usually do," the Secretary said with a confident air. "We have a cabinet meeting scheduled for Wednesday, so I'll be telling everyone about our success down here."

I bet you will, she thought. She turned to Estelle. "I'm sure you've been kept pretty busy through all of this."

"Oh yes," Estelle said. "Um, Mr. Secretary, could you excuse me for a moment? I want to speak to Jessica about something."

"You girls run along," Leventhal said. "I want to go talk to the vice president. I see he just came in."

Jessica and Estelle moved away, and each of them snatched a glass of wine from a passing waiter. "What's up?" Jessica asked.

"Oh, I don't know how much I should say, but things got even worse after you left the bar last night," Estelle whispered.

"Last night? It was almost one o'clock when I left. What happened?"

"Leventhal had left a message for me, and I figured I'd better answer it. He told me he was working late and told me to come up to his room."

"Oh no. What happened? Was he at least dressed this time?" Jess asked.

"Sort of. He had a bath robe on. He asked me to come in. He offered me a drink. I said I didn't want one. Then he tried to get me to sit down on the couch next to him. I backed away. Then he grabbed me and said I was a pretty young girl, that I was smart, and he would be happy to help me get ahead in the State Department."

"What did you do?"

"I got over to the door, said that it was late, and I still had some work to do. I got out of there and back to my room. I couldn't sleep much, though. Jess, I don't know what to do now. I can't work like this. I think

I'm going to have to quit and look for another job," Estelle said in a low voice.

"Let me think about this," Jess said. "Maybe we can find you a spot in one of the other agencies, or even in the White House. It'll take a bit of time. Do you think you can manage in there for another week or two when we get back?"

"Yes," Estelle said. "In the office I can usually finesse the situation. There aren't any more trips on the schedule, that is unless some part of the world blows up and he has to get on a plane again. He does travel a lot, but if it's a national security situation, I can't imagine he would pressure me to come along. And if he did, I guess I could always call in sick."

"Okay," Jess said putting her hand on Estelle's arm. "Hang in here as best you can, and we'll keep in touch." She started to look around the room, hoping to see Bill. But he wasn't anywhere in sight. At least not yet. "I'd better go mingle."

"Right. I can't tell you how happy I am that we met on this trip. Now, I think I'll try to find an hors d'oeuvre."

• • •

Bill hurried into the dining room and found Chet over in the corner. "They should be opening the doors for the dinner any minute now," he said. "Have you seen Jessica?"

"Hold on. She's probably still in the reception area. Before we talk about which security guards will be where, I just got further word from the Rio Chief," Chet said excitedly. "In addition to arresting Pazio and two of his men at the Barro hotel it now turns out that with the information Jessica gave me this morning, they had a whole team canvassing the Rocinha favela in a mile radius from that girl's address. That girl is Christina, who took Jess back to the Copacabana."

"Thank God she did that," Bill said.

"Anyway, they found the tunnel and the lab. Got some files and equipment and sealed it all up. Nobody's going to be using that facility ever again. Well, not for drugs anyway."

"And what about Domingo and that other guy?" Bill asked.

"Got them too from the other warehouse. In fact, in exchange for a slightly more lenient sentence, Domingo is singing like a choir boy. They're going to be able to round up most of the network in the next few days. I'm sure of it."

"This is incredible news," Bill said. "How will they announce it?"

"They'll let the president take credit, of course. And they know not to tie Jessica or you to any of this. The president will simply say that they followed up on a number of tips from concerned citizens, and an efficient police force was able to crack the entire Pazio ring. Or some such."

"'An efficient police force'?" Bill said, giving a slight shake of his head. "I wonder what'll happen to all the ones who were on the take from that ring?"

"Guess they'll have to cut down on their spending habits," Chet said. "All in all, it's been quite a day. But . . ." He scanned the ballroom, "we have more work to do tonight. Let's see where the major players will be sitting. I guess that's your job," Chet said with a slight grin. "Well, yours and the Social Secretary."

"One of them," Bill said, ignoring Chet's last remark. He started working his way through some of the tables. "I see they have the president here at the center table. Number one, of course. He's sitting with Leventhal and some other top foreign ministers." Bill moved to the right. "Vice President Serra is at number two. I managed to get the Argentine Ambassador assigned to his table. He was a last-minute addition. Remember?"

"Yeah. I see they even gave him a steak knife. Your boss would be pleased," Chet said, chuckling.

"The vice president's Chief of Security—that emaciated fellow named Rabelo—is seated right behind Serra at number three along with some of his other staff," Bill said. "I'm at number four, so I've got this side covered. They've got you and some of our other embassy people on the other side of the room," Bill continued. "Jessica and the rest of the State department contingent are in the next row behind the President. As for Mendez's security detail, we talked about how they'll be dispersed around the room with a few of them standing against the wall, and two more on the stage, over in the wings. What do you think?"

Chet looked around. "This set-up is about as good as it's going to get. All we can do is keep watching the players and pray for the best."

"By the way, I know you gave me a summary of your meeting with Jessica but do you think she really bought it?" Bill asked. "I mean, the part about how Pazio might have sent her picture to the hotel manager to get a ransom?"

"I have no idea. She was so wound up telling me all about what his goons looked like and how she used the WD-40 to get the tape off and then the nail gun to get away, I have to say, that is one gutsy lady."

"That's not all she is," Bill said.

"Yeah, I get it. You've got the hots for her," Chet said, raising one eyebrow. "So how are you going to handle her from now on?"

"I'm not sure. I need some private time to try and explain why I left her that night."

"And what, exactly, are you going to say? That you had an urgent meeting about seating charts?" Chet said with a laugh.

"I'll have to think of something, but I don't think I can do that here. We've got too many other things to take care of tonight."

"We have just one more thing to take care of tonight," Chet said. "And that's protecting the life of the President of Brazil."

CHAPTER FIFTY-NINE

Alvorado Palace—Brasilia

Waiters began hitting a series of chimes, urging the delegates to move into the dining room. Jessica was talking with the woman from Canada who remarked, "I do love your dress. That aqua sheath is stunning." Then, with a slightly sad look, she said, "I can never seem to find formal clothes in Ottawa that fit that well. Then again, I'd have to lose a few pounds to wear one like yours."

"I think that navy taffeta is perfect for this occasion." Jess was being diplomatic. "By the way, what did you think about Secretary Leventhal's pitch this morning?"

"He made some excellent points that I intend to go over with my Prime Minister. We'll take them up right away and see what we can do to push this trade proposal along."

"I appreciate that," Jess said. "Now I think we're supposed to find our tables."

They wandered into the gigantic ballroom where members of the Social Secretary's staff stood at the doorway with seating assignments. Jess was directed to a table toward the front of the room. She marveled at the colorful tablecloths set with gleaming sterling silver, large candelabra that were so tall, the candles were above eye level so people could talk across the table and not be staring into the flames. There were sprays of multi-colored orchids wound around the bases of the candelabra and linen napkins to match. *This rivals our White House State Dinners*, she thought as she found her place next to the Assistant Secretary of State in charge of the Bureau of Western Hemisphere Affairs.

The dinner began with a first course of crab and lobster on a bed of radicchio and endive fanned out across the plate, served with a pinot grigio. Jessica tried to maintain a decent conversation with her dinner partners, but she couldn't help scanning the ballroom from time to time, trying to catch a glimpse of Bill. She surveyed the back of the room. No luck there. She looked to the left and saw a pair of doors that she figured led to the kitchen. There were security guards stationed on either side, keeping a close eye on the dinner guests.

Before she could look anywhere else, one of the Assistant Secretaries asked her opinion of Brazil. She wasn't about to complain about luggage thieves, purse snatchers in the shopping mall, or kidnappers in Rio. She remembered that Chet had asked her to keep that incident quiet for now while they rounded up the perpetrators. He also said that whenever they arrest drug dealers, they like to give the president a chance to release the information. It was the same in Washington. The president announces good news. Some bureaucrat from an obscure agency announces the bad stuff.

She answered the question, saying that the architecture was quite futuristic and fascinating. He agreed but said he preferred classic styles. A bevy of waiters swept the salad plates away and served a main course of beef tenderloin, haricots verts with pine nuts, and some sort of potato pancake that was infused with a light cheese mixture. To complement the main course, the waiters offered a Casa Valduga Gran Reserve cabernet sauvignon. She took a sip and thought it was full-bodied, a bit heavier than her usual fare. So, she decided to stick with white wine and water.

As she glanced over at the vice president's table, she saw the Argentine Ambassador sitting there. She had met him at an embassy party in DC not too long ago. When she studied the entree, she mused that the ambassador should be pleased with the steak, but he was probably comparing it to the prized beef they have in his country, hoping his was better.

Then she looked toward the next table over to the right and finally saw Bill. There he was decked out in a handsome tuxedo. She wanted to go over and talk to him, see his smile, talk to him about Saturday night. But she could hardly get up in the middle of the dinner.

She noticed that he wasn't talking to the people on either side of him. He kept looking at the president's table, then over to the sidelines. She couldn't follow his line of sight too well because there were several guests seated between them. She had to lean over a bit to even get a glimpse of him, but she wondered who he was looking for. *Maybe he's looking for me. At least that's a good sign.* But she couldn't catch his eye.

She vowed to go over to his table when the dinner was over. *Although he left me, I'm sure there's some plausible reason. I should give him a chance to explain. After all, he's probably been trying to call my cell, which I don't have any more, but he doesn't know that.* She turned back to her dinner companions.

After the dessert course, the waiters came around again to pour champagne. This was the cue for Vice President Serra to get up from his table, take three steps up to the stage, and ask for everyone's attention. "Ladies and gentlemen from throughout the Americas. We are delighted to have you as our guests here in the Capital. The meeting of the Organization of American States may have set a milestone when it comes to new agreements, but I will let our president focus on these accomplishments. At this moment I would like to raise a toast to all of you and also to President Roberto Mendez. May we remain the best of friends and neighbors."

As he raised his glass, shouts of "Hear, hear!" burst from the crowd. The vice president retreated back to his table, and President Mendez took over the microphone.

"Ladies and gentlemen. On behalf of my entire government, we have been delighted to have you as delegates and guests in our country, and we hope you have enjoyed the sights and balmy temperatures. I am also very pleased with our discussions at this OAS meeting about the desirability of lowering and eventually eliminating tariffs, enhancing trade, reducing tax rates to expand our economies while at the same time refocusing our efforts on education and job training.

"However," he continued, "I have another important announcement to make. Our police forces have just broken up a major drug ring this very day. It was a big one that had been operating not only in Brazil but in several neighboring countries." The room erupted in loud applause, and Jessica felt a warm glow thinking that she had played a part in the whole drama. When President Mendez gave his final thanks to the delegates for coming to his country, everyone began to stand up and clap.

Bill stood with the others, all the while scanning the crowd. His gaze took in the people closest to the president, those at table number one. All were smiling and applauding. Then he looked at each person at Antonio Serra's table and stopped when he focused on Edwardo Rabelo, the vice president's gaunt security chief. He saw the man reach into his pocket. Bill thought it was probably time for more pills. Instead of pills, Bill caught a glint of metal. He knew he couldn't pull out his Glock in this crowded ballroom, but it looked like Rabelo had a gun in his hand.

Bill jumped toward their table, his chair crashing on the floor. In one fluid motion, he shoved the Argentine Ambassador aside, grabbed his steak knife, leaped over, and plunged the knife into Rabelo's arm just as the man pulled the trigger. The bullet went wild, hitting a candelabra, sending the flaming candles down onto the tablecloth.

People began screaming as dinner guests threw their water goblets to douse the flames. The president's security guards materialized, surrounded President Mendez, and hustled him out a door at the side of the stage. In the pandemonium, Bill had Rabelo pinned down as Chet and four other guards rushed over. As a group they dragged the shooter out another door while the vice president quickly slipped out through the kitchen.

Jessica stood transfixed as she realized Bill was the one who had stopped an assassination attempt. She was shocked, stunned. What just happened here? Who was that man with the gun? He was sitting with the vice president. Why would he want to kill the president? Why would he do it here, with all of this security around? He would certainly be caught in the act. It would have been a suicide mission. And how in the world did Bill manage to jump on top of him and stop the attack? The president could have been killed. And God, *Bill* could have been killed. She wondered where he was now and when she would see him again?

"Ladies and gentleman," the president's chief of staff almost yelled into the microphone. "Please remain calm. There has been a terrible incident, but I want to assure you that everything is now under control. We all saw that a man, someone we know and had trusted, evidently had an evil intent to harm our president. But I want to assure you that President Mendez is fine. We are all thankful that he has been taken to a safe place, and the perpetrator of this heinous act has been apprehended. The threat is over, and a full investigation will be underway, of course. Right now, for everyone's safety and comfort, please leave the ballroom quietly and accept our profound apologies for a difficult ending to what had been a very successful conference."

The delegates were anything but quiet. Cries of astonishment were heard at every table as the shocked and shaken delegates pushed and shoved their way toward the exits. Jessica watched the shoving matches, then turned and hurried over to Secretary Leventhal.

"Shades of John Hinkley," the Secretary muttered. "I can't believe a member of the vice president's security detail had a gun aimed at the president. This doesn't make any sense."

"You're right," Jess replied. "What can it mean?"

"I have no idea. I hope to hell they get to the bottom of it."

"Did you see Bill Black take down the shooter?" Jessica said.

"Sure did. Never saw anyone move that fast. Damn proud that it was a member of *my* staff who saved the day. When we sort this out, I'll have to give that man a medal."

CHAPTER SIXTY

Alvorado Palace—Brasilia

"The doctor's got Rabelo all stitched up," Chet said. "You sure stopped him cold with that knife trick."

"It wasn't a trick," Bill said. "It was desperation. I thought I saw a gun. I just reacted."

"Well, it was a helluva good job. I don't know how much longer the palace security detail will be in there questioning him. They asked us to stay. Looks like it could be a long night."

"Guess I could use some coffee," Bill said, walking over to a sideboard along the wall of a secure conference room on the top floor of the President's Palace. He poured a cup and looked over his shoulder. "Want some?"

"I'll wait a while. I had coffee and everything else at the banquet. It was a nice dinner. Before the disaster," Chet said. "Why do you suppose Rabelo did it?"

"We only saw the guy twice in our meetings, but remember how he kept popping pills all the time?"

"Yeah," Chet said. "So?"

"So, let's say that he's got some terminal disease," Bill speculated. "Cancer, brain tumor, whatever. And let's say somebody that hates the president pays him a bunch of money to kill the guy. Rabelo's going to die anyway, so maybe he cut a deal with someone who promised to stash the funds in an offshore account to take care of his family when he's gone. What do you think?"

"Kinda makes sense. Everyone around here has an offshore bank account. As for why it was tonight, Rabelo knew he would be at the banquet along with the target. He knew he could get close. He knew he was allowed to carry a weapon. So, you could say he had means, motive, and opportunity. But who do you think wanted the president dead?"

"Who the hell knows?" Bill said. "Pazio was steamed about the way Mendez was cracking down on his business. Pardon the pun," Bill said.

"They've got Pazio's whole gang locked up. Maybe they can confirm if he orchestrated the deal," Chet said. "On the other hand, just taking out Mendez doesn't mean the raids would stop. Even though we have DEA agents working with the locals trying to stem that trade, I don't see it stopping no matter who lives in the palace. Especially with the Olympics coming up. The whole government is working their asses off trying to clean up the cities before the tourists arrive. We all know that."

"If Pazio didn't pay Rabelo, then who?" Bill pressed, taking a sip of coffee, and settling back down at the conference table.

"That's what we need to get out of Rabelo. Come to think about it, the news shows must be going ballistic with this whole assassination story. The headlines in the morning will be speculating about everyone. Conspiracy theories abound in this country," Chet said.

"I'm sure we'll get a full dose of it when they let us leave," Bill said. "I wonder when that will be."

Chet looked at his watch. "At this rate, it could be days."

CHAPTER SIXTY-ONE

Royal Tulip Hotel—Brasilia

"Can you believe that scene last night? I wonder who the shooter was and why he wanted to kill the president," Estelle said breathlessly as she stood with Jessica in front of the hotel check-out desk.

"I heard it was a man named Edwardo Rabelo. He was in charge of the vice president's security detail. But how in the world could one of his security people be involved in an assassination attempt?" Jessica asked.

"My question exactly. It's all so crazy. And to see that guy, Bill, from our department stop the whole thing, it was absolutely surreal."

"You got that one right," Jess said. She motioned to the desk clerk who looked like she was finishing with another guest. "I'll just be a minute here, then we'll talk some more. I have to settle something." She turned back and said, "I'm checking out. I would have used the online system, but I had a quick question about one of these charges on my bill." She pointed to a line item.

The woman checked and said, "That is for a cocktail in the Old Barr Sunday night."

"I just had juice," Jessica said. "It's not a big deal, but it looked a bit expensive."

"Only juice? Then you are most correct. I apologize," the clerk said. She made a calculation, printed out a new bill and said, "Here is a corrected copy. We have your credit card, so you are all set. Will there be anything else?"

"No, thanks," Jess said. She muttered to Estelle, "I guess it's the economist in me. I always have to check numbers."

"Hope mine was right," Estelle said. "I checked out from my room. Now we'd better get to the shuttle. There's one outside to take us all to the airport. I assume you're on the same flight with the rest of us."

"Yes, I am," Jess said. "It's just that I was . . ."

"Looking for someone? Our whole delegation should be on the return flight," Estelle said.

"I wonder about Bill Black," Jess said, checking around the vast lobby.

"Yes, the hero," Estelle said. "He's probably tied up with the authorities. They said they were doing a big investigation. I doubt if we'll see him for a while. He certainly had some great moves last night."

"For sure," Jessica said, dragging her roller bag out to the curb. *That man has lots of great moves*, she reflected. She certainly wished she could see him before she had to leave for Washington. She thought about trying to call his hotel room this morning, but Estelle was probably right. He was with the security people, sorting it all out. He could be delayed for days over the whole situation. *The question is, will he call me or try to see me again?* The more she thought about it, the more she was determined to let him contact her. Not the other way around.

CHAPTER SIXTY-TWO

Washington, DC

"I couldn't believe the headlines about that assassination attempt in Brazil. And you were right there!" Kay Heller exclaimed as she pushed through the door of Jessica's condo. "I've been trying to call you all day, but I'm sure you've been swamped. When I got your text about dinner tonight, I couldn't wait to talk to you." She swept in, tossed her purse on the entry table, and walked into the living room. "I have to hear everything. And I mean everything."

"You will," Jessica said. "Yes, I was there, and yes, I saw it all. I've been in debriefings all day with J. L. and others from State. It's been crazy, and I didn't get much sleep on the plane back. I'm still kind of wound up. I could use a glass of wine."

"I'm just so glad you're back," her friend said. "What a horrible scene, to be right there when some crazy gunman tries to kill a president. It's been all over the news all day."

"I know. And that's not all that happened when I was down there. We have a ton to talk about. But let's do that over dinner. Where should we go?"

"Why don't we head over to Georgetown? We could splurge and go to Café Milano or get a booth at Martin's Tavern," Kay suggested.

"Café Milano is always so noisy and jammed with political wannabes, if you know what I mean. I guess it's fun once in a while, but it's awfully hard to talk in there. I'd opt for Martin's."

"Good idea," Kay pulled out her phone. "I'll give them a quick call and make a reservation."

During their drive to Wisconsin and N Streets, Kay kept peppering Jessica with questions. "I not only want to hear about that incredible dinner scene, but I'm dying to know about you and Bill Black." Her friend found a parking place around the corner, put money in the meter and they walked to Martin's. Once inside, the Maitre d' showed them to a booth on the right side by the window.

"Look," Kay said. "They gave us the Kennedy booth. See this little plaque here? It says that this is where Jack Kennedy asked Jackie to marry him."

"That's kind of sweet," Jess said, settling onto the wooden seat. "That reminds me. I used a Kennedy quote in my remarks at the conference. He had some good lines."

"As I said, what I want to hear about are the lines this Bill Black used on you. Well, that and the gunman at the banquet and everything else. From the texts you sent earlier, it sounds like Bill turned out to be more than a boring bureaucrat, right?" Kay said.

"Did he ever," Jess said with a sigh. "I'll get to the shooting in a second, but first, I'll admit it."

"Admit what?"

"That Bill and I spent an incredible weekend together in Rio," Jess said.

"Does that mean what I think it means?"

"It does," Jess said. "The trouble is, I haven't talked to him since."

"Wasn't he at the same conference? I don't get this," Kay said.

"I don't get it either. But before I go through it all, I want to get a glass of wine. This is going to take a while."

"Good evening, ladies. Here are your menus, but what can I get you to start?"

"I'm going to stick to fish tonight," Kay said. "So how about a glass of your Sonoma Cutrer chardonnay?"

"And for you?"

Jess opened the menu and glanced at the wine list. "Let's see. I think I'll go with your Hob Nob pinot noir. Thanks."

When the waiter scurried away, Kay said, "So did you 'Hob Nob' with the great and the near-great in Brazil? Besides Bill Black that is. I want to hear more about him."

"We did have a whole collection of diplomats, ambassadors, foreign ministers. It was a big deal this time. Secretary Leventhal gave a good presentation, but he also presented himself as quite the ladies' man."

"Yes, I've heard that. Word gets around. Wait, does that mean he came on to you?"

"No. It was Estelle. She had a hard time keeping her clothes on and fending *him* off."

"Jeez. Is she going to stay on at State with that kind of pressure?" Kay asked.

"She doesn't want to. I put in a call to White House personnel this afternoon to see if they can find another slot for her."

"Good move. Now, get back to the assassination. You know I always want details."

Jess held up her hand in a wait-a-moment gesture as the waiter approached.

"Here you are ladies, chardonnay for you and the pinot over here. Have you decided on dinner?"

They both examined their menus. "They have such great comfort food here," Jess said. "Shepherd's pie, pot roast, meat loaf. Sounds like home."

"Martin's has been here for eighty years, you know," the waiter volunteered. "We have a lot of dishes that have been popular for ages, but the chef has some new additions as well. Of course, our lamb chops are my favorite."

"Good idea," Jess said.

"They come with fingerling potatoes, roasted apples, and plums." He turned to Kay.

"I think I'll have your grilled salmon," she said. "But hold the pilaf and just bring extra broccoli if you would, please." The waiter nodded and walked off.

Jess took a sip of her wine and leaned forward. "Okay, I guess I should start at the beginning because it all sort of ties together. Well, not really, but sort of."

"What do you mean? You're talking in riddles," Kay said, tasting her wine.

"It all started on the flight down to Brasilia. That's when I met Bill."

"The protocol guy," Kay prompted.

"Right. And at first, he gave me this rather boring tutorial on the Greek origin of the word *protocol*, how John Quincy Adams had his own definition, then he went on about whether you bow to royalty and all of that."

"Sounds like you at least listened," Kay said.

"I had no choice. I have to say that in the beginning I thought he was sitting there looking like an envelope without an address on it," Jess said and added, "I think Mark Twain said that once."

Kay chuckled as Jess continued. "Then when we got to the hotel, he kept hanging around, telling me about street crime and how he had been told to keep an eye on me. I spent the first day trying to avoid him."

"And then?"

"And then I was in a shopping mall because all my cosmetics were stolen out of my luggage, and I had to replace them."

"Wait, someone stole your stuff?" Kay said.

"That was the least of my worries. It evidently happens a lot down there. When I was in the mall, there were purse snatchers around, so when Bill showed up, I started to feel better about having him with me. It kind of evolved from there."

"Evolved?" Kay said with a grin. "Where and when?"

"As I said, we both went to Rio for the weekend and spent the most incredible time at the Copacabana Palace," Jess said dreamily. "But the next morning he was gone."

"Gone? Gone where?"

"I don't know. I'm still not sure. He showed up later at the banquet, and I'll get to that in a minute. But when I saw that he had left me alone in the room and had only scribbled the word 'Later' on a business card, I was pretty upset. I decided to take a walk, and when I left the hotel, two thugs grabbed me, threw me in a car, stashed me in a drug lab and tied me up."

"*What?*" Kay exclaimed in a loud voice.

Jess shushed her friend, trying to keep her calm. "Yes," she said in a low voice, "I was kidnapped. It was so awful, so scary, so unbelievable. I had no idea what to do."

"My God, did they hurt you? Did they want a ransom? What happened? Who rescued you?" Kay asked anxiously.

"Here you are, ladies. Salmon for you, ma'am, and the lamb chops for you." The waiter set the plates down and asked, "Will there be anything more? Another glass of wine, perhaps?"

"Absolutely," Kay said. "I need one, and I think my friend here does too."

"Coming right up."

"Now, tell me the whole story," Kay said. "You're kidnapped in Rio de Janeiro by bad guys, and now you're here looking calm, cool, and collected. I don't believe this."

Jess cut a piece of lamb and continued her story. She described the lab, the men, their conversations, the photos, and finally how she was able to use the solvent, nail gun, and compressor to attack them and make her escape.

"Wait a minute. You got *yourself* free and shot the kidnappers?"

"I didn't kill them," Jess said. "I shot them with the nail gun, and it stopped them long enough for me to get out of there." She described the ride with Christina, her flight back to Brasilia, alone, her meeting with the station chief and their round-up of the drug ring.

"This is incredible," Kay said, waving her fork in the air. "You were able to tell our agents where the lab was and help them take down a bunch of drug dealers? Does J. L. know all about this?"

"Of course. I've been in meetings all day. That's why I was late tonight, remember?"

"Who else knows what happened to you? Is this going to get out?" Kay asked.

"They've asked me to keep it under wraps, so you can't tell anyone, okay?"

"Sure, but why?"

"Our embassy people in Brasilia are working with the locals to wrap it all up. The drug dealers, the whole assassination plot, whether there was any connection—all of it. There have been a lot of drug raids and arrests, especially since they're getting ready for the Olympics. They're trying to tell the world that things are safer, so the fans and tourists won't get spooked. The assassination was enough to get the whole country riled up. While my situation was a minor story, if word got out that someone on the White House staff was taken off the street and held for ransom, that wouldn't make a very good headline either."

"I see their point, although I don't think your kidnapping is a minor issue," Kay said. "But I guess you don't need that kind of publicity either."

"I hate seeing my name in the paper," Jess said, drinking more wine and starting in on the potatoes. "But I haven't told you the rest."

She explained searching for Bill, finally spotting him at the banquet, and seeing his incredible leap over a table to stop a skinny, weird-looking man with a gun who was obviously trying to kill the president.

"*Bill Black* is the one who saved the president's life? His name wasn't in the papers or on the news."

"I know. I think they're trying to keep our people out of this or something. I'm not sure. I told J. L. about everything and, of course, everyone at State knew it was Bill who stopped the bullet from hitting the president," Jess said.

"So where is Bill now?"

"I don't know. They're still investigating the whole thing. He might still be down there. I haven't talked to him, and he hasn't called or anything." She hesitated and added, "I suppose he might have called, but they took my phone when I was kidnapped, so I really don't know."

"I'm sure he'll call you when he can," Kay said. "Think about it. He stopped a killer. Sounds like a real hero to me. Certainly not a boring bureaucrat."

Jess sat back, took another sip of wine, and said, "You know, when I was assigned to the conference, all I could think about was whether I could add a little excitement to my life."

CHAPTER SIXTY-THREE

Planalto Palace—Brasilia

"We've got another informant," the president's security chief announced to Bill, Chet, and a host of additional agents and analysts gathered in the war room of the Capital building. "Our Rio people had a call from a lady named Irena."

"She's the vice president's mistress," one analyst ventured. "Isn't she?"

"I think she's his latest," another said. "Lives in Rio. What does she know about any of this?"

"That's what we're finding out right now. She's being questioned by our people over there. What they've heard so far is that when the news broke first about Rabelo trying to kill Mendez and then Pazio's network being taken down, she decided to come forward with an interesting connection."

"What connection?" Bill asked.

"And why would she come in?" Chet asked.

"We're not sure, but she said she was mad at Antonia Serra. He had evidently promised he'd divorce his wife and marry her."

"Oldest promise in the book," one agent observed. "What's she spilling about him?"

"It turns out she was in Serra's penthouse in Rio when he had a meeting with Pazio."

"She *saw* Pazio there?" Bill asked.

"Yep. She was hiding in the kitchen, and says she saw Pazio give what she believes was a suitcase full of money to Serra," the chief said. "We should be getting another update pretty soon, but this throws a whole new light on it."

"This, in addition to Rabelo's statements, means we may have found who's really behind this whole thing," Chet said. "Rabelo hasn't said much so far, just that he knew he was dying and needed money for his family." He turned to Bill. "This is the whole motive you sketched out earlier. Looks like you may have nailed it."

"But Rabelo hasn't said who paid him to kill the president," the chief said. "And it's hard for me to process this. I mean, we all worked with that man for years."

"Look at it this way," Bill said. "It's possible that Pazio paid Rabelo to do it, but I think it's even more plausible that the vice president was the one who gave the order. We now know that he was on the take from Pazio, probably to tip him off about the raids, so he had the funds to pay Rabelo."

"But why kill the president?" an analyst asked.

"The best reason in the world," Chet said. "He wanted to be Number One. Mendez dies, Serra becomes president. He pays Rabelo, who takes the job because he knows he's going to die anyway, and Serra runs the whole show from now on."

"Where is Serra now?" Bill asked.

"We still don't know for sure that it was the vice president who paid Rabelo," the chief said.

"No, but you have to admit it all makes sense," Bill said. "We need to find Serra and question him."

"I have to consult with the president about this," the chief said, getting up from the table and rushing out of the room.

The deputy of presidential security detail took Bill aside. "Thanks for all your help on this case," he said. "I'm sure President Mendez will want to commend you for everything you've done here, but we'll need you to stay in town for a little longer. There's still more to get out of Rabelo, maybe more from Irena, as well as a lot of other people. I'm sure your government will allow you to remain here for a few more days, right?"

Bill exchanged a look with Chet. "I do have a lot of work in Washington, but I've been checking with the Undersecretary of State about this whole affair, and he has already told me to stay and help in any way I can. At least for a while." Bill wasn't sure what had been told to Alicia at Protocol, but he couldn't worry about that now.

"That's good. I'll check on the president's schedule about a possible meeting, and I'll also get back to you about the next steps in the investigation," the man said.

"All right," Bill said. "In the meantime, I would strongly recommend that you find the vice president and at least detain him for questioning if you can."

"And one more thing," Chet added. "I want to make a formal request that you continue to keep our names away from the press."

"Yes, we understand the sensitivity. It's going to come out that Bill is the one who stopped Rabelo, even though we didn't use his name in the initial press briefings. But you know our reporters down here. They are clamoring for every detail they can get and since everyone in that ballroom saw what Bill did, I'm surprised his name hasn't surfaced yet," another agent said.

"I realize that," Chet said. "But if his name gets out there, tell your press secretary to be certain that he is simply identified as 'William Black, Assistant Chief of Protocol for the US Department of State.'"

CHAPTER SIXTY-FOUR

Washington, DC

Jessica poured a glass of wine, took it over to her coffee table and stretched out on the couch. She had a book in her hand and told herself that after spending another busy week at the office, she was simply going to relax tonight. Alone.

Hal had come back to work and looked pretty good after his bout with pneumonia. She had filled him in on the entire Brazilian escapade, and he had spent an inordinate amount of time apologizing for assigning her to go in the first place. She had assured him that she managed and was actually glad that she could help the authorities find the lab and the drug dealers.

She had also told him a lot about Christina, the plight of her family and thousands of others in that dreadful favela. Hal told her the poverty and problems had been there for as long as he could remember, but with the new agreements she and the Secretary had proposed as well as the cooperation and gratitude of President Mendez for an American saving his life, things would surely improve over time.

Jessica still wanted to do more for the teenager. She had written out a personal check and sent it to Chet Osborn, asking if he could arrange to get the funds to Christina through one of his agents stationed in Rio.

She took a sip of wine and leaned back against the down-filled pillows.

Seven days. Has it been seven whole days since that night I spent with Bill Black? In some ways it seems like moments ago. I can still see his dark eyes and feel his light touch.

The more she thought about Bill, the more depressed she became. He had never called or even sent a text or email. He certainly knew where to find her. Anyone could call the White House. The number 202-456-1111 was probably one of the easiest numbers to find anywhere. There had to be a reason he was giving her the silent treatment unless that weekend just didn't mean anything to him. But she refused to believe that.

She took another sip of wine and glanced at her watch: 9:00. She could read a while longer. Even though she had early morning meetings, she'd try to enjoy her solitude right now and try to concentrate on the story. When she got to the third chapter, she heard the front door buzzer. Who in the world would be coming by at this hour? Kay would have called first. Besides, she said she had a date with some guy she met when she checked out a library book. At least he sounded better than the flagpole straightener.

Jess got up from the couch, went over to the intercom and pushed the button. "Yes?"

"Uh, Jessica, it's Bill. Can I come up?"

She was stunned. Bill Black was here at her apartment? He was downstairs? Right now? She took a deep breath and answered, "Bill? It's been so long. I mean, are you okay? Um, yes, I guess you can come up. I'll release the door."

She raced into the bathroom, ran a brush through her hair and glanced down at her sweatpants and T-shirt, but there was no time to change. Her bell rang. She hurried to the door.

"Hello, Jess," Bill said. "It is *so* good to see you. Can we talk for a minute?"

She hesitated, staring at the good-looking guy clad in a suit and tie. "You're all dressed up and I'm . . ."

"You look great," Bill said. "Who cares what we're wearing? I have some important things to tell you."

She motioned for him to come in "I just opened a bottle of wine. Would you like some?"

"Sure, wine would be good," he said, following her into the kitchen.

She reached into a cabinet, pulled out a wine glass and poured some Beaujolais for him. "Let's go into the living room," she said, leading the way and pointing to the couch.

He sat down next to her, took a drink, set the glass down and ran his fingers through his hair. "I just got back to the city this morning. Had an overnight flight, and I've been in debriefings all day."

"You must be . . ."

"Tired? Yes. But I had to see you. I probably should have called, but I really need to do this in person."

Do what in person? Let me down easy? I'm already down. I've been down ever since he left me in Rio. She took another sip of wine and held her breath.

"Look, Jess, I've been tied up with this whole investigation, the assassination, the drug dealers, the interrogations, the meetings. But I haven't stopped thinking about you. Not for one minute."

"But why . . ."

"Why didn't I call you before? I tried. I left messages, but then we found out that Pazio had taken your cell phone. Then later, I know I could have called you at your office or something, but, as I said, I really wanted to see you, talk to you, try to explain."

"Explain what?" she asked. "Why you left me last Saturday with that one-word message? 'Later.' What did you mean by 'later'?"

"Let me explain." He leaned forward to take another sip of wine, turned to her, and touched her hand. "I had a meeting today with our Undersecretary of State. I had to get his permission."

"Permission for what?" she asked.

"Permission to read you in," he replied.

"Read me in to what?"

"Look. When we first met, I told you I was the Assistant Chief of Protocol at State."

"Right. And that *is* your job. I know that," she said.

"The thing is, it's not my *only* job," Bill said.

"What other job do you have?"

"I had to get permission to tell you that I'm actually with the Agency. Being detailed to State is just my cover," he said. "There are only a few people who know that. The Undersecretary arranged the position at State. Chet Osborn knows because we've worked together on a number of missions, and J. L. and the National Security Advisor were the only ones at the White House. And now you. With your level here and all you've been through, I was able to get you added to the 'need to know' list. So, you see . . ."

"My God, you weren't sent to Brazil to arrange seating charts. You were sent on a mission," Jess said, staring at him.

"Precisely. We had picked up chatter about a possible plot to kill President Mendez. I had worked in Brazil before. I knew the language. Chet wanted me down there, and the OAS conference was the perfect opportunity. Then I met you." He reached over and once again ran his finger down her cheek, sending tiny shock waves through her system just like the first time he did that.

"So, let me get this straight," Jess said, moving closer to him on the couch. "You went there to help protect the president. When we were together, were you called back in the middle of the night for some reason?"

"Actually, I got a message that there was going to be another drug raid there in Rio. I had been part of one of those a year ago. I knew some of the DEA agents, and they asked for my help, so I had to leave you. I thought it would be over and I could get back. But then I was called back to Brasilia."

"That's when I went out and . . ."

"Yes, I know. Pazio sent me the pictures of you in that lab. You can't believe what that did to me. To see you tied up like that."

"He sent the pictures to you? But why?"

"He had your cell phone. My number was in it. He sent them to me because he didn't want you. He wanted me."

"What do you mean 'he wanted' you? Why would he want you?"

Bill explained what happened a year ago when Pazio's brother was killed, and he got the blame. He told her how Pazio had vowed to get his revenge and told Bill he would only release her if he traded himself for her freedom."

"Oh no!" she cried out. "He would have killed you!"

"Well, he didn't. I had backup. I figured I could take him."

"But he always had other guys with him," she protested.

"Not the two you nailed. Literally," Bill said with a slight grin. "I have to say when Chet told me how you got out of that situation, I laughed out loud. I don't mean to make light of it. I was just visualizing you holding a nail gun, surprising Domingo and his buddy and making your escape. It was positively brilliant. How the hell did you pull that off?"

"I used to work in my dad's hardware store. Remember?" she said, taking another drink of wine. "So, when I got away, you didn't have to come rescue me. I'm so glad of that. Pazio was awful. I have no doubt he would have killed you," she said with a shudder.

"It didn't exactly go like that," Bill said. "He tried to keep me thinking he had you and was moving you around. I did go back to Rio to find you, but when you met with Chet, he got hold of me. We took Pazio. I got out of there, and the rest of the Rio agents and police took them all down."

He came to find me? He was actually going to try and trade his life for mine? She tried to process it all as she took a deep breath and gazed into his eyes. "This is all so mind-boggling; I'm trying to take it all in. You were ready to risk your life for me?"

"Jess, please," Bill said, stroking her hair. "I couldn't stand the thought of those guys having you as their prisoner. I would have worked it out. I simply *had* to find you."

"You are amazing! Talk about finding, I wanted to find you too, but I didn't see you until we were at the banquet. I saw you tackle the guy with the gun. It was so wild."

"Just happened I was the one who saw him draw the gun, I guess," Bill said.

"I still say you were incredible," she said.

"Everything happened so fast. They got the president out of there. We got Rabelo out."

"Yes, I heard more about him on the news. But you weren't mentioned until later. There was a report from *Rede Globo* in Brazil that gave your name as the person who stopped Rabelo and saved the president. The reporter said you were a State Department employee who worked in the Protocol department. That's all there was."

"We asked them to keep it that way," Bill said. "I've been trying to dodge the State Department press corps all day."

"Then just this morning, I heard they arrested Vice President Serra and accused him of masterminding the plot against Mendez."

"Yes. They first got him on corruption. Then they were able to trace deposits in one of Rabelo's bank accounts and connect it to Serra. They wrapped up the whole thing pretty quickly as these things go," Bill said. He leaned closer and cocked his head to one side. "Now with all of that behind us, do you think we could start over? Or, rather, pick up where we let off in Rio?"

He tipped her chin up. When she murmured, "I'd like that," he put his arms around her and lowered his mouth to hers. The kiss was deep, urgent. She felt his grip tighten as his body pressed against hers. She put her arms around his neck as he whispered, "I've missed you, Jess."

"Missed you too," she murmured.

He started to kiss her again, then hesitated and said, "Is there a better place for us . . ."

She nodded and pointed down the hall. He got up from the couch and held out his hand, and when she stood up, he lifted her in his arms and began to walk toward her bedroom. She had a vivid memory of the first time he picked her up outside the Copacabana Palace and carried her inside. She put her head on his shoulder and said, "I just have one question."

"Go ahead and ask," he said, taking her over to the bed.

"How in the world did you get assigned to two jobs anyway?"

As he set her down and took her in his arms once more, he gave her a slow grin and replied, "Besides helping to protect the President of Brazil, I was sent to protect you, Jess, as well."